FOR

Love from

Noel & Peter

The Eye of the Everlasting Angel

By the same author

The Redemption of Elsdon Bird
Among the Animals: A Zookeeper's Story (non-fiction)
Then Upon the Evil Season
In the Country of Salvation
Always the Islands of Memory

Noel Virtue

The Eye of the Everlasting Angel

Peter Owen

London & Chester Springs PA

PETER OWEN PUBLISHERS
73 Kenway Road London SW5 0RE
Peter Owen books are distributed in the USA by
Dufour Editions Inc. Chester Springs PA 19425–0449

First published in Great Britain 1992

ISBN 0 7206–0863–5

Printed in Great Britain by Billings of Worcester

Contents

For Michael J. Yeomans,
who is much loved

Grateful acknowledgement is made
to the Queen Elizabeth II Arts Council
of New Zealand, for their generous grant.
I am indebted also to John Zeigler, of
Charleston, South Carolina, and to the
late Edwin Peacock, for their consistent
encouragement and practical support, which
has helped sustain me in my writing.

N.V.

1 Gran and the Gypsy Line

The morning after Alice Todd left for America, Toby and Gran found huge piles of elephant dung along the street outside the house. It was Saturday. The Bingling Brothers Circus was back in town. They rested their animals in a nearby meadow between seasons. Before the neighbouring women got their hands on the dung Gran got Toby to collect every bag and container he could find, and together they hurried out to shovel it up. Gran believed the dung would be a blessing for Alice's dahlias, even if she wouldn't see the benefit. It took them almost two hours. After they finished it began to rain. Gran's arthritis began to play merry hell with her. She went back to bed with a cup of tea and a hot water bottle.

The elephant dung lay all over the kitchen floor, in plastic bags and tin buckets and even in Alice's pink washing-up bowl. Gran was delighted, despite her aching joints. She smiled at Toby from her bed. 'We'll have a special supper tonight,' she told him. 'We can call it the elephant's surprise. George will hate it. I'll cook everything he won't eat.'

Gran had moved in with George and Alice Todd, her son and daughter-in-law, after she had given up her life as a gypsy. Toby was her only grandchild. After her husband Bert had died of a brain haemorrhage brought on by the death wish, she'd muddled on, still travelling with the gypsies until she became too lonely. George couldn't stand her living with them. He hated it. Alice had been adamant at the time. Since Gran had turned up there'd been years of hell for George. Now Alice had gone off to America on her own for three months, leaving Gran in charge. George thought life would become an even greater misery, so he was planning to be off down to the Hare and Hounds every night once he'd finished work.

Gran told Toby that they wouldn't see much of George while Alice was away. Grumpy old bastard, Gran called him. George was her only son. He had run away to sea when he was fourteen. He'd got on a ship at the docks and didn't come home for years. Once he was back he met Alice and married her. She'd been a barmaid at the Hare and Hounds, the pub in the same street where George had found digs. Gran told Toby that Alice had married George out of sexual melancholy. Toby was the only result. According to Gran, George was ashamed that she and Bert were gypsy folk. Gran, whose name was Nesta, and Bert, came from a long line of gypsies. The line stretched back for hundreds of years, so Gran claimed. George had managed to cut the line. Gran despised him for it. George despised her for everything. Just as well Alice liked Gran, and that Gran liked Alice, and that Gran loved Toby. She stuck up for Toby. Gran was getting to be frail now, she'd been claiming lately. She believed she wouldn't live much longer. 'I've got the death wish coming,' she'd told Toby every day for years. 'It's in me like it was in Bert. I want to join him soon. Though he's probably in Hell.'

Toby never said much. He'd smile his slow smile and let Gran hug him. He was Gran's boy. George despised Toby for that as much as he feared and despised Gran. Yet they all got along somehow. At least they had done. Alice had yelled at George a lot but they'd never really fought. George had never hit Alice. Mostly they'd ignored each other in the house. They'd gone their separate ways whenever they could. They had carried on so that Toby would have a home, so Gran had said. To the world outside the house they'd been no happier or more desperate than anyone else.

Empire Street where they lived was in a quiet area of Southampton. Toby had been born in the council house, unlike George. George had been born on the road. Inside a caravan in the middle of nowhere, Gran told Toby. Gran didn't know where she'd been born. Alice never talked of her origins except about her American relatives in South Carolina. It was them she'd gone off alone to visit. She hadn't wanted George along. She'd told him that he would moan about America like he moaned about everything else. Alice had been saving up from her housekeeping money for two years. There hadn't been enough for anyone else to go with her even though Toby had wanted to.

Gran had talked Toby out of the idea. 'You don't want to go there,' she said. 'They're a silly pack of beggars. They've no sense. Look at their history. You must have learned about it at school. They shoot their presidents, they've more money than they know what to do with. It's criminal. And that president they have now! At least we're not barmy about our prime ministers. We ignore them once they get into Number Ten. Me, I've never voted for any of the wasters.'

Sometimes Gran would talk to Toby for hours. Toby was the only one who listened to her. He'd sit beside her on the sofa and he'd smile and sometimes he'd nod. He never needed to say much. Gran said it all. Toby took in most of what Gran told him but forgot a great deal of it.

He didn't remember anything he'd been taught at school. He'd fared badly there and passed no exams. He'd been working in a job for six months now. George had found him the job through a mate. He said it was about all that Toby was capable of doing. Toby sat on a hard chair in a spare-parts factory eight hours a day every week using a machine that put holes into pieces of copper tubing. No one had ever told him what the tubes were for. Toby had never asked. As soon as the crate at the side of the machine was filled with tubes, it'd be hauled away to the packing-room by Fred. Fred was from Jamaica. He was Toby's best mate at the factory. Toby had grown to love Fred, who was old like Gran and laughed a lot. He had cracked teeth and talked of travelling home to Kingston one day.

Toby didn't like the women in the factory very much. There were a lot of women. They were always talking about sex. In the canteen they talked of nothing else, making jokes about the men and picking on Bill, who was sixty-four and waiting to retire. Bill's wife had died of cancer and sometimes he talked to Toby about how much he missed her. Bill kept to himself most of the time. One morning he'd had enough of the women yelling dirty things out to him across the canteen. He walked over to their table, unzipped his trousers, took out his cock, shoved it in one of the women's cups of tea and stirred it. He was sacked on the spot. Fred told Toby that Bill would be all right, he'd been looking forward to retirement. Fred was always cheering Toby up. He never stopped smiling. He had brilliant white teeth, never mind they were cracked.

'He'll probably have the Angel in him,' Gran told Toby when he talked to her about Fred from Jamaica. 'There aren't many about like that. I've the Angel in me. As well as the death wish in my blood. When I die you'll soon see something special, my lovely. You'll only need to keep your wits about you and you'll see it. You'll see the Angel when I die. She'll be there. And one day that Angel will help you out from bad times. She'll watch over you all your life. You remember that. She watches those with gypsy blood.'

There were many things that Gran told Toby when they were

alone. Toby tried hard to take it all in. He loved to listen to her as much as he loved her. He loved George and Alice too but hadn't had much chance to show his love. George was usually bad-tempered when Toby was about. Alice once told Toby that love was for folk who had plenty of money, not for the likes of them. Or it was for the birds. Yet Toby felt that, underneath, his parents must love him. They'd tried to do their best for him. At least that was how Toby had viewed things. Even if Alice and George hadn't let him call them Mum and Dad. It made them feel too old, they said. Toby had been using their Christian names to their faces for years.

George made Toby drag all the elephant dung out into the back garden once Gran had gone to bingo. On Saturday night Gran usually went off to bingo with her best pal Betsy Molesworthy, who ran the local florist shop. Betsy had never married. Toby had once heard her telling Gran that for years she'd thought she must be a lesbian because she was hairy. But Betsy Molesworthy had never been attracted to either man or woman and had eventually discovered that she loved her flowers instead. She was an ideal pal for Gran.

George went off to see Maureen Stokes on Saturday night. George and Maureen Stokes had been having sexual intercourse for over six months. Gran knew about it. She'd even told Toby. Betsy Molesworthy had seen George and Maureen rudely fondling each other in the back room of the Hare and Hounds, and then coming out of a bed and breakfast holding hands. She told Gran this with relish. It was uncertain if Alice had known. If she had, she'd pretended otherwise right up until she'd gone away.

Maureen Stokes owned a bungalow somewhere up North. She came down every weekend and stayed at a bed and breakfast called Mon Repos. George paid for the room. Every Saturday night Maureen was a stripper at the Pink Kitten Club for Working Men. After her performance there she went back to Mon Repos with George and performed for him. George hoped it would become serious with Maureen so he could get away from Alice and Nesta as well as from Toby. He'd finally had enough. He had been waiting. He'd watched Maureen strip and he'd made love to her and he'd hoped for a stroke of luck. George had often spent all weekend at Mon Repos with Maureen. Alice going off to America had given him a chance to escape and start up a new life with a new woman, so he privately hoped.

Every Sunday Gran and Toby went hiking in the nearby woods. The woods and heathland covered several hundred acres. There were lakes and wild ponies, babbling brooks and dozens of birds to look at. Toby took binoculars. Gran packed a lunch of sardine sandwiches with plum seed-cake and a flask of tea. Toby carried the binoculars and the lunch in his rucksack that Gran had given him a few years ago. The binoculars belonged to George. Before they left, the day after Alice's leaving, Gran got Toby to help her spread the elephant dung over the back garden. They dug it into the earth, then weeded Molly's grave.

Molly had been Gran's beloved dachshund which she'd brought from the gypsy life. Gran was certain that Molly had died of a broken heart. She'd pined for Bert. She'd pined for the freedom she had once enjoyed. Molly the dachshund had worshipped Bert. She'd hated everyone else. Molly had had only three legs. Her left hind leg had been amputated after a farmer had shot at her years before Bert died. One fine sunny morning Toby had found Molly lying dead beside the compost heap. They'd buried her nearby. 'She was the last straw,' Gran had whispered to Toby over Molly's freshly dug grave. 'With her has gone all memory of my Bertie.' After that, as far as Gran was concerned, it'd been downhill all the way.

Hiking in the woods was the highlight of the week for Toby, though Gran walked more slowly now, as she had her arthritis to contend with. Most days they didn't go far. If it rained they sat in the shelters. They stared out at the landscape, eating sandwiches and drinking tea from the flask. Gran told Toby about her past life as a gypsy. She had an endless stream of stories. Toby had heard them all dozens of times. When the sun was out or when at least it wasn't raining they tramped through the undergrowth and across peat bogs and around the edges of lakes.

Gran stared at Toby in a strange way as they walked that Sunday. 'It's come on me like a rash, my lovely,' Gran told him. 'The death wish. I feel it stirring in my juices. Just like it came on to Bert towards the end. It runs in our veins. There won't be much time left now. You've got to be prepared. Things will change once I'm gone. George cut the line.'

'What change, Gran?' Toby asked. 'What will change?'

Gran stood stock-still, staring out across the lake they were walking past. She drew her arms upwards, reaching out. She closed her eyes tightly. 'You have the gypsy blood,' she said slowly. 'It's there, it's inside you. And the line of gypsies I come from, and Bert came from, will mingle together in you for evermore.' Then she stopped, opened her eyes and said brightly: 'Don't you worry, my lovely, the Angel of the light will be watching over you. Look out for her, watch for the light. You will see her sooner than you think, when I die.'

'I don't want you to die, Gran,' Toby said quietly. He went across to her and hugged her tightly.

'Oh, my lovely, you'll have to expect it. It'll happen. It'll happen very soon. But you'll see the Angel there in the shining light. You must watch for her always. You'll see her in folk's eyes as they come near you. Those will be the ones that you must trust. All the rest will be selfish bastards.'

They walked a long way that Sunday. Gran said she was filled with energy because the Angel was close and getting even closer. They tramped through the woods for a longer stretch than they had done for months. Toby worried about Gran's arthritis. He could see on her face that she suffered pain. Her face got flushed. Her arms trembled. Yet in the boots and the clothes she wore that had belonged to Bert she acted as if this hike was no different from all the others they had made together. Gran went over and over with Toby the names of berries and seeds and plants that she had shown him down the years. She made Toby repeat everything she'd taught him a dozen times. She told him how to tell a diseased rabbit from a healthy one. How to skin rabbits and squirrels and what to do when cooking them to eat. How to tell if water was too stagnant to drink, and never to swim in lakes or in rivers, as bad spirits might drain him of his special juices. She taught him where to find the tastiest birds' eggs.

Toby tried his hardest to remember everything. Though he didn't know why he had to learn all the facts, he trusted Gran. He felt in his heart that she couldn't really be crazy as George often said she was. Behind her back George called her the one-woman-nutter-brigade whenever Gran had gone on about gypsy folklore inside the house. George had no time for any of it. It made him angry. George once told Toby that Gran made up everything out of her head. What she told him had nothing to do with how gypsies really lived. It was all a pack of lies. Gran was nuts. Yet Toby sensed that George was scared of Gran.

'The death wish will be in you too, Toby,' Gran told him. 'Never forget that it's there. It's sleeping inside your heart, passed through the blood. When you're alone out in the world, you remember what your old Gran has told you. The death wish might pass you by if you're lucky. But you come from a line of gypsies whose blood runs in a queer way.'

'Are all gypsies like that?' Toby asked her.

Gran shook her head. 'Just our line,' she said. 'We were a special breed. Most of us are gone, we're scattered, we're dead. You may be one of the last.'

They had moved away from the lake into deeper woodland where few locals ventured. It was a place that Gran claimed was special. A place where witches came to on All Saints' Eve. Where goblins and fairies gathered to dance away the summer nights, to create new spells that they sold to gypsies. There were clearings, she said, where the Devil himself appeared, to fornicate with kidnapped women. Many of the local women had borne Devil children who would grow up to be politicians and bankers. There were places like that all over England.

Toby did sometimes wonder if Gran was all there. He wasn't good at deciding about anything so he just listened to her and tried to believe. He saw nothing in the woods that made them seem different. The woods were peaceful and filled with bird-song. Alice had told him that the whole area was what England should be like all over. No one went there, she said, as they'd become too lazy to appreciate it. She never went there herself. She was far too busy.

As usual, on the way home from their hike, Gran recited the Lord's Prayer backwards under her breath, which she said would protect Toby from evil.

While Gran and Toby were off hiking in the woods George was entertained by Maureen Stokes at Mon Repos. Maureen cooked him roast beef and Yorkshire pudding in her room. The owner of Mon Repos was one of George's mates, so there were no complaints from other guests about the cooking smells. Maureen gave George rub-downs with a special alcohol after they ate. Then they made love until it was time for Maureen to catch the coach home.

Before she had gone off to America Alice had spent her Sundays in the local hospice where she'd been working as a voluntary aid for the past three years. She'd cleaned out toilets and mopped floors and comforted the sick and dying. She'd been given a gold-plated watch before she'd given up the work.

Gran had never talked about her gypsy life to Alice. Not directly. For years Alice had denied that Gran had lived the way she'd lived with Bert. All those years Alice had denied it, Gran had told Toby, because she hadn't wanted to accept the background of the family she'd married into. She didn't have the blood in her, as George had and now Toby had. George had backed Alice to the hilt in her denial. He'd almost denied it himself. Probably did, Gran claimed, behind her back.

'He's a rotten apple, Toby,' Gran said. 'There's usually one or two get born every so often down the line. I had a bad confinement with George. My blood was thin. Something went wrong. That's why George has problems, I believe. After Bert was gone the rest of the clan never treated me right. It wasn't the same. They blamed me for George breaking away. A cloud hung over me and Molly. My arthritis was just my excuse to come to you. Your blood wasn't tainted when you were born, it would've purified. Now my time is near. The death wish squirms inside me. It got Molly. Now it wants me.'

Toby spent all his free time helping the locals in their street. He liked to help people, to do things for them. After work he would walk down to Cyril's house and help him clean out his pigeon-coops. Cyril had only one arm and was quite old. He'd lost his right arm in the war. He doted on his pigeons and spent all his time with them. He told Toby they gave him more happiness than his late wife had. Toby scrubbed out all the food- and water-bowls and raked out the coops. Cyril never paid him for the work. He was always grateful. 'You're a rare treasure, son,' Cyril would often say. 'Other young lads your age are usually selfish little blighters. All out for themselves they are these days.'

Cyril was lonely and seemed to have no friends except his pigeons. Sometimes if Toby had a day off and Cyril was due his pension they'd walk together to the post office to collect it. 'You're me minder,' Cyril would joke. 'One day I'll get you a badge with words on it. Toby Todd the minder.' And he'd laugh and wheeze until he started to cough and went red in the face.

Toby washed Betsy Molesworthy's florist shop windows once a week and swept out her yard at the back of the shop. She never paid him either, but Toby didn't mind. He shopped for groceries for old Mrs Kent, who was to be a hundred in two years' time and was planning a street party when she got her telegram from the Queen. He shopped for Mrs Green, who was too scared to leave her house. She was certain that Hitler was still alive and out to steal away all English ladies and turn them into sex slaves. Mrs Green had told Toby all about it on his visits. She had a picture of Hitler on her wall so she'd recognize him. She said boys were all right. They were as safe as houses.

Then there were Mr and Mrs Ramsdean who lived at The Cedars. Their house was the only one in the street which had a name instead of just a number. Alice had often said they were snobs, but Toby cleaned their windows and cut their hedge once a month and they were always friendly to him. Mr Ramsdean had a piano accordion and would often stand out in the street playing songs on it to get away from Mrs Ramsdean, who nagged at him. He had promised to teach Toby how to play the accordion one day. Toby loved listening to the music. Mr Ramsdean played old Vienna waltzes, as that was where they had come from just before the war. He and Mrs Ramsdean both spoke in heavy accents and were always going off to a club where other Viennese got together and played cards. They'd changed their name when they came to England.

Toby washed cars for some of Cyril's neighbours. He tried to get them to visit Cyril, to view his pigeons. None of them ever did. Some days he scrubbed tiles that people had laid down in their front yards instead of grass. He used to look after young Mr Grundy's garden, but he'd been put into a home when he turned eighty-seven. Young Mr Grundy had started to act a bit queer. Toby had once found him wandering along the street without any clothes. He had a hard-on. He told Toby he was looking for his wife so they could make another baby. Mrs Grundy had been dead for fifteen years and their daughter had run off with a Bible salesman. The council had pulled down young Mr Grundy's house and built a block of flats after he was taken away. The detached house had had rotten foundations, the council claimed. Alice had talked for years about their getting one of the flats. They were at the far end of the street overlooking the cemetery. Alice thought they were posh.

Toby didn't help many of the neighbours in other streets. Alice said they were all nobs and snobs. She'd always had a lot to say about them and what they got up to, just as she'd moaned about everyone in Empire Street. She thought Toby helping people was a complete waste of time.

'You're a bit like an Angel yourself, Toby,' Gran had told him one day to cheer him up when Alice had been moaning. 'The Angel of Empire Street, that's who. No one appreciates it. You help the needy, those who have it rough. It might be your vocation one day. Though I'll have a word with Betsy, my lovely. She could afford a few shillings a week for your work. She's always winning at bingo, bless her cotton socks.'

A few weeks went by. Alice sent a postcard from Washington, DC. It said that she was having a grand time. She was on her way by coach down to Charleston, SC. The postcard was of the White House after dark. Over it Alice had written I WAS HERE in huge letters. Toby pinned the card up on the kitchen wall. When George saw it he pulled it down and shoved it away in a drawer.

Gran talked about her death wish. Toby worked overtime at the factory. Fred from Jamaica handed in his notice, as he'd saved enough money to go home to Kingston. George had the flu and was in bed for three days. He lay about downstairs afterwards, moaning, in his dressing-gown and slippers. The day after George went back to work Toby heard that Fred had been run over and killed by a bus in the High Street. It was the weekend by then. Gran and Toby stayed home from their hike. Gran cooked a huge ham and roasted some Jamaican sweet potatoes. Toby cried for Fred. They played consequences in the front room after supper and George joined in but fell asleep in the middle of the second game. He snored so loudly that Toby sat there grinning despite feeling gloomy about his mate, Fred. Gran fetched a wooden clothes-peg from the kitchen and tried to attach it to George's nose. She was trying to cheer Toby up. George woke with a yell and called Gran an interfering old hag and a rotten bitch. Gran just laughed.

By the time the next weekend came round George, not having seen Maureen Stokes while he was sick, was in a foul mood. He even scared Gran, the way he acted and spoke. She told Toby that they should set out very early on Sunday morning and have another extra long hike, having missed out last weekend. She packed even more lunch than usual. She'd baked two apple tarts. There were Cornish pasties, home-made chocolate chip biscuits and a bag of boiled sweets. Gran told George that he could fend for himself from now on, until Alice came home. She'd done enough for him. George just shrugged and gave her back a queer grin once she turned away. Then he noticed Toby staring at him and glared. George had not mentioned Alice once since she'd left them. Toby had been waiting for him to mention her.

'I'll be over on the estate, then,' George said to Gran's back. 'Trevor's place. His wife'll look after me. Don't you bother yourself. I only live here.'

'I shan't bother myself, then,' said Gran, and winked at Toby before leaving the room.

Toby and George stared at each other then George made a loud grunt. 'Flaming Gran's boy,' he muttered. He went off to lock himself in the toilet with his newspaper.

Gran and Toby set off soon after a late breakfast. It was a beautifully sunny day. The sky was clear and there was a warm breeze. Half the town seemed to have set off into the woods. They stood on a small bridge that spanned Kingfisher Brook and played Pooh sticks for a while. There were so many others playing the same game Gran got fed up so they carried on towards the deeper woodland away from the noise. Most of the Sunday trippers would be too lazy to trek as far as they'd trek, Gran said, to where the real woods lay. Striding across the heath, over mounds and hillocks, Gran and Toby sang songs and watched out for birdlife. The day grew warmer. Gran said she could smell the summer days ahead, even though it wasn't proper spring yet. 'We'll have a bounty of summer days like this one, Toby,' she said, staring up at the sky. 'There's no place like England for balmy days. It's heavenly. I wish my Bertie was here with us. You'd have loved him. He would have wanted to eat you, my lovely. He'd always wanted a grandson to spoil.'

Toby had never met his grandad. Grandad Bert had hated George and while Bert was alive he and Gran had never come to visit. Toby had an old black and white photograph of his grandad that Gran had given him.

They'd reached the first part of the woodland where Gran claimed witches danced, when she had a funny turn. She went pale and clutched at her chest and began to wheeze. Toby helped her to sit down on a log while she got her breath back and some of her colour. She was wearing a pair of Bert's old trousers, so she put her head down between her knees. Toby stroked her back. There was no one else in sight. Gran got Toby to undo her corset and pull it off, which helped her feel a bit better. Toby fetched Gran's cloth cap. The cap had fallen off Gran's head and it lay on the path. He used it to fan Gran's face. The cap had also belonged to Bert. It was badly stained.

Once Gran had recovered she said: 'I'd like to go home, Toby. I don't feel it's a good day. There's an aura in the air. I feel rather queer, my lovely.'

They took it slowly, all the way back along the dirt path, until they'd returned to the green where most of the Sunday trippers were sitting about having picnic lunches. Gran had stuffed her corset down the front of her trousers. She worried aloud that someone would notice she wasn't wearing it.

She perked up a bit by the time they reached the corner of Empire Street. The street was quiet. No one was to be seen. A few collared doves strutted about in the middle, cooing. 'It used to be like this in the war,' Gran told Toby as they neared the house. 'Quiet everywhere. Peaceful. In the daytime it was, wherever we were camped. That rotten Mr Hitler made certain we never got no peace at night. I could've strangled him at night. The noise of his blessed bombs was a disgrace.'

Toby opened the front door and helped Gran up the steps. She had begun to tremble and gone pale again. She seemed so worn out that Toby sat her down on the chair beside the hall table. On the table sat a jug with dead dahlias in it. After she'd rested, Gran went to pick up the jug. A letter had been stuffed behind it. It was opened. Gran picked that up instead. The letter was addressed to George. It had an American stamp on it. Gran said nothing as she pulled out the single sheet of paper from inside the envelope. She grinned sheepishly at Toby.

Gran read the letter out loud. It was from Alice. In it she told George that she wasn't coming back. She was planning to live in Charleston, SC, from now on. George could go to the dogs. Alice had stopped even liking him years ago. She was having a grand time in Charleston, SC, and had met a real man there who'd swept her off her feet and had proposed. A man with more guts and money than George would ever dream of. She'd be wanting a divorce. The letter did not mention Gran. It didn't say a thing about Toby and what was to become of him or Gran. It was signed *Alice Trimble*. Trimble was Alice's maiden name. There were a dozen x's at the bottom.

Gran got to her feet and drew her arms upwards, holding them out. She closed her eyes. Toby thought she was about to have another turn. He rushed forward. The letter fell to the floor.

'You'd best get me upstairs, my lovely,' Gran wheezed. Her face was as white as a sheet. She was covered with perspiration. Then she whispered: 'How old am I, Toby Todd?'

'You're one hundred and four,' Toby whispered back. 'You're only a youngster.' It was a little game of pretend they played when Gran felt upset. Toby's reply, which Gran had made up, always got her feeling better. She made Toby put the letter back behind the jug with the dead dahlias.

Half-way up the stairs, Toby supporting Gran and Gran clutching on to the handrail and wheezing softly, they suddenly heard a queer sound. It was like a trapped animal, the sound, coming from beyond the landing. The stairs were dark and the landing above was even darker. The sound stopped, then resumed. Gran stopped wheezing. They both stood very still, looking upwards.

'What is it, Gran?' Toby whispered.

Gran put her arm out and covered Toby's mouth with her fingers. After a time, slowly, they carried on up to the top, Toby's arm round Gran's waist.

Toby's bedroom door was wide open. The other doors were closed. The sound was at its loudest now.

On the linoleum, in Toby's room, squatted Maureen Stokes. She was stark naked. She was on her hands and knees facing away from them, her head pulled back and her huge flabby bottom in the air. Her dyed red hair was jerking up and down. Underneath her, wearing only his socks and a cowboy hat, was George. He had a pillow underneath his bottom and his legs were thumping on the linoleum. He was thrusting his hips up against Maureen Stokes as if he had St Vitus's dance. It was George making the animal sound, crying out and moaning so loudly that neither he nor Maureen Stokes heard Gran's shriek and then the thud as she fell down on to the landing in a faint.

2 Calcutta Mansions

On the night Gran died Toby saw an Angel standing at the top of the stairs. He'd been sitting on the bottom step listening to Gran yelling out. 'I can see him! I can see him!' she'd shouted from the front room.

George had been out for hours, drinking at the Hare and Hounds. Toby had just looked up the stairs and there was this silver light and then a face. The Angel smiled at Toby and her arms reached down towards him. She didn't say anything. Her eyes were huge. Toby smiled back. Then the Angel moved, gliding down the stairs. She moved so fast that Toby didn't even have time to stand up. The Angel paused at Gran's door and the light around her grew brighter. Then she entered. Toby thought he heard a cry of joy. After a minute he got up and walked into the front room and there was Gran propped up on the bed with her eyes and mouth wide open, staring at the door.

The Angel left.

After catching George and Maureen Stokes cavorting on Toby's bedroom floor Gran took to her bed. She got Toby to shift her bed downstairs into the front room. She hardly spoke for three days. George kept well clear. He came home only late at night to sleep or to change his clothes. Neither Toby nor Gran knew where he'd been staying on the nights he didn't come home at all. George said nothing to Toby when they met in the kitchen at breakfast time. Toby cooked sausages, bacon and eggs for George every morning he was there. George ate the food standing at the kitchen sink. While he ate he kept his back to Toby. Then he left, not having uttered a word. Toby didn't see him until the next morning unless he stayed away from the house. Toby made Gran a pot of tea and washed her before he went off to the spare-parts factory. On the fourth morning Gran told him she would be dying any day. She'd be joining her Bertie. Toby must be ready. She had left him a letter and some money wrapped in plastic, hidden in the toilet cistern where George wouldn't find it. 'Don't fetch it until I've gone,' Gran told him. 'And don't tell that wretched dad of yours about it. He can rot in his own juices. Call it payment for all the pay-packets Alice took off you.'

Apart from that Gran stayed quiet except for mentioning Alice again. 'I knew she wasn't planning to come back,' she told Toby. 'She always was hard-hearted where you were concerned. She's never deserved you, my lovely. George hasn't either. You'll have to steel yourself. You'll be on your own after I'm with Bertie.'

Late one night Toby found Gran at the window staring up at the sky. She was mumbling. Toby reckoned she must be looking for Bert, as she was mumbling 'Where is he?' He helped her back into bed. Gran was weak and shaky but seemed cheerful. She didn't want a doctor. She said there wasn't much a doctor could do. The death wish was growing stronger every day. She reached up and stroked Toby's hair before he left her.

All through the next day she kept yelling out every so often. Toby stayed home from work after telephoning to say he had caught the flu. He sat in the kitchen and listened to the floorboards creaking as Gran moved about the front room. 'Is he there?' she yelled. Then she cried out: 'I can't hear you!' It was late afternoon when she first started to yell out 'I can see him!'

Gran ate all her supper as usual and had become quiet by then. Toby cooked her favourite pork sausages and mashed potatoes with gravy. There was jam roll and ice-cream for pudding, with a pot of tea. Gran ate all her share and wanted more. George hadn't come home and it was quite late when Toby, sitting on the bottom step of the stairs, saw the Angel. He knew Gran had died before he even went into the front room. When he leaned down to move her head up on to the pillows, her dentures fell out. They'd always been loose. A deep sigh and a smell came from her. Half-way down the candlewick bed-cover was a dark, wet stain. Toby sat beside her in the dark until George came home rolling drunk.

At Gran's funeral, held two days later, only five people turned up, including Toby and George. None of the neighbours came. Toby was the only one there who cried. He'd loved Gran more than anyone else in the world. George stood with a face like a piece of boiled cod. He kept licking his fingers and flattening his hair. The only other woman there turned out to be waiting for a different funeral. She patted Toby on the arm afterwards. She whispered words he couldn't hear. No one else bothered to say anything to him. The vicar hadn't even known Gran. He called her Vesta instead of Nesta when he spoke about her. He went red in the face twice and coughed a lot. He talked of how Gran had worked so hard as a matron at the hospice, healing the sick. He said how much she would be missed. Nobody said a thing to correct him. Not even George spoke up to tell the vicar he was talking about Alice and not Gran.

After everything was over and they'd been to the cemetery for the burial, George took his mates off to the nearest pub. He'd brought along a couple of mates to boost the numbers, he said. He told Toby to go on home. It had begun to rain. 'There's no use blubbing,' George said at the cemetery gates. 'It won't bring your Gran back.' He patted Toby on the shoulder before walking off.

Toby ran all the way home. He tried to think of everything Gran had ever taught him but his mind was blank. The rain fell heavily until he reached the house. Then it stopped. The sun came out.

George didn't bother to announce Gran's death or tell anyone about the funeral. He didn't try to contact Alice. He had Gran's body taken off to the funeral parlour in the back of a mate's van. And he didn't plan a get-together afterwards at the house. He thought that a waste of effort too. Gran had left a little money to pay for a few lines in the obituaries of the local paper. George pocketed the money and ripped up the note she left him. While Toby sat in the front room staring at Gran's empty bed George got drunk celebrating with his mates and then spent the rest of the night at the Pink Kitten Club for Working Men, playing darts.

Two nights later Gran's best pal Betsy Molesworthy, who hadn't known that Gran had died, turned up from her flat above the florist shop and threw a brick through the front-door glass. Toby watched her from a window but didn't say a word about it next morning to George. George had a good swear before he covered the hole with a piece of plywood.

'Now the old bint's dead there's no use us pretending,' George told Toby after he'd covered the hole. He stood staring, licking his fingers and flattening his hair. He kept blinking. His face had gone crimson. 'I'm going to push off out of it now, boy,' he added after a while, when Toby just stared back at him. 'I'm not hanging about any longer. You're old enough to fend for yourself.'

George went to his bedroom to pack his bags. He said he was off to live with Maureen Stokes, as she'd asked him to move in with her. Maureen was going to give up work and settle down to look after George. Maureen Stokes didn't want Toby living with her, as the bungalow up North was too cramped.

George gave Toby a fiver and shook his hand before he departed. 'There's plenty of food in the freezer. The rent's paid up until the end of next month. Alice'll be back by then. You're on your own till she gets back. She'll look after you. Well goodbye, boy. Have a nice time of it.'

Toby didn't say that he knew Alice was gone for good. He wanted to but he didn't know how. He just stared at George's face. George stared back, his face still so red Toby knew he was feeling guilty. Then George made a choking sound and walked out of the kitchen into the hall. After a long silence he closed the front door behind him with a thump.

And that was that. George set off down to the bus station carrying his suitcases and Toby sat at the kitchen table, the sausages and eggs he'd cooked untouched and growing cold. He didn't try to follow George. He sat there holding on to Gran's letter that he'd fetched from the toilet cistern. Inside the letter was a hundred pounds in five- and one-pound notes. The letter told Toby that he'd always be loved by Gran. It told him to get off on his own away from George. To do all the things Gran had taught him about how to survive. He could become a gypsy, Gran said, but only if he wanted to be one. He could go up and have a look at London if he liked. Toby had never been there. It was a grand place, Gran said. He'd have a bounty of happy days ahead of him and a good life if he did his best. The end of the letter was covered with kisses and was damp where water from the cistern had seeped inside the plastic wrapping. Outside the kitchen windows Toby could see clouds scudding across the sky. After a while, in the silence, he tried to recite the Lord's Prayer backwards the way Gran had done.

Toby was still in the house a week later. Some men had showed up to take away most of the furniture. George had told them the house would be empty, that no one would be living there any more. He had let the council know. The three removal men were a bit shaken when Toby told them that he was George's son and he still lived in the house. They went off in their van and didn't come back until the following day. Then they took the furniture out without saying much except they were sorry. Toby watched them driving off. In the sky beyond them was a pink sunset. The street, as usual, was empty. No one had come to see what was going on. He'd seen Betsy Molesworthy a few times. She just turned her face away as if she didn't know who Toby was. He saw no one else. The fiver George had given Toby went with the furniture. Toby had left it in a bureau drawer by mistake.

He packed extra clothes and his things into the rucksack that night, with some food. He'd cooked and eaten most of the food in the freezer. Once he'd tidied the rooms and made sure all the windows were locked tight he sat and wrote a note to Alice and pinned it to the kitchen wall. He knew she wouldn't be coming back, but the note helped. He didn't feel as if he was the only one who'd been left stranded. But then, rushing across the room, he pulled the note off the wall and ripped it up into dozens of pieces and kicked the pieces all over the floor and jumped on them. He stayed awake all that night, sitting on his bed waiting for the sun to rise.

On the morning of his own departure the sun shone and the sky was clear. As he left just after sunrise there was no one about except the milkman, who didn't see Toby leaving anyway. Toby Todd walked off down the street with his rucksack on his back and Gran's money in his duffle-coat pocket while the racing pigeons owned by one-armed Cyril flew in circles across the sky. As he reached the corner of the street he looked back, but the street was still empty. The early sunlight shone down on the puddles of water that filled the pot-holes.

At the cemetery, which stood behind a supermarket at the end of Empire Street, Toby couldn't find Gran's grave. He looked at all the new headstones but none had Gran's name on it. Then he remembered that her grave didn't have a headstone. He wanted to say goodbye to her. For a while he stood under a conker tree. He stared across the cemetery. There was no one alive there to ask where Gran's grave sat. All the pathways and the graves looked the same. Toby couldn't remember where they'd stood on the day of the funeral. So he stayed under the conker tree to say goodbye to Gran, who had been his best pal, who had long ago been a gypsy as Toby reckoned he might be from now on. He and Gran had enjoyed life for all those years. He thought about Jamaican Fred and about all the days he had lived in the house. He thought about George and Alice and Molly the dachshund and wondered if he would always remember. He breathed deeply and walked fast as he left the cemetery, heading for the motorway. He'd decided to go up to London as Gran had said he could in her letter. As he moved away from town he remembered something that Gran had once told him: 'I never gave up the ghost, my lovely. Not when I was young like you. Never. Went straight ahead and blew raspberries when the road got rough. You'll do the same. You've got our gypsy blood in your veins. Good luck to you, I say.'

Toby started to walk faster and above him the sun was moving higher into the sky.

By night time Toby was lost. He hadn't found the motorway. He had walked for miles and eventually found himself on a long, straight road with thick copses of trees on either side. Every so often he saw a driveway leading off into darkness. The only cars that came along the road didn't stop. He saw distant lights, but they were too far back and the driveways weren't lit. He was too tired to get off the road to look for someone. He just kept on walking. He'd walked so far he thought he should have reached another town, but he hadn't. It was bitterly cold. A wind blew straight through his duffle-coat and the two vests he was wearing. After the road turned right and narrowed he saw ahead of him a bus-shelter. It was an old wooden shelter with no seats and a dirt floor. Once he'd reached it he stood there for a long time. Then moving inside he lay down in the corner, curling himself up. He rested his head on the rucksack after eating some of the food he'd brought. Rain began to fall. Apart from the sound of the rain and the water dripping from the eaves it was quiet. Toby felt sleepy. His feet throbbed. He heard Gran's voice.

'All the blessed gypsies thought I'd never survive after Bertie went,' Gran had often told him. 'But here I am and here we are, you and me, my lovely, all my bad times blown away. We're as cosy as a couple of bugs in a mattress.'

Gran's voice seemed almost real, there in the bus-shelter as Toby lay on the dirt floor. He listened to her voice for a long time. The rain carried on falling. Water carried on dripping from the eaves. Sometimes a car went past, spraying water. Yet Toby soon felt warm, curled up in the corner. He smiled to himself and whispered: 'Good-night, Gran, sleep tight. Hope the bugs don't bite.' He thought about seeing the Angel at the top of the stairs and how beautiful her eyes had been. How she had glided downwards past him, to meet Gran in the front room.

With the Angel's face in his mind and with Gran's voice like an echo in his head, Toby fell asleep. He dreamed that he was standing at the edge of a vast wood, looking at a river. The river was still. As the sunlight around him faded and darkness moved towards him up from the river, Toby called out. In the dream he was the only person alive in the whole world. He cried out for somebody to appear. There was no sound except of wind.

He woke up early the next morning. The rain had stopped. The sky was grey and heavy with cloud. The dirt floor of the shelter was covered with pools of water. Toby ate what was left of the food in his rucksack, remembering the dream. And after combing his hair with his fingers he set out along the road, listening for cars that might stop to offer a lift. It seemed a little warmer once he'd got going. Cars and vans and lorries began to pass him. He stretched out his arm, holding up his thumb, smiling his slow smile whenever a car went by.

By the end of that day, Toby had reached London. He'd managed to hitch three different lifts from people who stopped. They'd all three been men. Toby told each of them that he was off to meet his dad. He thought that sounded best. Two of the men weren't that friendly. One asked Toby to help out with the petrol. Toby offered him a pound note. The man handed it back after a while and said that it was hardly worth taking. The other man just moaned the whole time about his wife who slept all day and never did any housework. He kept picking at a scab on his chin and sniffing.

The third lift was in a van which took Toby the longest way. It was driven by a man from the Salvation Army. He gave Toby a lecture on morals before he left him outside a YMCA in the West End. Toby didn't understand half of what the man said. He shut the car door quickly when he climbed out of the van and didn't look back as he walked away.

Toby sat down on some newspaper, his back against a wall outside the YMCA. All about him in the street there were people rushing up and down. Cars were parked bumper to bumper everywhere he looked. He watched an endless stream of faces as people walked past. Most of them looked as if they were about to scream. After a while a light, drizzling rain began to fall. A wind sprang up, blowing rubbish in circles. There was rubbish everywhere. Old newspapers, empty tin cans and food wrappings lay about where he sat. The air smelled something like metal. It was a stale smell. The number of people about him grew as Toby sat there. It was getting dark. There was more noise but fewer cars and the lights grew brighter. Someone threw a coin on to the newspaper Toby was sitting on. The young woman didn't even look at Toby as she threw the coin and hurried on. Toby stood up and stretched. He bent down and picked up the coin. He put it in his pocket.

Having never been to London before, Toby had no idea which part of it he was in. So he just walked. He felt excited by the lights and all the people. Half of them looked like foreigners and wore the oddest clothes he'd ever seen. They were laughing and talking to each other in loud voices. There were groups and couples and people on their own like he was. He was jostled and bumped and one time had his rucksack knocked off. No one took much notice of him. Everyone seemed to be in a hurry, all going somewhere else. No one spoke to him. After a time the noise started to make his head feel tight. He'd got earache.

That night Toby slept in a doorway. He discovered a huge railway station first, after walking away from the crowds. He went in and found the toilets. At the hand-basins he saw men with their shirts off, washing themselves. There was an old man having a shave who'd taken off all his clothes except his underpants, which were bright red. Toby had a wash too but didn't take off any of his clothes except the duffle-coat. No one spoke to anyone else. It was as if each man was alone in the vast toilet. The man with the red underpants kept belching, then started to sing a song with foreign words.

Afterwards Toby sat on a seat in the main hall, looking at the people queueing up for trains. Some were appearing from gangways carrying luggage. The station was called Euston. There were a lot of people standing about with no luggage at all. One woman dressed in a filthy, ragged coat and with bare feet was asleep across two of the seats. Her feet were black with dirt. A man came up and asked Toby for a cigarette.

'I don't smoke, mister,' Toby said.

'Have you a few pence on yer, then?' the man said. 'For a cuppa. Down on me bloody luck, mate. The wife's left me, she has.'

The man was unshaven. He wore a woollen hat pulled down low over his face and he rolled about as he tried to focus his eyes. He smelled of beer. Toby handed him a pound note and the man quickly walked off, staring at the money in his hand as if he'd never seen a pound note before. He joined a group of others all dressed like him. They talked and started laughing. Then they began to stare across at Toby. After a few minutes all of them began to amble across towards where Toby sat. They looked drunk. Toby picked up his rucksack and headed off to the long line of glass doors.

He knew it was late now, though he didn't have a watch. The streets outside the station were quieter. There were only a few people about, walking fast, heads lowered. Wandering on down even quieter streets filled with what looked like warehouses, Toby found a doorway. The doorway went far back into the building. It was dark and dry and out of the wind. For a time he stood outside the entrance looking up and down the street. He felt hungry and tired, so tired that his eyes kept closing. Seeing no one in sight he moved into the doorway and curled up in a corner. Wrapped in the duffle-coat that Gran had bought him from the Co-op he fell asleep straight away.

He didn't wake up until the first light of dawn when a man came out of the double doors and told him to clear off. Toby didn't argue.

During the next few days he discovered many new sights. Places he had seen only on television or heard being talked about by George, who'd once been up to London with Alice. He wanted to see Buckingham Palace but got lost after someone gave him the wrong directions. He found Piccadilly Circus almost by accident. He watched an old woman there standing on the steps below a statue. She was singing. She sang in a foreign language, like an opera singer. She held her arms out, her face screwed up and her eyes closed, and her voice was so beautiful that Toby stayed near her to listen. When the woman had finished the song, tears were pouring down her cheeks. Picking up the overflowing plastic bags that lay at her feet, she crossed the road and disappeared from sight.

Toby watched people queueing up at the huge cinemas. There were buskers who sang or tap-danced or played accordions, while a mate went along the line with a hat. Few people handed over any money. Some of the buskers were women. One of the women played a harp, sitting on the pavement. She wore paper flowers in her hair. Her face was lined and raw-looking. One old man made Toby laugh at first. He placed a matchbox down on the pavement very carefully, beside a queue of people. Then moving away from the matchbox, backwards, he rushed forward, jumped over the box and then held out his arms to the crowd. Most of the people watching just kept on watching and didn't respond at all. A few laughed. The old man jumped over the matchbox again and again, each time holding out his arms and grinning. He had no teeth. His grin made him look as if he was in pain. He had a bottle of whisky in his coat pocket and kept taking it out to drink from it. The man hadn't shaved for days. His clothes were worn and filthy. When the people had all gone inside the cinema the man sat down on the pavement against a low wall. Drawing his knees up, he wrapped his arms round them. His face slowly lost its grin. To Toby the face became grey and very old. The man's eyes looked bloodshot and sad as they roamed the square. He glanced at Toby once, but then quickly looked away. For a while the man just sat there. Then he lowered his head, stretched out his legs and went to sleep. Toby went closer. He pulled out a five-pound note from where he kept Gran's money in his coat pocket. Reaching the man's side, Toby bent down and put the money into his lap. The man didn't move for a moment. Then he opened his eyes. When he raised his head and his eyes met Toby's, Toby quickly stood up and began to hurry away, not looking back. In the man's eyes had been a stare of anger, as if he hated the whole world.

Each night once the streets had emptied Toby returned to sleep in the same doorway near the station. Most mornings he found he could stay there until the coldness of first light had gone. He lived on hamburgers and cans of soft drink during the daytime. He ate bags of crisps and ready-made sandwiches he bought from kiosks. He used the station toilets. He noticed many people he thought were also living like he was. Toby hadn't figured out what else to do yet. He did wonder where all the other people like him slept. After dark few spoke to him except to ask for money or directions. When Toby said he didn't know where places were, he was glared at. After a while, as his clothes became dirty and crumpled, no one spoke to him at all. During those few nights and days he met no one who showed him any kindness.

After a week wandering the West End streets and sleeping in the doorway he set off in a different direction one morning, finding areas where the people did not rush about with so much noise. The people looked a little more like ones he'd been used to back home, though few of them smiled when he smiled. No one seemed to look each other in the eye. There was even more rubbish lying about in the streets and in the gutters. Cars were parked half-way across pavements. Huge piles of black plastic bags lay in front of the shops. Toby saw stray dogs wandering about. Outside an Underground station called Camden Town sat an old man with silver hair and a beard. Just as Toby was ignored, no one took any notice of him either. The man wore several overcoats that were stained and ripped. Around him on the ground were plastic carrier-bags filled with old clothes and newspapers. The man sat with his legs stretched out as if he was dead. Some people just stepped over his legs to get into the station. Toby stared at the old man for a long time. He moved every so often, though he kept his head lowered. Sometimes he drew up his hands, shook them and rubbed them across his face.

In the window of a newsagent's further along Toby noticed a display of cards. Most of the cards offered things for sale, typewriters and prams and electric blankets. Along the bottom were cards offering flats and rooms for rent. None of the cards said how much the flats cost. He went inside and bought a can of drink, asking the woman if the flats would be cheap. She wrote down an address without saying anything. She stared him up and down. The house was two streets away, she said. The landlord there might have something for him if he had the money to pay.

Toby clutched the piece of paper to him as he left. He thought that if he found a place to live, he could stay in London for a while. He had Gran's money to use. Gran wouldn't have minded that. Toby felt quite excited. He kept thinking about having a bath, sleeping between clean sheets. He might even find a job if he was lucky. Gran had said he didn't have to be a gypsy if he didn't want to. He hadn't thought much of living like a gypsy here in London. No one wanted to be friendly. The streets stank.

The house was at 17 Mimosa Crescent. No one knew where Mimosa Crescent was, when Toby stopped people to ask. He hadn't thought to ask the newsagent woman, who'd stared at him as if he was dirt. But the street wasn't far away and when he did find the house he stood outside and stared up at the windows. It looked old and crumbling. There were three floors and a basement. The basement windows were boarded up, the boards covered with faded posters. In front, in a concrete yard, sat a row of black bins. The bins were overflowing with bottles and rubbish. Toby walked up the steps and rang the one bell. Above the bell was a small sign. The sign read: *Calcutta Mansions. Weekly rates. No children, No pets, No unemployed.*

The landlord told Toby he was from India but that England was his home. He wore a purple turban and a green suit. He didn't have a shirt on under his jacket. His chest was very hairy. He grinned all the time. After Toby had explained who he was and that he'd just arrived in London but didn't have a job yet, the landlord stared at him for a while then asked him inside. The hallway was unlit. An old fridge lay on its side by the stairs. The carpet was full of holes. Toby was taken up two flights of stairs that had no carpet on them at all. Without speaking, the landlord opened the door at the far end of the landing. 'You are just the sort of tenant I am looking for, Mr Todd,' he said once he'd beckoned Toby through the doorway. 'This is a special flat. It is just right for you. It can be your home away from home.'

The 'flat' consisted of one room. There was a sagging bed in the corner, an old gas cooker covered in grease, and there were rugs on the floorboards but no curtains. There was a wardrobe, a kitchen chair, and a small sink with one tap. The only window was dark with dirt. The walls had long ago been white but were now stained with damp and what looked like cooking fat. A sour smell hung in the air. It made Toby feel a bit sick.

'I will provide for you some curtains,' the landlord told Toby. 'It will make your flat homely. My last tenant, he was a very dirty man. I made him clear off. He was not nice.'

Toby stared about, saying nothing. He wanted to leave. The landlord had moved. He was standing in the doorway blocking the way. He stared at Toby, still grinning. 'My name is Mr Braithwaite,' he said after a silence. 'I am a good landlord. I ask no questions once you move in.' Then he said the flat was Toby's and he wouldn't even need a reference, but he'd like two weeks' rent in advance.

Toby was shocked at how much it cost. He said it was too much money.

'I make you a deal, Mr Todd,' Mr Braithwaite said, not grinning now. 'I'll charge you much less if you help me take down all the rubbish. We have much rubbish here. It is jolly hard work, isn't it? I am not a strong gentleman.' Many of his other tenants were lazy, good-for-nothing foreigners, Mr Braithwaite told Toby. Toby was English, so that was all right. He liked the English.

After Toby had handed over the rent, Mr Braithwaite smiled even more. He pointed out the electric and gas meters on the floor beneath the bed. He opened the wardrobe doors. There were hooks on the wall, he said, for Toby to hang up his kitchen utensils. 'You will be very much at home!' Mr Braithwaite said brightly.

When Toby tried to talk about himself, about Gran and George and Alice and where he'd come from, Mr Braithwaite said he was very busy. He had no time to listen. 'There is so much to do, Mr Todd,' he said. 'Always much to do! I work my fingers to the bone for these people. No one is grateful.'

Then, shutting the door, he left Toby on his own. Toby heard him talking loudly to himself all the way down the stairs. The front door slammed.

The floor creaked loudly as Toby moved across it. He sat down on the bed. On the bed were sheets and blankets and a stained pillow. The house was quiet but he could hear voices coming from above him, then a loud thud. Water was dripping from somewhere outside. After a few minutes, too tired even to get up to look out of the window, Toby lay down on the bed and fell asleep.

3 Two Ladies of the Town

Toby sat on the bed in his room at Calcutta Mansions. It was still early in the morning. He stared at the ceiling. Two nights before there'd been a flood somewhere above him. Water had trickled down on top of him while he was asleep. No one had done anything about it. In the middle of last night pieces of plaster had fallen down on to the bed and across the floor. Toby was under the blankets listening to Annie screaming. Annie lived in the room above, with her son. She was always screaming out of her window. Sometimes she stayed up all night drinking vodka and screaming out of the window, clomping about and singing at the top of her voice.

Toby had cleared away most of the plaster and was shaking out his bedding when Annie knocked on the door. He let her in when he saw who it was.

'Jesus,' she said, looking up. 'Are you all right? I heard the noise.'

Annie had her son Adam balanced on her hip. Adam was two years old. He had ginger hair. He had one of the ugliest faces Toby had ever seen. Adam screamed a lot too. Toby had been up to their room once. Annie had asked him to help move her furniture. She had ripped up all the carpet and moved most of the furniture out into the landing, except for a mattress. She didn't like furniture, she told Toby. When Toby went up there Adam was crawling over the bare boards dressed in only a vest. While Toby watched, Adam stood up on his short, stubby legs and peed. The pee ran down his legs and soaked into the floorboards. Annie just laughed when she saw it. There were wet stains all over the room, even along the skirting-boards.

'This house is the pits,' Annie said, standing in Toby's room, looking at the plaster lying in a pile on the floor. 'That bloody landlord should be taken to court. He's as mean as the Devil.'

She didn't offer to help Toby clean up the mess. She'd had to get up early to go collect her dole, she said. They wouldn't post it to her here any more. It kept getting stolen. As usual Annie's right eye was twitching. It had something wrong with it. Sometimes she wore a black patch over it.

Mr Braithwaite gave Toby a brand-new, two-bar electric heater after the flood. He didn't say much about the flood except that it could have been worse. 'It is the best heater money can buy, isn't it?' he said, grinning at Toby. 'It will dry all your flat for you, Mr Todd.'

Toby kept the heater switched on all day, using a lot of money in the meter. Yet it didn't stop the ceiling plaster falling. After the plaster fell, he didn't see Mr Braithwaite. The landlord stayed away for nearly a week. Toby began to hear Annie and Adam even more loudly than before. He put cotton wool in his ears when he went to bed. He slept every night in fits and starts, his head buried in his blankets.

Annie was from Northern Ireland. She had come over with her son to look for work. She hadn't found any but had stayed anyway and signed on for the dole. She was over six feet tall and told Toby she weighed eighteen stone. When she walked about her room the sound was like the beating of a drum. It was quiet in the mornings. Annie never usually got up until noon. She had a double mattress and blankets on the floor and nothing else except the cooker and a sink. Though Adam had dozens of broken old toys. He would throw them about across the floor when he wasn't screaming. Toby would find toys left on the stairs. Annie said she'd found all Adam's toys in skips along Kentish Town Road.

During the day she took Adam off in a push-chair she kept in the hall cupboard on her floor. She never said where she went. The push-chair wheels were always clogged with mud. Toby washed the push-chair once, but Annie said nothing about that. She told Toby she hated Mr Braithwaite. She was forever calling him names. She claimed that Indians were the reason England was in such a mess. She hated the English even more. For a while she chatted to Toby each time they met. She told him she was a vegetarian. She ate only vegetables and rice. People who ate meat were damned. She never explained why she screamed. Now she ignored him a lot of the time. Toby had complained about her noise. When he'd politely asked her if she could be quieter at night she had said she would be and had smiled at him and blinked. After that she got even noisier and banged on the floor after midnight with some sort of stick. She still smiled at Toby whenever she saw him, her right eye twitching.

One of the other tenants, Peter, told Toby that Annie had caused the flood. Adam had left the tap running in her sink with the plug in and Annie had forgotten or hadn't noticed. She'd gone off to friends for a day and a night with Adam. That was how the flood happened. Mr Braithwaite discovered the overflowing sink. No one else had been bothered by it. Mr Braithwaite was too scared of Annie to say anything to her.

Peter was from South America. His real name wasn't Peter. He used that name to make it easier for people to be friendly to him, he said, because the name was English. 'I am a dancer of ballet,' Peter told Toby. 'I dance with the best ballet troupe in France. But when I come to England I fall in love with London town. I love the English mans! The English mans are beautiful!'

Peter had a bicycle. He told Toby that on fine nights he rode the bicycle out to motorway cafés and had sex with truck-drivers in the toilets. 'It is beautiful!' Peter said.

When Peter said the word beautiful his voice went up high and he threw his head back and waved his arms about. Peter was tall like Annie. He had straight, black hair which was so long it reached half-way down his back. When he went off bicycling he tied the hair into a pony-tail and wore leather trousers and a tank top. He was very strong. Every morning in the back garden he did dance exercises. He told Toby that he had really learned how to dance in Bali. When Toby asked him where Bali was, Peter invited him up to his room. He told Toby all about his life. About every place he had ever lived in across the world, including Bali.

Peter's flat was at the top of the house. Like Toby's, the 'flat' was just one room. Facing the door inside it was the back of a wardrobe. On the wardrobe Peter had hung a life-size drawing of himself without clothes. Toby's face went pink when he saw it. The drawing was rude.

'Am I not the beautiful, Toby?' Peter asked, throwing his head back. 'Do not be shameful! I have beautiful body, I have beautiful cock. The English mans love me! They are so very passionate! Those drivers of trucks, they cannot get enough of myself. They are so wild!'

Peter spoke in his strange accent about his early life in a village in South America. A rich man had taken him off to New York and then on to Paris and paid for him to learn to dance. Then he had gone to Bali with a rich lady. He had been famous there for a while, in Bali. In Paris he had danced for near-royalty, he said. He'd loved Paris as much as Bali.

'What about your mum and dad?' Toby asked, staring at Peter's fingernails. They were long and pointed. The fingernail on each of his little fingers was about two inches long. They were painted red. Peter laughed and leaped into the air, throwing out his arms and legs. He usually went about in bare feet inside the house. He wore silk clothing that looked to Toby like Alice's pyjamas. Except they were purple and had rude words stitched over them in gold.

'I am a child of all the world!' Peter told Toby. 'I am my own! I have family everywhere who love myself!'

Tacked to Peter's walls were posters of Bali and Hong Kong and Paris. Toby thought that Peter might be lying about his life but he said nothing. He didn't think anyone who'd been famous could be living at Calcutta Mansions. He thought Peter's eyes looked lonely and sad. Peter talked and talked that first time. Toby sat on a chair and just listened. He smiled his slow smile. Peter didn't ask Toby anything about his life. Toby didn't mind.

Peter said he had sex with other men almost every night if it wasn't raining and he wasn't at work and the truck-drivers weren't on strike. Sometimes he found travelling salesmen who enjoyed a good time. Toby wasn't very shocked at what Peter told him. He'd heard about men having sex with other men. Gran had explained all about it to Toby once. 'It's called buggering, Toby,' Gran had said. 'It's quite common. One of the gypsies was like that. He was happy enough, bless him. He had lots of friends. Some of them wore pretty dresses in the summer and carried handbags.'

Peter didn't seem like the sorts Gran had gone on about. Toby liked Peter too. He was tough as well as muscular. He didn't seem to be afraid of anything. The only question Peter asked Toby about himself was how old he was.

'Sixteen,' said Toby. 'I'm nearly seventeen. My Gran, she's . . .'

'Sixteen!' Peter cried out, interrupting. 'You are much too much young. I should not be telling you this things! You act older than sixteen! How old do you think am I, Toby?'

Toby shrugged.

'I am thirty-five years! No one thinks I have passed twenty! I am so beautiful. My body is like the peacock!'

Toby started to like Peter more and more. He was kind and seemed gentle. Toby went up to Peter's room some nights and was given exotic fruit to eat like mangoes and lychees which Toby had never eaten before. Sometimes they ate spaghetti on toast. Afterwards Peter would dance for him.

Peter told Toby that Mr Braithwaite was a fine gentleman. He had let Peter live here for almost nothing once because Peter had been a famous dancer.

'I pay now, Toby. I have a job. I am assistant chef. I use my charm, I use sometimes my beautiful self to make happy people. I dance for customers! I am not a bad sort, as Annie tells me. I am not a prostitute. I give my love, I give my beautiful body freely because I have love. I have the love in the heart for the English mans. The English mans need it badly.'

Peter asked Toby not to tell Mr Braithwaite about where he went on his bicycle at night time. 'He would not much like this, Toby. He would put me out of his fine house. I am certain Mr B is a deep, holy man in his heart. He would not like the sex that I do. Some people do not know it is good for us.'

During the daytime Toby looked for a job. He bought a newspaper every day and read it carefully in his room, sitting beside his window. Once Annie was awake above him and clomping about he would go out and use the public telephone at the end of the crescent.

There were no factory jobs offered. Most were in offices and meant doing work that Toby had never heard of. Everyone told him over the telephone that he had to have experience. It was hardly worth his bothering to come along for an interview if he had no experience. No one wanted to hear that Toby would work hard, that he'd learn. He was too young, some said. There were too many other applicants. Toby kept on trying. There were dozens of jobs in the paper every day. He wasn't offered an interview at any of the places. He tried lying about his age and experience. He wasn't very good at lying. He kept getting caught out. After a few weeks he telephoned less and less. He sent a few letters off when the advertisements asked for letters. Each letter took him an hour to write. He didn't get any replies. He'd begun to worry about Gran's money. He was using up the hundred pounds fast.

He ate cheap food and used the gas and electricity as little as possible. He paid his rent every week and didn't say anything to Mr Braithwaite about his money. After a while Mr Braithwaite stopped asking him about work. He'd stare at Toby with a strange grin when he took the rent. 'You are my best tenant, Mr Todd,' he said once. 'You are an example. I tell everyone. I tell them that Mr Todd pays. This is good, isn't it? You stop paying and you have no home! Calcutta Mansions is a grand house.'

Toby took the rubbish out to the bins as often as he could. It was left in the downstairs hall in black bags. Sometimes he helped Annie down the stairs with her push-chair after he'd put out the rubbish. Sitting in the push-chair Adam would stare with his mouth wide open. Adam's face was always covered with chocolate from the biscuits Annie gave him. Adam would point at Toby and scream. Annie would laugh.

There were a lot of other tenants in the house. Sometimes the house was like Euston Station. There were people coming and going all the time. Most didn't even bother to shut the front door properly. There were a few old men who never said anything when Toby said hello. There were some foreigners who couldn't speak English. One always spoke to Toby in his own language and grinned. An old lady called Toby 'my ducks' whenever they met. She lived on the ground floor. Sometimes Toby would help her up the stairs to the bathroom and back. She had a false hip, she told him. She couldn't walk very well up stairs. Toby would see her peering out of her window as he left the house, or when he returned. He'd wave and she'd wave back. She never invited him into her room. She said her name was Mrs Cranks. She had a budgerigar called Ringo who was nasty to strangers. Toby never saw her in the street. Twice a week a nurse came to visit her. On those days Mrs Cranks would yell her head off. She told Toby that the Health Department employed sadists to look after old people in London. Nobody gave a hoot for old folk these days. Old folk were a waste of time. A drain on resources. That was politics, she said. Toby thought she was a brainy person, the way she spoke. He wondered why she lived in the house all alone.

After a few weeks Toby had begun to leave little parcels of food outside her door. He wrapped the parcels in brown paper and wrote her name on the top. One week he bought Mrs Cranks a dressing-gown from a charity shop and left that for her. When he saw her next she was wearing the dressing-gown over her old one. She didn't say anything but she grinned and winked. Her eyes sparkled. Toby thought he could see the Angel in Mrs Cranks's eyes. He waited for her to invite him into her room, but she never did.

The only bathroom that worked properly was on Toby's floor. Everyone used it. Toby often had a bath in the middle of the night, as there was usually somebody in there with the door locked during the day when he tried to get in. Mrs Cranks spent hours in the bathroom. None of the toilets worked very well. They were usually blocked up. There were three toilets, one on each floor.

When Toby told Mr Braithwaite about the blocked toilets the landlord gave him a grin and said that Toby could use the sink in his room. 'I have so much to do, Mr Todd. All the time I work hard. I am a very busy gentleman. I try to do my best for you. In my own country, Mr Todd, I had nothing of luxury. England is paradise!'

Peter told Toby that he should try to sign on for the dole. 'It will give you the money, Toby. They will pay the rent! They won't give to me the dole. They say to me I am not enough English. But I work now. That is beautiful!'

One morning Toby set out for the unemployment office. Peter drew him a map, showing him how to get there. Toby couldn't make head or tail of the map but he found the place quite quickly after asking someone. The office wasn't far from the house. It was a huge building with several doors. Each entrance had a sign over it with a row of letters. A lot of people stood about outside reading newspapers. Toby kept going into the wrong entrance. Eventually he found the right entrance and was given forms to fill in and told he had to wait. The woman wouldn't lend him a pen. She told him to go out and buy one. Hers were always getting taken away. The place was full of young women with babies, and elderly men. There were Jamaicans like Fred and a few drunks. Many of the people had dogs. Toby sat there for an hour. One of the dogs squatted on the floor in front of a sign and relieved itself. The sign read *Please Wait Your Turn*.

When a woman began screaming her head off and then started a fight and began throwing chairs, Toby got up and stood by the door. The woman kept shrieking 'You're a pack of bloody mean bastards!' In the end when no one took any notice she threw herself on the floor. She kicked anyone who came near her and swore. Others began joining in and shouting. Toby left.

Mrs Cranks was coming out of her flat when Toby let himself back into the house. He'd ripped up the forms and thrown them into one of the rubbish bins. Mrs Cranks told him that she was off to stay with her sister in Bognor. Ringo her budgerigar had died. Toby helped her down the steps with her luggage. A taxi was due, she told him. She had Ringo's body in a cardboard box and said she was going to bury him in her sister's garden. She had buried all her budgerigars there. She was crying and her lips trembled. She had loved Ringo with all her heart, she told Toby. She'd had seven budgerigars and they'd all died. Toby tried to give her a hug, but

Mrs Cranks pulled away from him and stared at him as if he was mad.

That same night Peter came to Toby's room to tell him that he was moving out. 'I have meet the Englishmans who loves me!' Peter said. 'He is accountant with much money. It is beautiful! He wishes for me much happiness and grace. He gives me money for dancing again soon. He will take me to Bali where I again become dancing!' He was very excited, his words slurring. He gave Toby two mangoes, a bag of grapes and a photograph of himself as a parting gift. He kissed Toby on both cheeks as he said goodbye.

Peter was gone the next morning. Toby found his room empty, the door open, when he went up there. The posters had been taken down from the walls. Toby felt the whole house was becoming empty, with Mrs Cranks gone too. Though there was Annie above him, still making a racket and keeping him awake at night. He could hear other voices up there now on some nights, and a lot of singing.

In the early hours one morning, a few days later, Annie began screaming right out in the hall. It was long before dawn. Toby got up from his bed, unlocked his door and peered out. Annie was standing on the stairs leading up to her floor. She was brandishing a bread-knife. A man was backing away from her towards Toby. Annie was shrieking. 'You come in my flat again and I'll shove this knife in you, you English bastard!' she yelled.

Toby slammed his door and locked it when the man turned and ran towards him. Just before the time-switch light went off he saw that the man had a deep cut across his face. Blood was pouring down his chin. There was more noise and shouting and thumping. Then it went quiet.

After that for a few days Toby kept seeing the man coming and going from the house with a bandage across his face. Annie became quieter at night. She didn't scream. Adam started screaming even more than usual.

Weeks went by. Toby still looked for a job. He was given no interviews. He had little of Gran's money left. More plaster fell from the ceiling.

During the daytime Toby went on long hikes. He didn't want to meet Mr Braithwaite inside the house. He owed three weeks' rent. Mr Braithwaite didn't say much when Toby told him that he was waiting for some money to come and he'd pay the rent then.

Mr Braithwaite didn't like it. Toby didn't like lying. The landlord stared at Toby without smiling, each time they met in the hall.

Toby discovered Regent's Park and Primrose Hill, and then one sunny day he found Hampstead Heath. He had walked further each day, staying away from the house for hours. Some days he stayed in Regent's Park by the zoo watching elephants over the fence. Hampstead Heath seemed almost like the heath back home, except there were twice as many people and much more rubbish on the ground in some parts of it. A few people acted friendly. The trees and the grass and woodland made him feel close to Gran. He kept thinking he could hear her talking to him as he walked. There were ponds where people swam. There was a high hill where kites were flown and other ponds where men sat fishing. There were dogs everywhere, all shapes and sizes. Toby made friends with some of the dogs. He saw the same dogs each time he went back. Many had no collars and didn't appear to belong to anyone. A few people spoke to him kindly, about the weather. A lady in a black suit told him the place was called Parliament Hill. She gave him a sandwich. On wet days he sat, his duffle-coat hood pulled over his head, in an old wooden shelter. The shelter looked down on to a green and a stretch of woodland. Often on rainy days he saw no one there at all. He sat and thought about Gran. He listened to her voice.

'Life is like an old piece of bread, my lovely,' Gran's voice came to him. 'It's as hard as rock. You keep chewing on it and it'll get soft so you can swallow it.'

He'd never worked out what that really meant. Gran had said it so often he'd never thought about its meaning. But the words had made him feel calm.

During the next week he walked to Hampstead every day from Mimosa Crescent. When the sun was out he lay on the grass above one of the ponds and stared up at the sky. He'd fall asleep there. The sounds of voices coming to him were comforting. Some days the sun was hot. The soft calls of the ring-doves he kept seeing added peace to the quiet afternoons. On the Heath he felt that he was still with Gran and soon they'd walk home together and she'd cook hot soup and make toast in the kitchen. He could almost see her as well as hear her voice. 'It's your soul that keeps you going,' Gran would say. 'The body gets old and dithery. The soul stays the same, if you're lucky. In the end it flies off to a private place when the body gives up. The Angel comes.' Then she'd laugh. 'I'm a silly old sausage, my lovely, aren't I? I do talk a load of rot.'

Sometimes Toby stayed on the Heath all night. He slept in amongst the trees watching the moon when the sky was clear of cloud. He saw foxes and owls. He often saw other people wandering about. They were mostly men. No one bothered him. He walked back to Mimosa Crescent at dawn. The streets were quiet and empty. Toby walked slowly, listening to Gran's voice.

Mr Braithwaite began appearing at Calcutta Mansions every morning. He'd knock on Toby's door and try to open it. He'd call out through the keyhole. If he was in his room Toby would sit on the bed without moving. He sat quietly until the landlord went away. Mr Braithwaite was after the rent. There wasn't much Toby could do about that. When he went out he took his money with him. Now there was only enough of Gran's money left for food. That wouldn't last much longer. He knew Mr Braithwaite went through his things while he was out. The landlord had a spare key. At night, and when he was in his room during the day, Toby kept the door bolted from the inside as well as locked. There wasn't anyone he could ask for help. Peter had gone. Mrs Cranks hadn't come back. He couldn't ask Annie.

There was somebody else living in Mrs Cranks's flat, a young man whose face was covered in bright-red spots as if he had measles. He'd spoken to Toby only once and ignored him when they saw each other now. His name was Basil. Basil played pop music so loudly the whole house shook some nights. It was so loud that it drowned Annie and Adam's screaming. Basil offered Toby some pot and Toby said no. He didn't know what pot was. Basil laughed.

'I have had enough of you people!' Mr Braithwaite shouted through Toby's keyhole. 'I work my fingers to the bone! You are ungrateful!'

Late one night Toby was taking some bags of rubbish out to the bins. He had just walked down the steps and into the concrete yard. He'd put the rubbish down when he heard a noise at the far end, where the light from the street-lamp didn't reach. He could see two lumpy shapes pressed against the wall. All the lids of the rubbish bins had been removed. Some of the rubbish was lying on the ground.

'Who's there?' Toby called out.

The figures didn't respond. He heard one of them cough. After a moment the figures stood up and moved towards him into the light. They were two women. Apart from Annie, they were the oddest-looking women Toby had ever seen.

'What do you want?' Toby asked when they didn't say anything. One of the women was very tall. She was wearing a ragged fur coat and had a woollen scarf tied round her head. On top of the scarf was a straw hat with feathers sticking out of the top. The woman's legs were bare and she wore a pair of men's work boots on her feet. The other woman hid behind her, peering round her side. She seemed very short and large. She had a white plastic Tesco bag on her head. She wore men's boots too.

'How do you do?' the first woman said, moving further forward and holding out her hand. 'My name is Miss Lillian Pike. So lovely to meet you.' She spoke in a very posh voice.

'Hello,' said Toby. He shook Lillian's hand as she pushed it at him. Her hand was freezing cold and rough.

'We are two ladies of the town who do not wish to alarm you, sir. My friend's name is Olive Pinch. Pinch and Pike, that is us. We are a team.'

Under the scarf Lillian Pike's face looked pale and wrinkled. She had the largest nose Toby had seen on anyone. He liked her eyes. Suddenly Olive Pinch moved away from Lillian. She covered her eyes with her hands and started to giggle.

'Olive, molive, hold on to your knickers, sister,' Olive said loudly.

'My friend and I were seeking sustenance, dear boy,' Lillian said. 'We are not dangerous. We search, we find, we consume. Sometimes we flounder. We are ladies fallen on hard times. We are wanderers of the street. We are those whose lives are bruised and shaken.' Then she grinned.

Toby didn't know what to say. Olive, unseen by Lillian, poked her tongue out at him.

'Shaken, bacon, show us your jewellery, mister,' Olive muttered.

Lillian said in a loud whisper 'Quiet, Ollie' and patted her on the arm.

'Where do you live?' asked Toby, after the women had stared at him for a long time.

Olive took a step closer. She was screwing up her face and squinting at Toby, sucking her top lip. On her chin were two large sores. Her face was round and also pale. She was only about five feet tall and very thin. She was wearing several coats and other clothes that made her look huge. The coats were all different lengths. 'Food!' she shouted. 'Food!' Then she added: 'Food, mood, rude, crude, pop the question sailor and show us your goods!' And went into fits of giggling and coughing.

Lillian spoke as if Olive hadn't said anything at all. 'We live in the moonshine, in the sunshine. Wherever we hang our hats is home,' she said. 'We are rovers, sir, we are gypsy folk. The world leaves us to defend our honour! We have no home or roost in which to ruffle our feathers.'

'My Gran was a gypsy,' Toby heard himself saying. He kept staring at Olive.

Seeing him staring, Olive stuck her tongue out. She crossed her eyes and wiggled her tongue up and down. Lillian slapped her wrist. Olive turned her back and became perfectly still.

'She is often naughty,' Lillian whispered, leaning forward. She smiled. In her eyes Toby thought he saw the Angel. Her eyes were beautiful. They were large and very dark. Lillian looked tired and ill yet she had a face that reminded Toby of Gran. They were both about Gran's age.

'Where do you sleep?' Toby asked.

Lillian shrugged. 'Sometimes we walk. Sometimes we run. We sleep to dream, London is our home, the streets are our bedrooms,' she said. Then her voice changed and she winked at Toby. 'I don't always talk like I'm deranged,' she whispered. 'I do it for Ollie. Ollie appreciates it.'

Olive had sat down on the concrete. Crossing her legs, she rested her head against the wall at her side. She started mumbling softly to herself.

'You could come up to my room if you want,' Toby suddenly said. He didn't know why he said it. He just thought of Gran being there and the words came out of their own accord.

Lillian said nothing for a moment. She turned her face away. Then she sniffed loudly. 'You are too kind, gentle sir,' she whispered. 'Too kind.'

'Harridan begone!' Olive shouted. 'Sleep, beep, marry and weep, show us your rude bits, Rodney!'

Ten minutes later Lillian and Olive were sitting in Toby's room. They sat on the floor in front of the glowing electric fire. Toby had made mugs of tea. He had only two mugs. He pretended he didn't want any tea himself.

'You'll get warm by the fire,' he said. 'I like helping people. I used to when I was back home.'

Neither of them said anything to that. He sat on the edge of the bed not knowing what else he could say. Olive was tucking into a plate of bread and sardines. He'd given them a plate of food each, with two apples. Olive had grabbed both apples and shoved them into the pockets of an inner coat. 'Warm, storm, dorm, give us a hand-out, Harry,' she mumbled, spitting out breadcrumbs.

'Manners, Ollie. Manners, dear girl,' said Lillian, staring down at her plate of food.

They ate in silence, pushing the bread and sardines into their mouths so fast Toby thought they must be half starved. He wished he had more food to offer. Both women stared up at him from time to time. Lillian looked scared. She kept glancing towards the door and seemed to be listening.

Above them came a sudden heavy thumping on the ceiling. Olive jumped and Lillian yelled and Olive spilt tea down the front of her coats. She lifted up the edge of one coat and sucked on a damp patch. Then she muttered: 'Bombs, Lil, bombs. Doodlebugs, doodlebugs, rum tee tee.'

Lillian said nothing, her mouth full of food.

'That's only Annie,' Toby said. 'She lives here too, upstairs. There's a lot of people live here at Calcutta Mansions.'

Olive was staring at Toby with her mouth open. Half a sardine sat on her chin. It was squashed into one of her sores. She looked at Toby as if she hadn't noticed him in the room until that very moment.

'What is your name? What do they call you?' Lillian asked.

'Toby,' said Toby. 'Toby Todd.'

'You are an Angel of mercy,' Lillian whispered.

'Annie, fanny, canny, watching the blue roses grow,' Olive was muttering, squinting up at the ceiling.

Lillian leaned towards Toby and whispered: 'She's a mite vacant upstairs, dear boy. She has had the trials of the world on her dear shoulders.' Then she smiled. There was colour in her face now. Her eyes darted round the room. Toby saw that her hands shook all the time. 'Ollie used to live in this house. Her husband owned it,' Lillian whispered.

'Bums away!' Olive suddenly shouted and passed wind so loudly that Toby jumped in fright.

After they'd finished eating, Olive fell asleep. She just rolled on to her side, put her hands up beneath her head and lay there very still. Lillian moved over to her and kissed her on the cheek. Gently, she eased the plastic bag from Olive's head. Olive had only a little scattering of hair. The front of her head was bald and very white. Toby could see a white scar there. The scar was jagged and looked raw.

'She'll sleep anywhere, bless her,' Lillian whispered. 'I do trust you will not object, dear boy. She is an unwell lady. I do love her so.'

Toby shrugged and smiled. He couldn't take his eyes off the scar on Olive's head. Lillian saw him staring but said nothing.

Lillian and Toby sat there in silence for a long while. The house about them was quiet. Rain began to patter against the window-pane.

After a time Lillian began to talk about Olive. Olive had lived in the house throughout the war, while London was being bombed. She had lost the house years ago when her husband Gerald had died. Lillian wasn't sure of the details. She had brought Olive back to the house numerous times, trying to get Mr Braithwaite to let Olive and her have a room. He would never let them in. Lillian spoke to Toby in quite an ordinary way as she told Olive's story. Olive had told Lillian that she had been in and out of mental hospitals after she'd lost the house, until she'd run away. Lillian had found her on the street and the two had become friends. They'd come to rely on each other. They had found a love that only women understood. 'I don't think she fully comprehends where she is any more,' Lillian said. 'It gets worse. She would have been terrified of coming in if she'd known. Her mind's getting like mush, the poor darling. I don't think she will go on much longer. Winter is so hard. They took away part of her dear brain, you know, in hospital. She told me so. So wicked, so cruel.'

Lillian had been living on the streets for years. She had given up her life before, she told Toby. She wouldn't tell him why. 'We all have memories that crush,' she said. 'I ran away from mine, dear boy. Ran like the clappers. I've lived like this ever since. In London you can. No one bothers you. It's quite simple. No one bothers you because people here are far too busy to want to be bothered. But it would be so lovely to have a proper home.'

Lillian's hands didn't stop shaking as she talked. She looked so tired that her face seemed to sink in on itself.

At Christmas a charity took them in, Lillian said. They were fed turkey and roast potatoes and given new clothes. Newspaper reporters came and took photographs. Some of the others had been filmed last Christmas and the film was shown on television so that the people who had homes could feel there was something being done. The rest of the year she and Olive slept where they could. Mostly in doorways. Sometimes they went to a Salvation Army hostel, but Olive hated having to sing hymns before she was given any food. Lillian had lived on the streets for so long she knew no other way to live. She had met so many others who had not begun living on the streets through choice as she had. Many had had no choice at all. Yet she and Olive did all right together. They got by. 'We have life. We have life in our bodies yet,' she whispered, hanging her head. 'The world leaves us to it. London is a cold, dank place for us ladies of the town.'

Outside, the rain was falling more heavily. Toby could hear Annie up above, moving about her room. The sounds seemed muffled. He stared at Lillian, who was falling asleep where she sat. Soon she too lay on the floor beside Olive, in front of the heater. Toby sat on the bed staring down at their faces as they both slept. He thought about Gran. He thought he had seen the Angel in Lillian's eyes but wasn't sure now as her eyes had been filled with pain. He couldn't understand why people had to live so long without a home, without shelter. He sat there for a long time. Towards dawn he lay back on the bed. The room stayed quiet.

Toby woke up suddenly. It was morning. The room was freezing cold and it smelled. Olive was still asleep on the floor. She was sucking her thumb. Lillian wasn't in the room. Toby had been woken up by someone shouting, and when he saw that his door was slightly open he got off the bed and tiptoed out into the hall. Lillian was standing with her back against the wall at the top of the stairs. She was facing Mr Braithwaite. Her arms were raised and her hands were clenched into fists. Mr Braithwaite turned, as Toby appeared.

'What is this, Mr Todd? This is not good. This person, she is a blessed tramp! She says you are having her stay here with you. I want an explanation!'

Toby started to speak, when Olive suddenly appeared in the hall behind him. She leaned round Toby, holding on to him and squinting. When she saw Mr Braithwaite she pointed at the landlord and shrieked: 'There he is, that's the man! Leave, heave, on your horse you sodding darky!' Then she pushed past Toby, nearly knocking him over, and tried to hit Mr Braithwaite with her fists. She carried on shrieking, hitting out with her arms in all directions.

Lillian rushed forward and pulled Olive away. Olive had torn off Mr Braithwaite's purple turban. He was bald underneath. Lillian started kicking Mr Braithwaite as he had hold of Olive by her wrists and was trying to shove her down the stairs. He didn't say a word in the struggle. He looked so angry that Toby tried to get between the three of them. Lillian managed to drag Olive with her and in a moment they were running down the stairs across the hallway and out of the front door. Mr Braithwaite ran after them, shouting now in his own language and in English. Before Toby caught up with them Lillian and Olive were half-way down the steps into the crescent.

Mr Braithwaite grabbed hold of Toby so roughly as he tried to get past him that Toby fell against the door. 'I will not have this!' Mr Braithwaite was shouting. 'I will not have such goings on in my house!'

Toby clambered to his feet and ran down the steps. He couldn't see Lillian or Olive anywhere. Mr Braithwaite stood very still on the steps. He had covered his eyes with his hands. He was weeping. His shoulders shook and he was moaning as if he was in pain.

When Toby got back to the house Mr Braithwaite wasn't to be seen anywhere. The front door had been left open. Toby had run down two side-streets looking for Lillian and Olive. They had simply vanished.

It rained for the rest of the day. The sun which had come out in the morning became covered by cloud. A wind had begun to blow along the crescent, dragging newspapers and plastic bags high into the air. Late in the afternoon Toby went out again, hoping to find his new friends. Mr Braithwaite had not returned. Toby saw no sign of Lillian and Olive, though he walked for miles in the rain. On the way back he felt so upset he pretended that he was going home to Gran, who would have cooked supper in the kitchen. Sitting at the table would be George reading his newspaper and Alice would be washing her hair in the bathroom and singing 'I Can't Get No Satisfaction'. Thunder was sounding from the sky. The late afternoon had become grey and bleak. Mimosa Crescent looked empty as if everyone had moved out of the houses. Toby was soaked through from the rain. He was shivering and very cold.

His key wouldn't turn in the lock when he tried to let himself in. It turned only a little and the door wouldn't open. Toby pushed at the door but it wouldn't budge. He rang the bell but nobody came. When he looked down he saw his rucksack sitting in a corner on the top step. On the rucksack was pinned a note. He picked up the rucksack and slowly read the note. It was signed *E. Braithwaite, Landlord*. It told him that he did not have a flat at Calcutta Mansions any longer. Someone else would be getting it. He had let tramps in. He owed many weeks' rent. Some of his things had been taken towards payment of his great debt. It is a very sad state of affairs, the note ended.

Toby sat down on the steps. He read the note again and again. Nobody left the house or came up the steps to go in. He heard no sounds from inside. From time to time he rang the bell, keeping his finger on it. Once he thought he heard a voice inside, shouting. He stared up at the windows but could see no lights. Several hours went past. He couldn't understand why no one appeared. The rain began to fall more heavily and the sky and the street in front of him seemed very dark now that night had fallen. Eventually, having tried to sleep, Toby picked up his rucksack, rubbed his face with his hands and walked down the steps into the street. The rain, being blown across Mimosa Crescent as if it was alive, fell so solidly that he lost sight of the house behind him as he left it, when he turned to look back.

4 The House in Pudding Lane

Toby walked all the way to Hampstead Heath after he left Mimosa Crescent. Eventually the rain stopped. The wind died down. The pavements glistened under the yellow street-lamps. Along Haverstock Hill he thought he saw Lillian and Olive, but when he hurried across the road to get closer to them it was not them at all, just two old women standing outside a baker's shop in the dark, talking. They both stared at him as if he'd made a rude noise, before he carried on. As he walked he kept thinking about Annie and old Mrs Cranks as well as Lillian and Olive. He thought they might have all become his friends if things had been different. As one-armed Cyril had been his friend, and old Mrs Kent. Even Mrs Green, who'd been scared of Hitler.

He'd never had any friends his own age. He'd never got to know anyone very well at school. Everyone at school seemed to have had special friends except him. There'd been gangs and clubs but he'd never been asked to join any of them. Gran had told him that she was his best mate. He hadn't needed to be in a gang with her around. He'd never thought that he'd been missing out. He'd been happy being with Gran, helping Cyril and helping Betsy Molesworthy and young Mr Grundy before he'd been taken away. Toby had enjoyed doing things for them, looking after them. They'd liked him being there. He'd made them laugh and feel young again. He knew Gran had approved of that. As he walked, their faces whirled about inside his head.

Toby hadn't planned to go back to the Heath. He just walked, remembering how he'd lain on the grass there and felt peaceful and watched old men fishing in the ponds. He thought it might be the best place to go until he could decide what to do. In one of the small pockets of his duffle-coat he had found a five-pound note he hadn't known was there, and felt lucky. He could buy sandwiches. He could live on sandwiches for days if he had to. He'd be all right. He reckoned that Gran might be watching out for him from wherever she had ended up with the Angel. He felt that she was close to him and inside his head saying all the things she used to say that he'd heard so often. Her voice always calmed him. He kept on walking without stopping, his rucksack over his shoulder, crossing streets and turning corners and looking ahead as if he knew where he was going. After a while there were few people about. A light, drizzling rain began to fall. He sheltered under an awning for a while, crouched down so that no one would notice him. His duffle-coat kept him warm.

Finally, wet and tired, his legs aching, he found the Heath almost by accident. It had stopped drizzling by then but the night was dark. Cloud lay low and heavy across the sky. For a time he walked in amongst trees, trying to recognize which part of the Heath he had entered. Too tired to really care, he lay down in amongst some bushes on a dry patch and, wrapped in his duffle-coat, he fell asleep. He did not wake up until the first light of morning.

Being on the Heath during the next couple of days did give Toby a sense of peace. The days were warm and mostly sunny. He found a café and bought sandwiches and cartons of flavoured milk and he ate and drank at the place called Parliament Hill, overlooking the ponds. He walked and lay on the grass staring up at the sky trying not to think about anything, sun-bathing in the afternoons as if he was there for only a couple of hours. No one took any notice of him. The trees were already covered in leaves and the grass was lush and it smelled sweet. There was a quietness everywhere. He liked being there. It felt right, and even safe. At night time he found places to sleep where he was not disturbed, except for the sound of foxes. He saw several hurrying past at a distance. Sometimes he spotted stray dogs, which kept out of his way in the moonlight.

Toby felt lonelier than he had ever felt before. He missed his room at Calcutta Mansions. Sometimes at night he would hear Gran's voice so clearly. Waking up with a start and calling out, thinking that she was close by, he kept trying to see her face in his mind. But she was just a blur. He could hear only her voice talking to him, whispering to him from the trees when he lay below them. In his dreaming she was always there. He kept feeling that he was waiting but didn't know what he was waiting for.

During the day he began to notice an old man. The man wore a long tweed coat that trailed to the ground. He never took the coat off even when the day was at its warmest. What was strange about him was that around him on the ground was gathered a circle of pigeons. There were six of them. The man was usually standing under trees when Toby spotted him. He never moved out into the open. Whenever anyone came near to where he stood, the man would move back into deeper cover until the people had gone past. No one seemed to take any notice of him, just as nobody took any notice of Toby. Toby did not see the man in any of the areas where there were a lot of people but he kept sighting him. The man stayed in shadow most of the time. Toby would suddenly see him as if the old man had just appeared by magic. The pigeons followed the man wherever he went. They stayed about him in a circle and did not fly off or even try to. Sometimes he fed them with pieces of bread he pulled out from the pockets of his long coat. The pigeons would peck at the bread on the ground and, while they ate, the man would peer up into the sky as if he was looking for something there. He began to notice Toby watching him. He would point to the sky and mouth words that Toby could not hear. He did not smile at Toby. His face was pale and deeply lined as though covered in scars. His eyes were jet black. On his head he wore an odd purple cap that had tassels hanging down its sides. His hair was long and a dirty grey colour. Toby started to think that only he could see the old man. The people who did walk past him acted as if they could not see him at all. Toby began to follow the old man, trying to get closer to him.

For a while the man would hurry off whenever he saw Toby coming after him. He'd disappear into thickets and when Toby got there there'd be no sign of him or his pigeons. They were not racing pigeons, as one-armed Cyril had owned. They looked like wood-pigeons. One of the birds limped badly and seemed thinner than the others. The man kept reaching down to touch it and shaking his head. The bird didn't try to get away from him as it was touched. Late one afternoon at dusk Toby spotted the old man bent over on the grass at the side of a wooden shelter where Toby had often sat when he had come to the Heath from Mimosa Crescent. Toby walked slowly across to where the man was crouching. Nearby, the pigeons were standing in a line, not moving. They didn't even stir when Toby reached the man's side. He looked up and stared at Toby and then nodded his head. Up close he had crossed eyes and a long scar that stretched from below his right eye to his chin. At his feet one of the pigeons lay dead.

'You have the vision,' the old man said. His voice was low and deep and he spoke with a foreign accent. Then, looking away, he held his hand over the pigeon's body, lowering it until it rested on the dead bird's breast. The pigeon lay on its back. Its neck and head were twisted. It seemed to have been strangled. 'The time draws closer,' the man said. 'It comes with all the signs.' He stood on his feet and backed away from Toby as if he was suddenly scared, still staring at him, a frown on his face. 'Are you the redeemer?' he asked. 'Have you finally descended? Are you the saviour? You are too early. It is not the hour.'

'Are those your pigeons?' Toby asked.

The man didn't answer. His head jerked and he blinked. He looked away, moving his lips. He was talking to himself. His eyes darted back to peer into Toby's face. He whispered: 'Perhaps you are the demon. He plots my death.'

Around them the light was fading. It seemed so quiet that Toby thought he could hear the man breathing. After a moment he pointed up at the sky and made a stabbing movement with his hands. Then the man said softly: 'They fail to deliver the prophet. He must come before the true night. Five are left. Who will guard, once life has finished? Jehovah does not listen.'

The old man let his arm fall down to his side. He hung his head. Turning away, he started to hurry off. The pigeons followed him, fluttering about him so that they again formed a circle at his feet. Toby looked around. There was no one about in any direction. He and the old man seemed to be the only people on the Heath. The day had grown dark, but as the figure moved away from him, surrounded by the pigeons, the light around Toby slowly got brighter. People who had been sitting on the grass, or walking their dogs, had disappeared. When Toby looked for him, the pigeon man had moved out of sight. Toby ran forward, looking in amongst the trees behind the shelter and up the low rise, but there was no sign of him at all. In the distance he could hear several dogs barking and then a woman crying out. Toby was alone beneath the trees. He went back to where the dead pigeon lay on the ground, its body cushioned by leaves. The bird's neck was broken. On its breast was a small circle of dried blood. Toby dug a hole in the earth with a stick and buried the bird. The corpse was still warm when he lifted it up.

Toby did not see the pigeon man again after they had spoken. He looked for him everywhere he walked but there was no sign of him. Toby wondered if he had imagined the whole thing. It hadn't seemed real. He didn't understand what the pigeon man could have meant. He'd spoken as if he was reciting a poem. It was an hour before Toby started to see people dotted about across the Heath. They were all a long distance away. For the rest of that day the air had stayed very still and close, without any breeze at all.

Toby hurried away from the area, feeling the whole time that someone was watching him.

He'd been having a wash in one of the ponds very early one morning, close to where he'd spent the night, when he saw a woman coming towards him from a distance. It was only just beginning to grow light. There was a mist lying across the surface of the pond. Toby had made his mind up to leave the Heath. He had used up the money he had found in his coat pocket on sandwiches and drinks and he hadn't eaten for almost a full day. He knew he couldn't stay on the Heath any longer. He'd tried not to think about where he might go. He'd searched for berries and plants and even rabbits, trying to remember what Gran had taught him. But he'd found nothing that he thought he could eat. He hadn't been able to sleep at night, thinking he could hear strange noises and voices when no one was anywhere near. He was scared the pigeon man would come back, appear out of nowhere when Toby wasn't expecting him. During the dark hours the Heath had suddenly become a place where he didn't want to be. The strange silences that lasted for a long time kept him sitting up under trees and watching, in case something happened. He kept seeing the pigeon man's eyes. They had seemed to have had no pupils in them, just a blackness.

Toby had taken off his shirt and vest and was drying himself with the shirt when he looked up and saw the woman. He'd never seen anyone on this part of the Heath so early before. Toby stayed squatting at the edge of the pond and stared at her. The woman looked quite ordinary. She appeared not to have noticed him. She was looking around her and calling out something he couldn't hear. She was wearing a light-brown mac but her feet were bare. In the near-dark her face seemed to shine. She didn't look old or young. She looked frail. She was walking slowly and carefully. Just as she went to move out of his sight she suddenly slipped on the wet grass and fell sideways, down into a ditch she'd been walking alongside. Toby heard her cry out. The woman didn't appear again as he thought she would. Then he heard her calling out for help.

Toby pulled on his clothes. Looking about him he still couldn't see anyone else in any direction. Picking up his rucksack he began to walk across to the path and along it towards where the woman had disappeared. Just as he neared the spot a small black and white dog appeared. It growled and showed its teeth when it saw Toby, then started to wag its tail. It was trailing a lead and acted excited.

The woman was on her side in the ditch. She was lying in a few inches of muddy water, struggling to sit up and gasping. Toby, ignoring the dog, which was barking loudly, slid down into the ditch beside the woman, taking hold of her arm.

'I'm afraid I've injured myself,' the woman said in a shaky voice. 'I'm terribly sorry. I'm so clumsy.'

When Toby tried to lift her the woman managed to get up so she was sitting in the water. The dog was frantic. It raced up and down along the top of the ditch, barking and whining.

The woman said in a loud voice: 'Bella, would you stop that this instant!'

The dog sat back on its haunches, watching them with its tongue out, its tail wagging. Toby helped the woman up out of the ditch. She sat on the edge trying to brush at her mac with her hands. After that she looked up, staring Toby up and down. 'I thought I was done for that time,' she said. 'You must be an Angel. I've never imagined anyone else wanting to be out here at this time of morning.'

Toby just smiled his slow smile.

The woman stretched out her arm to him, smiling gently back. 'Well, I am most grateful,' she said. 'Most grateful, my dear. I believe you've saved my bacon. The name's Wickham, Alicia Wickham. Who are you, out here at the crack of doom?'

'My name's Toby,' said Toby. 'Toby Todd.'

Alicia Wickham stared at him for a while. 'Jolly good,' she said. Then she added: 'Well, my dear, I think I've injured my ankle. If you'd be so kind as to help me home I shall make you a cup of tea and whatever else you might fancy. You look as though you need something.'

Alicia Wickham lived just outside the Heath, she told Toby, in a small street called Pudding Lane. Toby supported her as she limped along one of the paths in the direction she'd pointed. The path led upwards out of the Heath and through an open gateway. Her house was the first on the left along the small street, which she told him was private. It took them a long time to reach it. Alicia could hardly walk at all, even with Toby's arm round her waist. She was very tall. The dog Bella belonged to her, she said. She had been looking for Bella when she'd slipped and fallen. Bella had pulled out of Alicia's grip and run off.

'She does it all the time. She assumes it's what I want her to do as if it were some game,' Alicia told Toby as they struggled towards the house. 'Stupid animal. She gets the wanderlust. No sense at all.'

The house was very large and old and built of dark-red brick and tile. There were statues of weird animals on the chimneys. The house stood behind a high brick wall which was covered in ivy. It looked run-down and neglected. Alicia got Toby to open a small side-gate that led into an overgrown garden. The garden was choked with tall weeds and stumps of dead trees and bushes gone wild.

'My old gardener died on me, would you believe it,' Alicia said in a breathless voice as they moved along the narrow path towards the front door. 'Though the dear man was just as neglectful when he was alive. He had dreadful arthritis.' Then she laughed. She acted cheerful though Toby sensed that she was in pain.

She handed him the key to open the front door after fumbling for it once they'd climbed the steps. On either side of the steps sat two concrete lions covered in moss. Toby opened the massive door and helped her into the hall. Alicia was breathing heavily. Her face was very pale. She gestured for him to help her through to a room leading off from the right. The room was dark. Bella had followed them from the Heath and had raced into the house in front of them as soon as Toby had the door open. She disappeared down the hallway at the side of the staircase.

'Put me down on the sofa if you will,' Alicia asked Toby, her voice sounding weak. 'There's a rug somewhere. There, on the floor.'

After he had made Alicia comfortable Toby found the kitchen and made a pot of tea. Alicia told him where everything was kept. She asked him to fetch a bottle of aspirins from a cupboard beneath the sink. The kitchen was enormous. It was long and narrow and seemed empty. Along the windows which faced out towards the Heath were rows of plants in pots. The plants seemed to have been dead for some time. The floor of the kitchen was dirty and stained. The room smelled. Bags of rubbish and newspapers were piled up in one corner, half-way to the ceiling. Bella had followed Toby into the kitchen and watched his every move. She hadn't growled at him again and stared with her head on one side. Toby patted her and she licked his hands, thumping her tail on the floor. The kettle took ages to boil, on an old gas cooker that was filthy with grime.

Alicia was leaning back on the sofa with the rug drawn across her legs when Toby carried in the tea-tray. Her eyes were closed and she had a hand over her mouth. She tried to sit up when Toby entered the room. Bella had followed, leaping up on to the sofa and settling down with a loud whine. Alicia ignored her.

'Bless you, my dear,' Alicia said. 'What would I have done without you?'

'I could call your doctor,' Toby suggested. 'Your ankle looks swollen.' Alicia had started to examine it.

'No, no, my dear, that won't be necessary. I'll be fine once I've taken some aspirins and had a little rest. I don't wish to delay you any longer than necessary. I do apologize about all this. I'm such an old fool. You're being most kind. I'm growing clumsier every week that passes. Never let anyone tell you that getting older brings harmony. It brings nothing but discomfort and other non-sense. I detest it.'

'You're not old,' Toby said, and grinned.

'Am I not?' Alicia asked, and laughed.

The room they were in was filled with books and piles of magazines. There were shelves from floor to ceiling along the walls, stacked with books that looked very old. Alicia had got Toby to open the curtains. The room, like the kitchen, was huge, with cobwebs across the corners of the ceiling. It was cluttered with furniture, half of which looked broken. On small tables there was a mass of china figurines and huge ornaments. In the fireplace, which was almost as tall as Toby, sat a pile of blackened logs. Ash spread out across the hearth on to the carpet.

'I detest doctors almost as much as I detest feeling ill,' Alicia said, after she had sipped her tea and swallowed several aspirins. 'Half of them are senile. They charge ludicrous prices.' She stared at Toby as he looked about him.

'I live mostly in this room, my dear,' she added. 'I must apologize for the state it's in. I used to have a woman who did, but she decided one day that doing was too beneath her so she upped and left. I haven't bothered since. Dreadful, isn't it?'

'It's a nice house,' Toby said. 'I've never been in such a big house before.'

'Have you not?' Alicia said. 'It is a mausoleum. I'm part of it, I fear. I suppose I should have sold up years ago. Lord knows, it's worth selling. Draughty old place. But it is home. It holds all memory for me. My son will inherit it one day when I'm gone. He'll be welcome to it.'

Alicia had a son called Antony, she told Toby. He was living abroad, somewhere in the Middle East. He travelled a lot, she said. She hardly ever saw him. 'And what were you doing on the Heath so early at your age, child?' she asked after a second cup of tea.

Toby had fetched more hot water from the kitchen. Bella had not stirred from her place at the foot of the sofa.

Toby shrugged. 'I was having a wash in the pond,' he said. He felt his face grow hot.

'Jolly good,' Alicia said slowly. She looked at him with a small frown. After a moment she added: 'Forgive me, but you are homeless, aren't you?'

Toby nodded.

'I thought so,' Alicia said. 'Thought that the moment I spotted you. I did see you, you know, before my fall. Wouldn't have called out otherwise. I don't miss much over there, know it too well. Told myself you were living rough. I've been reading about it, you know. In *The Times*. You're far too young, of course, but there it is. The world has become quite incomprehensible. Not as it was in my day. Listen to me going on. Tell me, if you don't mind my asking, have you run away from home, child?'

Toby started to answer but then looked away from her out of the window.

'I'm sorry, my dear. How insensitive of me. I don't mean to pry. So crude. I'm alone so much that talking to someone, anyone, becomes a little like interrogation. Questions jump out and manners are forgotten. Would you like something to eat before you go? There are some eggs, I believe, and what's left of a leg of lamb. I'm sure you must be ravenous.'

Toby looked over at her and smiled. Alicia smiled back, and kept nodding. Her eyes began to narrow as she looked at him, then they opened wide. Somehow she reminded Toby of Lillian Pike. She had Lillian's large nose and the same eyes. He could see only kindness in her face. He couldn't tell if she had the Angel in her eyes. They looked at each other for a long time, Alicia smiling gently, reaching down to stroke Bella's head.

'I can see you have had hard times,' Alicia said eventually. 'It's there, so clearly. I see such things. The eyes do mirror the heart.'

In a moment Alicia had fallen asleep. Her head drooped and her eyes closed and she let out a long sigh. Toby sat near her in one of the armchairs. He stared about the room. He tried to count all the books but there were too many. His eyes blurred from staring at them. Quietly he got up out of the chair and wandered about the room. Bella watched him from the sofa. Every time he glanced at the dog she would wag her tail and let out a little whine. Alicia Wickham didn't stir. She lay sleeping so soundly that Toby worried if she was all right. Her face had got back some colour. She looked peaceful and smiled in her sleep. He didn't want to disturb her. He thought it might be best if he just left, but something kept him there in the room. He walked along the bookshelves and stared at all the titles. Some of the books seemed to be in a foreign language. Their spines were ripped. Most of them were covered in a thick layer of dust. There was a moving set of stairs at the far corner, attached to the shelves. Toby had a sudden urge to use it but was too scared he would wake Alicia up. A pair of french windows led out on to a concrete patio, on which sat dozens of plants in tubs. Many were lying on their side and looked dead like the plants in the kitchen. He could see parts of the Heath from the windows and a small area of a pond over the top of the brick wall that surrounded the house. The garden was so overgrown it looked as if it hadn't been touched for years. The curtains at the windows were frayed and dusty. Cobwebs hung down behind them. On an old piano on the far side of the room sat photographs in silver frames. There were two photographs of a young woman dressed in fancy costume, standing on a stage in what looked like a theatre. When he looked closely he saw they were signed with Alicia's name. There were photographs of a little boy who, Toby reckoned, must be Antony, and others of a man. Toby couldn't see any photographs of anyone else. In the corners of the room lay folded-up sheets, a huge pile of them. The air in the room smelled musty.

Toby sat down again in the chair watching Alicia's face. Bella watched Toby. The dog did not take her eyes off him. The chair Toby sat in had wings on its sides. After a while he rested his head and fell asleep.

When he woke up the room was empty. He could hear a dog barking outside and thought it must be Bella. As he sat there Alicia put her head round the half-closed door. She smiled when she saw he was awake.

'Well, there you are. With us again,' she said. 'Look at me, on my feet. I feel so much better.' She hobbled into the room, using a wooden walking-stick. She had a bandage tied round her ankle. The bandage looked like a piece of ripped sheet. Her feet were still bare. 'A little rest does wonders, my dear,' she said. 'I feel quite renewed. I've prepared something to eat. You slept for quite a while. I could not bear to disturb you.'

'I didn't mean to fall asleep,' said Toby.

'Of course you didn't! You must have been exhausted, helping me back here. Come, I've made some soup and toast. It's all ready.'

Toby followed her out along the hall and into the kitchen. Alicia had set out the toast and soup on an old rickety table which stood just outside the back door. 'You can have this as a starter,' she said, smiling at him, beckoning him out through the door. 'It's the least I can do. I've poached some eggs and there's cold meat. You shall feast and tell me all about yourself. I feel you've been sent to me. Things do happen for a reason.'

Toby didn't talk as he ate. Alicia sat and sipped at a cup of tea but ate nothing at all. Bella had rushed round from the front of the house and sat at Toby's feet, staring up at him with her bulging eyes.

'What sort of dog is it?' Toby asked once he'd finished the soup. Alicia had brought him a plate of poached eggs with slices of cold mutton.

'King Charles spaniel,' Alicia told him. 'Or she's supposed to be. I doubt she would win any prizes at Cruft's, bless her. She stops me from going insane. We never normally entertain visitors. Bella's my life blood some days.'

Toby found himself telling Alicia all about Gran and George and Alice going off to America. He couldn't stop talking about them once he'd started. Alicia watched him without saying a word, nodding every so often. She thought it an omen, she said, when Toby finally stopped, that she and Toby's mother had almost the same name. Toby didn't tell her about Calcutta Mansions. He didn't think she'd want to know everything. There was too much to tell.

'Have you found out if your mother has returned?' Alicia asked after a time.

Toby shook his head.

Alicia sighed. She kept wiping her mouth with a handkerchief and stared up at the sky. 'Jolly good,' she said eventually.

It was warm where they sat. It was so quiet Toby thought he could hear voices coming from the Heath.

'I feel as though I've lost touch with the world,' Alicia told him. 'My days are rather cloistered, my dear. Nothing changes. Nothing happens. Sometimes I think I am just waiting until my own door shuts. I have had a most fortunate life. I shouldn't grumble. I was an actress for most of it. Damned good at it too, if I may be so bold.' Then after a moment she added: 'I really do not know what to say. I don't understand how your own father could have just upped and left you. So cruel. So very unkind. Thoughtless. I'm afraid I have little time for what passes as family these days. I suppose I hide from life in this mausoleum. Behind my walls I sleep and dream. Dreadful, isn't it? However, you should be able to get away with solitude if you choose it.'

'If I had a house like this I'd never leave it,' said Toby.

Alicia leaned forward, staring into his face. She was frowning. She patted him on the arm. 'Bless you,' she said. 'Bless you for saying that.'

For a few minutes neither of them spoke. Alicia stared into the garden as if Toby wasn't there at all. When she looked back at him she said: 'Oh my goodness, I'm being so rude. I'm not accustomed to company. I find company rather difficult. You must forgive me.'

'Does your ankle still hurt?' Toby asked.

Bella, once Toby had stopped eating, had moved away and was lying on the grass in some shade, stretched out on her side.

'Only a little,' Alicia said. 'I've learned to be resilient. Never mind me. We have to decide what to do about you, don't we? I cannot possibly allow you to just walk off. I know you're thinking about it. It's in your face. I meant what I said. You've been sent.'

She stared at him, holding her handkerchief in her closed fists on the table. The table was so old its paint was peeling from having been in the sun for too long.

'Do forgive me,' she said. 'You might wish to refuse, but would you consider staying here for a while? I have so many rooms. You could do some work about the place if you felt you had to. I'd pay you, of course. Goodness knows, the old place needs some youth, and care. I can't let you sleep another night on the Heath. It's too dreadful to think about. Do you think you might tolerate a vague old battle-axe like me?'

Toby shrugged. Then he nodded and gave her a smile. 'You're not a battle-axe,' he said.

Alicia grinned. 'Well then, it's settled! Let's just suppose you stay here for a day or two, until my ankle gets better. I'll need help. There's no doubt about that. Will that suffice?'

Toby nodded. 'I don't want any of your money,' he said.

'Fine, then I shan't give you any. You can earn your keep. You can become my servant. I can order you about and treat you with disdain. I'd enjoy that.'

Toby stared at her for a minute until she began to laugh. 'You look altogether too serious, my dear,' she said. 'Do relax. I was making an attempt at humour. I want you to stay. I think it might be rather delicious. You don't have to do a thing if you don't wish to. Except cheer me up. You can read, I take it?'

'Yes,' Toby said.

'Well then, you can read aloud to me in the evenings. I adore having Dickens read aloud by candlelight. Only way to hear him.

There, that shall be your duty.'

'I could clear up your garden,' Toby said. 'I used to help my Gran in the garden.'

'We'll see, shall we?' Alicia said. She stared at him with a grin. 'You look worried. You'll be quite safe here. Have no doubt about that. What are you worrying about?'

'I don't know,' Toby answered. Then he said quietly: 'It might be too much. You said you're used to being on your own.'

'Nonsense. You've bucked me up already. I'll employ you officially as my new gardener if it'd make you feel more relaxed. We could work out a proper contractual arrangement. We could be boringly formal. But I'd rather you just stayed as my new friend. I think you and I would get along famously. Look, we've hardly stopped talking. I need company. You need a roof. Fair swap. It's perfectly acceptable. What better reasoning than that, child? You might like to sleep in the Blue Room, upstairs at the back. It has a glorious view of the Heath. Only room left with a proper bed.'

'It's very kind of you,' Toby said.

Alicia smiled vaguely and then she began to nod her head vigorously. 'Yes?' she said. 'Yes, yes.' She was looking away from Toby, again acting as if he was not there. She seemed to be listening, her head on one side. 'It is providence – yes, I do understand. Divine intervention? Yes, yes, I do know what that means, dear, but you are exaggerating. I knew something was about to happen, this morning. There's no need to shout.'

Toby realized that she was not talking to him at all but to someone else he couldn't see. 'I'll help you as much as I can,' he said, staring at her.

Alicia didn't take any notice of him, as if she hadn't heard. She still wasn't looking at him. After a while she shook herself and looked down at her hands. 'I was listening to you, Erihapeti,' she said loudly. 'I know I've not listened lately but I was listening then. Don't argue, dear, please. I hate it when you argue. I've been ignoring you, dear, I do know that. But you got through after all. You often do.'

Alicia had looked up to her left as she spoke but then she jerked her head round and stared across at Toby as if she had suddenly remembered he was there. 'Oh goodness,' she said. 'You must think me quite demented. I've done it again. You'll have to get used to my odd ways. I do apologize. I'm not sure I know where I am sometimes, when Erihapeti talks at me.'

'Who's Eri——?' Toby asked.

Alicia looked at him for a moment as if she didn't understand. She frowned, nodded, then reached over and put her hand on Toby's arm. 'You must indulge an old lady, Toby,' she said. 'Erihapeti? She is a spirit guide. With me constantly. Well, she has been. She's talking of going away, says I don't need her any more, or I shan't in the future. She stands beside me and watches after my soul, so she says. Half the time I ignore the poor girl. She gets so irate!'

'Oh,' said Toby.

'I'm not insane,' Alicia said. 'At least I don't think I am. Don't feel obligated to believe me. Erihapeti is a young Maori lass, from New Zealand. She was killed by a British soldier many decades ago during the Maori Wars. Somehow her spirit found its way to England and to me. She is a rare treasure. Everyone has a guide. Most people are not aware of them. I've had mine for donkey's years. Erihapeti talks to me inside my head. I was a spiritualist, Toby my dear, if you wish a name for it. I used to attend church. Too much effort now. I never got on with the congregation. So nosy and vulgar, most of them. I have my guide. Erihapeti has been my solace and friend. I dare say you find such an admission rather off-putting.'

Toby shook his head. 'No,' he said after a moment. 'Sometimes I hear my Gran talking to me. She told me that an Angel comes to help when you get into trouble. When she died I saw an Angel coming to get her, down the stairs.' He had not told her that before.

'Did you really? How absolutely fascinating.' Alicia's eyes opened wider and wider as she stared at him. 'Well, would you believe it,' she added. She reached over with her hands, touching Toby on the forehead. 'You have the most radiant eyes, my dear,' she told him quietly. 'You appear to have some sort of second sight. Most fortunate. Erihapeti tells me you have a strong aura. Your spirit shines. She's never wrong. You must tell me more about your Gran's Angel. We shall talk, you and I. We shall become like two of Priestley's good companions. Good chums.'

For a moment Toby thought he saw a shape moving just behind Alicia's shoulder, but when he blinked and stared at the spot there was nothing there. The sun was shining down through the branches of the oak trees in the garden, casting shadows across the overgrown grass at their feet. They sat there quietly after that and didn't talk again. In the distance they could hear a child laughing. The laughter sounded like the tinkling of a bell. After a while the sound faded away into silence.

5 Something from the Past

Alicia sat in an old deck-chair during the day wearing a straw hat and dark glasses. Toby worked in the garden. The deck-chair had come from Regent's Park, Alicia told him. It was very old. The canvas had been stitched and repaired so many times it was stronger now than when it was new. Her late husband William had stolen it.

Alicia never seemed to stop talking. 'William was frightfully mischievous, always acting the fool,' Alicia said. 'He was the only man I ever met who loved pranks. Peter Pan, I called him. He hated being an adult.'

Toby didn't talk much during the few days he'd been living in the house. Alicia reminded him of Gran. She never expected him to say a lot. He told her about Mimosa Crescent and Mr Braithwaite. Alicia said she'd never have just walked away as Toby had done. She would have hammered on the door and created bedlam until someone answered.

'Never mind, Toby,' she said. 'It led you to me, didn't it? Nothing happens without a reason. Erihapeti has often urged me to believe that.'

Alicia slept on the sofa in the room she called William's study. She rarely went upstairs except to check for damp. She kept all her clothes in the study too, inside a suitcase, because the wardrobes upstairs were rotting. Her ankle had troubled her for only a day. She had stopped using the walking-stick. Toby had helped her upstairs so she could see that his room was comfortable. The room was huge. It was filled with paintings stacked on shelves and lined up along the walls. Most of the paintings were of Hampstead Heath and local houses. Alicia had painted on and off for years after she retired from the theatre, she told Toby. The paintings were all her own work. She'd painted in oils but gave up when her husband died. Alicia stood and looked about the room for a long time. She acted nervous. Apart from the paintings the only furniture in the room was a bed. There were no sheets or blankets on the bed. Alicia didn't offer any. Toby used his duffle-coat to cover himself when he went to sleep.

'Life can change so abruptly Toby,' Alicia told him. 'I withdrew after William passed on. I had no desire to learn about the world. There was nothing there to paint. I could see only darkness. Eventually a kind of darkness took over my life. I'll tell you about it.'

Toby cleared the front garden. He worked for hours every day in the sunshine, piling the weeds and dead bushes against the perimeter walls behind the house. He used an old wooden wheelbarrow with a rusted metal wheel. There were no gardening tools anywhere. He pulled the weeds out with his hands. Once he had finished tidying the front garden he started working on the back one. He enjoyed the work and thought Alicia was pleased. She didn't say anything about it. She sat in her deck-chair watching him, smiling whenever he looked up at her. She kept moving the chair every so often, to stay in the sunlight.

In the afternoons Toby took Bella for walks across the Heath. Alicia said she would join them once her ankle was better. While he was out, Alicia washed and dried his spare clothes, underwear and socks and hung them outside to dry. She told Toby that the fairies had done it. She even brushed his duffle-coat and hung it out in the sun to air.

During the evenings they sat in the study and Toby read to her. Alicia did not have a television. Her radio had broken down and she'd not had it mended. The radio was old and had valves. Toby had never seen one like it before. It sat on the floor half covered by an old sheet.

'It's like me, Toby,' Alicia said, grinning. 'Ready for the scrap pile.'

Toby read Dickens aloud to Alicia for hours after dark. He had been out to the local shops and bought as many candles as he could pay for with money Alicia had given him. Every evening she would light a dozen candles, which she'd set about the study. Toby sat in the winged armchair with a lighted candle on each side of him on small tables that Alicia had cleared of china figurines. She lay back on the sofa to listen, a rug across her legs. She never once fell asleep. She did not take her eyes from Toby's face as he read. Every time he looked up she was staring at him. Toby had been reading passages from *David Copperfield*.

'They say it was his favourite, you know,' she told him once. 'It's supposed to be about his own life. How I'd love to have met that man. The greatest author in the English language, my dear.

There's been no one to match him anywhere in the civilized world.'

Sometimes she laughed gently as Toby read. She wept whenever Peggotty appeared in the story, clasping her hands and holding them up to her face. She told Toby that he read so well she felt transported back in time to when the great man was alive. She cursed Uriah Heep under her breath, despaired for little Emily. Ham's devoted love made her clench her fists tightly together in her lap.

Toby had never read Dickens before. He found some of the words difficult. He read slowly and carefully. Those evenings became a special time for him and Alicia. It drew them close.

When he had finished reading for the evening Alicia would tell him about her life. She didn't say much about her son Antony. She talked of the time before he was born. Toby didn't ask her any questions. He stared at the framed photographs sometimes, feeling Alicia's eyes on him. But she said nothing about them. 'William and I were always good chums,' Alicia said. 'We were never out of love. I cannot remember one day, child, when we quarrelled or misunderstood one another. William made certain of that. He was so calm. In those days we had a small house just off Richmond Park. I don't even know if it is still there. We luncheoned at two every afternoon when William returned from the City. We walked in the park, watching the deer. There was the theatre for me in the evenings, of course. I never played a leading role. I possessed no true longing to become successful. I did not desire fame. William was my focus. We were rarely apart. We never entertained. It was quite enough for us to be together, in our treasured world. Eventually William did so well in the City we sold the house and bought this one for a song. I can barely recall why. People were moving out here. It seemed a peaceful place to buy property. I began to paint. William employed a gardener. We had servants, of course, back in Richmond. Though they'd proved far too bothersome. Here there was only William and myself. And Antony. I never spoke to the gardener.'

Alicia stopped speaking. She covered her mouth with her hand for a moment and ducked her head. 'Oh my dear,' she said. 'I hope I don't sound too grand or stuck-up. We were never that. It was only money. Many call it breeding.' Then she laughed.

Toby sat quietly and listened, nodding his head or shaking it when she expected him to but saying nothing.

'I would come home from the theatre quite exhausted. William would light dozens of candles in every room. He would offer me chilled champagne, perhaps a plate of caviare. I never liked caviare, though I pretended to. I'm sure many people did. I thought it was ghastly. But we would sit out on the terrace if it was a mild evening and he would hold me in his arms and sing to me. He had a quite remarkable voice. Who else could claim they did that with their beloved after so many years of marriage? Our love grew deeper and bigger the longer we'd been together. I lived for William. There was never a time when he did not fill my heart with inexpressible joy.'

Toby sat and listened to Alicia for as long as he could keep awake. He thought her voice was beautiful, but she talked even more than Gran had talked. Sometimes during the night, as he lay on the bed in his room, he would hear her downstairs, singing. She had stopped asking him anything about his own life after he had been in the house for two days. All she wanted to talk about was William and the past. Toby started to feel that William was still alive, that one day he would walk in through the front door or appear in the garden. Alicia made him seem that way. She did not tell Toby how he had died. Toby wasn't even certain when he had done so. Sometimes it seemed to have been a long time ago. Other times the way Alicia talked it was as if he had died only a few months before. She acted muddled about time.

By the end of the first week Alicia was feeling well enough to join him on his walks with Bella across the Heath. They did not venture far, usually to the top of Parliament Hill and back again. Alicia always wore the same clothes, a long brown tweed skirt, a black blouse and a mud-coloured cardigan. She smelled a bit like Toby's Gran had smelled, a bit fusty. Toby didn't mind. He felt he was a different person, walking on the Heath with Alicia. She noticed everything around and about them. She made up little stories about the people they passed. She held on to Toby's arm and smiled while Bella romped and barked and ran in circles.

Alicia had food delivered, she told Toby. There was a laundry service she used in St John's Wood. The man would come once a fortnight when she asked him to. She would not allow any tradespeople into the house. The house was William's shrine, she said. Toby must remember that too. One day she would take him to where William lay in a Hampstead church graveyard. Famous people were buried there.

After they'd eaten lunch Toby explored the upstairs rooms during the early afternoons while Alicia took a nap. In each of the rooms stood furniture covered with sheets. Everywhere there were cobwebs and mouldy patches on the walls. Many of the floorboards had partly collapsed. There were tall, empty wardrobes standing leaning at angles with broken doors. In one room which was larger than the others stood a four-poster bed which was covered in cobwebs. There was no mattress on it. The springs had rusted. A huge dressing-table took up the opposite wall. It had tall mirrors that reached to the ceiling. The mirrors were brown with age and covered with dust. On the dressing-table sat a large silver picture frame, the glass in it cracked.

Everything seemed tidy in each of the rooms as if they had not been lived in for a long time. Toby was puzzled by their emptiness.

'Erihapeti never came to me until after William passed away,' Alicia said one night. Toby had just finished reading to her. They'd been sitting for a time in the candlelight without talking. 'She helped me recover from my grief. I'd been to the spiritualist church a few times by then. I was quite desperate to get in touch with William. The messages I did receive were most comforting. When they began to grow repetitive I kept wondering why on earth I went on attending. I'd made no friends there. One night, my dear, oh it seems so long ago, I was lying on my bed upstairs and I heard someone whispering. I grew so frightened. I searched the house high and low, finding no one. Erihapeti said she'd had to shout to get my full attention. She'd been so far away and was lost. She didn't like England, of course, in the beginning. It depressed her unutterably. She came to me night after night until I heard her voice clearly. It was perfectly agreeable after I could hear her and knew who she was. She explained everything. William was well. His soul was moving onwards and upwards and growing larger. Through her he sent little messages of love.

'I went back to the church to tell them. They were most polite. They acted as if they were pleased for me. Yet it really made no difference. I'd always felt the outsider there. I imagined I was being quietly snubbed. I stopped going altogether after that. Erihapeti stayed. She stood beside me, child. We talked for hours in those early days. Since then she has been my constant solace.'

Once Toby had tidied the garden and there seemed little work left for him to do in it, he and Alicia walked Bella on the Heath every day. Toby told Alicia about the pigeon man. He'd never seen any sign of him again while they'd been on the Heath together.

'I've no doubt he is a tortured soul,' Alicia said. 'There are so many in London. So wretched. One has to be compassionate.'

Toby took her to places where he had slept, to where he had seen foxes as well as to all the places where he'd seen the pigeon man. Alicia walked with her arm through his and smiled gently. Often people stared at her. Alicia's feet were usually bare. Her hair stuck up all over the place. She took no notice of staring eyes. Toby began to tell her about Lillian and Olive and about Annie from Ireland, but Alicia did not seem to want to hear. She kept changing the subject or she would say 'Jolly good' in a distant voice as if she wasn't really listening. She seemed to have forgotten Gran's Angel and wanting to hear more about Toby's seeing it. Toby didn't mind. Alicia talked enough for both of them, about her past.

'Do you know, I never had one acting lesson,' Alicia told him. 'Not one, my dear. My acting was pure instinct. A natural function, someone told me. Few have it. So many admired the way I walked on to the stage and lived my roles. I met such charming, lovely people. So kind. I wasn't really very good, but not one fellow-actor said a thing. Of course William helped enormously. He had many contacts in the City, those who financed the theatre. His position did help, I cannot deny that. William was always there. His love transported me to a higher plane.' Then she grinned. 'I must sound like some ghastly snob,' she said. 'Perhaps I am.'

Their days together were quiet. No one came to the house. Pudding Lane remained empty as if it was a forgotten place. There was never anyone in sight whenever Toby went out through the side-gate. Sometimes he heard cars at night, but they were usually just turning and going back the way they had come. Now and then Alicia took long naps during the day, complaining of headaches. Toby began cleaning the kitchen, tying up bundles of newspapers and gathering the rubbish together, leaving it all out in the street to be collected. Alicia would not let him clean the upstairs rooms or William's study.

Two of the cupboards in the kitchen were jam-packed with tins of food. There were cooked meats wrapped in newspaper. Some of the meat had turned bad. There were few pieces of crockery. Most of what was there was chipped and cracked. Alicia kept her cutlery in a plastic bag hanging beside the sink. The bag was from Harrods. Toby couldn't figure out why she lived the way she did, as though she was only staying in the house for a short time. It puzzled him every day. Yet Alicia explained nothing. She talked only of the past. Toby didn't ask any questions. He kept feeling that there was something wrong, something not quite right. Alicia acted calm and went through each day as if everything was quite normal.

One night, very late, after Toby had gone upstairs to his room, Alicia knocked on his door and came in. Toby had been reading from an old travel book on Africa he had borrowed from the study. Alicia loved reading so much that she'd made Toby promise to read for at least an hour every night before he went to sleep. She thought they could discuss what he read. She could help him to understand any words he didn't know.

Alicia was holding a lighted candle in her hands. She wouldn't use electricity at night. She'd told Toby that Erihapeti was scared of it. The spirit was scared of Toby too. Since Toby had been in the house Erihapeti had not made many appearances.

Alicia walked straight across to the bed and sat on the edge at Toby's feet. 'I feel I must tell you a little about Antony,' Alicia said. 'There are some things that aren't easily told. I shan't feel settled until you know what I want to say.'

'You don't have to tell me anything,' said Toby. 'Not if you don't want to.'

Alicia nodded. Toby smiled his slow smile and put his book on the floor. Alicia sat very stiffly on the edge of the bed. In the light of the candle her face looked older than Toby had seen it before. Her eyes glistened as if she had been crying. 'I never understood him at first, my dear,' she said quietly. 'Right from his birth he had a strange, withdrawn spirit. He never laughed like normal children laugh. So serious, always frowning. He wanted few toys back in the Richmond days. At times when he was small he'd whisper to himself for hours. I never told William. The whispering bothered me greatly. I did nothing to threaten William's love. That was unthinkable.'

Alicia stared at the candle. She had loosened her hair and it fell down to her shoulders. Underneath her long nightdress her feet were bare.

'When Antony was older he started to argue with William about everything. My poor beloved was so perplexed and troubled over that. He tried to hide his fears from me. They rowed bitterly when they thought I was out of hearing. The arguments were so petty. They were about silly, unimportant things. Missing ties or cuff-links. When Antony cursed his father, my blood would run cold. There were no reasons for such anger. William tried to be as affectionate and as tactful with Antony as one could expect a father to be. I think, looking back child, we had spoilt Antony to a regrettable degree. In the end, it was Antony who was the cause of William's death.'

Outside, a wind had sprung up. The whole house creaked. To Toby it seemed to sigh. He sat very still. Alicia spoke as if she was alone in the house and talking to herself.

'I was downstairs learning some lines for a new play I was to appear in at the Garrick. I remember that night so clearly. How could I ever forget it? I heard William shouting. He sounded so angry. I stepped out into the hall to hear more clearly. Antony was standing at the top of the stairs. William was just below him, leaning against the wall. They were arguing about money. Neither of them noticed me. Antony was quite distraught. His face was twisted. William had calmed down and was talking to him in a quiet manner when suddenly Antony made as if to rush off. William grabbed him by the arm to stop him. I remember calling out and rushing towards the stairs. William slipped and fell backwards. He fell and rolled. He bounced, his arms thrown out, and his head hit the banisters as he came down towards me. He landed at my feet. I knelt down and took him in my arms just before he died.'

Alicia dropped the candle, which went out. She covered her face with her hands and sat there leaning forward. Toby reached out with his hands and Alicia moved, clutching on to them for a minute and pulling them to her lips. She shuddered.

'There was an inquest. I had to attend, of course. Antony was excused. He was unwell for weeks afterwards. He blamed himself. The verdict was accidental death. I feared scandal, but it was all kept quiet. After the funeral Antony wouldn't speak to me, or couldn't. He said nothing and went his own way. He was filled with angry grief and guilt. I feared for his sanity. He did have his friends. They rallied round him. I had no one, I was very much alone. Antony moved in a circle of young men who had nothing better to do than throw parties and attend the opera. One night a group of them came with him to see one of my own performances. Someone in the cast told me she had seen him in the foyer. He never came backstage.

'We lived in the house like strangers until he eventually moved out. Now he travels. I made certain that he would never starve. I fear he has not recovered from his guilt. I love him dearly, yet he stays away. When he came home in the past he acted so differently.

He never wished to speak of his father. He looked at me with such pain it was all I could do not to weep in front of him.'

Toby didn't know what to say. Alicia didn't expect him to say anything. She stood up after glancing at him, patting him gently on the arm. 'There,' she said. 'Now I have told you. I needed to.' Her lips quivered. She didn't meet Toby's eyes. She moved across to the door and stood there for a moment, her back to Toby as if she was about to say something else. Then she went out, closing the door quietly behind her.

The next morning Alicia was cheerful and told Toby they should have a day out somewhere, some place they could take Bella with them, out of London. She would hire a car, she said, with a driver. They could drive out into the countryside and have a picnic. 'William and I often drove to places dear Dickens wrote about,' she said, smiling at him in the kitchen. 'We had a whole week in Rochester once. And Broadstairs, another year. William loved that man's work as much as I do. It was he who bought all those editions in the study. William did love me so.'

In the hall beside the telephone was a number written on a piece of card taped to the wall. Alicia told Toby the number was for her doctor, in case she fell ill. 'No one ever calls me, child,' she'd told him. 'But it is a link to the world. It provides a little notion of security. Who would wish to call me? I am quite forgotten. But one day Antony may telephone, from wherever he is. I live in hope. He hates writing letters. Lately I've been imagining that he too may be dead.'

Later that day, once they had finished their meal of baked beans on toast, and after Alicia had shut herself in the study to sleep, the telephone rang. Toby was in the kitchen. He listened to it for a full minute before going out into the hall. He couldn't hear anything from behind the study door and didn't know what to do. The ringing didn't stop. Then he remembered Alicia talking of her hope that Antony might call. Toby picked up the receiver and said hello.

'What number is that?' a man asked. His voice was very abrupt.

Toby read out the number on the dial.

'Who are you?' the man asked.

'Toby,' said Toby. 'I live here. Is that Antony?'

He could hear the man speaking to someone else in the background, then what sounded like a woman's voice answering. The receiver at the other end was slammed down. Toby went back to the kitchen and made some cocoa. He took a cup out into the hall and knocked on the study door, calling out Alicia's name. There was no response. He listened but couldn't hear anything. Alicia slept deeply. She had locked the study door. Toby didn't know where Bella was.

He was upstairs in his room when the front-door bell sounded. He peered out of the window but couldn't see anyone. It had grown dark by then. For some reason the street-lamps hadn't come on. He left his room and hurried down the stairs. The hallway was dark. Bella appeared to be shut in the kitchen. Toby was certain she hadn't been in there when he'd made the cocoa. Bella was barking furiously and scratching at the door.

The man at the front door was dressed in a brown coat with a dark velvet collar. He was wearing a trilby and carried a rolled umbrella. He stared at Toby before he spoke. 'Where's Mrs Wickham?' he asked. 'She is here, isn't she?'

It was the same voice Toby had heard on the telephone. Toby nodded and said she was asleep in the study. The man shook his head, pushed the front door open and stepped into the hall past Toby. He called out Alicia's name. Then he marched across to the study and opened the door, which was no longer locked. He went in, slamming the door shut behind him. Bella was howling in the kitchen now. Toby heard Alicia cry out, then the man's voice talking loudly, asking her what she was up to. Toby backed away and went into the kitchen to calm Bella, holding on to her and leaving the aoor open.

After a long time the man came out and stood in the hall. Toby stayed where he was, squatting on the floor. Bella was whining, thumping her tail on the floor. The man gestured to Toby to stay where he was, ignoring Bella. At the same time a woman appeared in the front doorway, which was still open. She stared at Toby through the gloom and didn't speak. Both she and the man began whispering. Then the woman marched across to Toby and took hold of Bella by her collar, dragging her across the hall to the front door. She didn't even glance at Toby. Bella seemed quite happy to go with her. After a few moments Toby heard the slam of a car door. When the woman came back she and the man went into the study together and shut the door, which had been left slightly open. Toby heard voices and then the man shouting. There was a thumping noise. The woman cried out: 'Oh for God's sake, let me handle it!'

There was silence for a moment until the man came rushing out of the study and picked up the telephone. He looked at Toby once, then turned his back. He spoke quietly into the telephone after he'd dialled. Toby didn't hear what he said. When he put down the receiver the man turned his head and nodded. Toby had stepped out into the hall.

'You'd better go back into the kitchen,' the man said. 'We can talk there.' He followed Toby and closed the door behind them. The man was hitting his leg with a clenched fist.

'My name is Henry Wickham,' the man told Toby. For a while he said nothing else but paced up and down, not even glancing at Toby, as if he was trying to decide what to say. 'There's been a misunderstanding, son,' Henry Wickham said. He stared at Toby's feet then peered at the kitchen walls. 'Alicia's had a slight collapse. Nothing serious. I've rung for the doctor. He'll be here directly. She'll be perfectly fine.'

He had stopped pacing the floor. He pulled one of the chairs out from the table and sat down. For a moment he rested his head in his hands, then rubbed his eyes. He'd taken off his coat. Underneath it he wore a dark suit. A white silk scarf hung round his neck. When he looked up at Toby his face had paled. His eyes were red. 'Alicia is my aunt,' he said. 'She told me what you are doing here, and your name. I'd appreciate it if you could confirm everything.'

Toby told him how he had helped Alicia back from the Heath and that she had asked him to stay, as he didn't have anywhere to live. The man kept nodding as Toby spoke but still didn't look at him. When Toby stopped talking the man said: 'Look, I'm sorry, but you cannot possibly stay on here.'

Toby shrugged and didn't answer. He felt he didn't like Henry Wickham at all. His eyes were cold and unfriendly.

'You are by law trespassing, you realize,' Henry Wickham said. 'I don't wish to involve the police.'

He talked as if he thought Toby was backward. Toby just stared at him.

'My aunt has a lot of emotional problems, son. What she has told you about herself isn't true. Oh, she's admitted what she's confided in you. None of it is true. She tells the same story to anyone who will listen. I know all about it. I've been away, off on business out of the country. I was delayed getting back. That was the cause of all this. My aunt has never been married. She makes up stories. She had no right to ask you to stay here, however you might be fixed. It's all most regrettable.'

William and Antony had never existed, Henry Wickham told

Toby. The dog Bella belonged to Henry's wife. His wife was with Alicia now. The house had belonged to the family and Alicia had lived in it for a while, long ago. He often had to go away on business, Henry said. This time his aunt had stolen the keys to the house from his bureau, came over with some of her belongings and pretended that she was living here. His wife would have come after her and taken her back, but she had been away with him. Alicia had lived with them for years after having been in a special hospital. The house was due to be demolished, once all the furniture had been removed. He'd had the telephone and the electricity reconnected a short time before. He'd been finally sorting the place out.

All the while as he was speaking Henry looked at Toby and tried to smile. Toby thought the smile was false. He wondered why the man was telling him so much.

'My aunt is not strictly mad,' Henry said. 'She's a mite touched, one might say.' He laughed, then stopped, and stood up. 'It's something from the past. I've been caring for her ever since she became . . . well . . . confused, shall we say. She has grown confused about the past. It's affected her mind. She was an actress for a while. That part of her story is true.' He paused, then added coldly: 'I don't know why I'm explaining all this to you. It has nothing whatever to do with you. I am trying to be fair. I realize she must have become fond of you. The way she's spoken of you at least requires some explanation. I understand you've been here some time.' He stopped talking and frowned. 'I'd rather my aunt didn't see you again, if you don't mind. She told me you were her son. She's insisting on it. She makes up such stories all the time. It has caused me and my wife considerable pain. There was little we could do about it. Perhaps, if you don't mind. . . .' He gestured towards the door. 'I think it would be best if you left now.'

Toby didn't know what to do. 'I've got my things upstairs,' he said. 'I've got my rucksack up there. Why can't I see her before I go?'

Henry looked at Toby and just shook his head. His face had now gone a deep red. He kept on staring.

'She was kind to me,' Toby added. 'I liked her.'

He wanted to say more, but Henry had turned away and was staring out through the kitchen window.

Henry Wickham stood in the hall and didn't follow Toby upstairs. Toby found his rucksack and his duffle-coat where he'd left them in the room. He tried not to think about anything. His head felt tight. He wasn't sure he believed what Henry Wickham had told him. He didn't know what to believe. There was no way he could find out the truth. He hurried back down the stairs. The woman had come out of the study and closed the door behind her. She was locking it with a key as Toby came down the stairs. She stared at Toby and without saying anything walked past him across the hall to the kitchen. She stood there in the doorway half turned away, peering in. She had a really ugly face, Toby noticed, with down-turned lips. One of her eyelids didn't seem to work. She looked like she was blinking.

'Look, son,' Henry Wickham suddenly said. 'If there's anything you need . . . this is my card, do take it. You had no reason to disbelieve my aunt. I realize that. I'm sorry. I could give you a lift somewhere, but the doctor. . . .' He stopped speaking, peering past Toby towards his wife. She was shaking her head at him. 'We should never have left her alone,' Henry added. 'My wife, you see. . . .'

At that moment the woman shouted Henry's name so loudly that Toby jumped. Then she muttered: 'For God's sake, just get rid of him.' She was glaring at Henry and ignored Toby standing between them. Her hands were clenched. Toby thought she looked like a crazy person.

Toby could hear no sound from the study. The house seemed as though it was empty, apart from the three of them. He'd taken Henry's card and put it in his pocket. Henry was about to say something else, then turned away. Toby crossed to the door, went out and stepped down to the drive. As he looked back up the steps the woman hurried across from the kitchen. She closed the front door without even glancing at him.

The sky was clear and it seemed warm. For a moment Toby thought he could see a face peering out at him from between the curtains at the study windows. He wasn't sure whose face it was. The curtain was pulled back quickly. He thought he heard Alicia cry out and then Henry's wife shouting something.

His rucksack over his shoulder, he walked up the short street away from the house. Opposite was a small car parked at an odd angle. He could see Bella sitting inside. The dog was watching him but made no sound. Toby walked until he came to the main road busy with cars going in both directions. There were a lot of people about. A crowd was coming out of a cinema on the corner. There was a queue of people standing at a bus-stop. He had no money to catch a bus anywhere, he'd have to walk. After putting his rucksack down on the pavement he pulled on his duffle-coat, which he'd been carrying under his arm. He didn't want to leave. He stood there for a long time near the bus queue looking up and down the street, pretending that he was waiting for the bus too. No one took any notice of him. The noise of the traffic seemed loud after the quiet of the house. He kept hoping that Alicia might come running out of Pudding Lane behind him and call out. He kept glancing back towards it. The bus arrived. People clambered on board. A woman carrying a huge bunch of white roses shouted out to him: 'Come on, ducky, these beggars won't hang about. Bloody union rules!' The clippie grinned at the woman, blowing her a kiss and laughing. He looked a bit like Fred from Jamaica. He stared at Toby and then shrugged, reaching up to ring the bell.

As the bus pulled away from the kerb Toby began walking in the same direction. Ahead of him the lights of the city had changed the darkness in the sky to a dull pink.

6 Under Waterloo Bridge

Toby sat staring down at the water. Along the edge lay empty glass bottles and pieces of plastic half buried in the mud. The tide was coming in. Further out in the centre of the river a long, low barge appeared, moving slowly forward from beneath Hungerford Bridge. There was just enough light for Toby to see an old man on the far side of the barge. The man was emptying a bucket of rubbish into the water. His head was turned. He was watching Toby with a grin. When he had finished emptying the bucket the man waved. Toby waved back.

There was no one else about. Once the barge had moved out of sight all Toby could hear was the lapping of the water and a sound of traffic. It was four days since he had left the house in Pudding Lane. He was sitting on steps that led down to the Thames, outside the Royal Festival Hall. It was just before dawn. He had been sleeping in doorways and in a small park by the Embankment near the Underground. He had walked away from Hampstead Heath without stopping until he had reached the West End. The first night he had tried to sleep on a park bench in Leicester Square, but the noise of the starlings in the trees kept him awake. The city seemed as busy in darkness as it did during the day. He watched people wandering about on their own or in groups. No one spoke to him. He felt lonelier than he had ever felt since Alice had cleared off to America and Gran had died and George had left home to live with Maureen Stokes.

Toby stood up and climbed the steps, turning left, away from the Festival Hall. There was still no one about except for a few pigeons and sparrows. It was too early for tourists. The day before, he'd found a wallet lying in a gutter in a quiet street just off the Embankment. The wallet had a few pieces of paper inside it with addresses written on them but no names. There were also two twenty-pound notes inside the wallet. He couldn't believe his luck. He took the money out and left the wallet where he'd found it. With the money he bought pasties and sandwiches and soft drinks, then ate and drank sitting beside the Thames, watching the river traffic. He walked, following the river, his rucksack over his back, looking at the sights and letting the sun warm him. It was almost full summer. The days were growing longer. The river sparkled in the sunlight even though it looked dirty and was choked with rubbish.

Toby didn't really know what he was doing in London any longer. He wondered why he didn't just set off back home and wait for Alice to turn up. Though he did feel deep down inside him that she might never come back from America. George couldn't have cared less about him either. Toby knew that. It'd been Gran who had kept them together. He saw that clearly now. As he walked he could hear in his mind Alice yelling at George before she left. They were both drunk.

'You don't give a monkey's shit about me and I feel the same about you!', Alice yelled at George. Toby was awake in his room. He'd opened his door so he could hear them more clearly and had then gone out into the hall. Alice started laughing. Gran had usually come out of her room to join him when Alice got worked up.

'You were a useless bag of dung when we got married! Why the hell did I bother, all those years? Washing your disgusting Y-fronts and your stinking socks week after week. You're the most disgusting bloke I've ever known, George Todd. Even your breath stinks! Well, I've had it. Understand? I'm finished with the lot of you. I want a decent life! I am going, George. None of you can stop me. You haven't the flaming energy to try, have you? Lazy bastard.'

Toby heard George say something in a quiet voice. There was a thud and then a sound like thumping on wood.

'I never wanted the kid, did I say that?' Alice yelled. 'I told you and told you I never wanted any brats cluttering up my life. I've had sixteen years of that dumb little shit! But oh no, you mucked that up too, didn't you? Cheap rubbers! You went out and bought rubbers that fell off a lorry so you could have your jollies. You couldn't even be bothered to buy decent ones! You're a cretin, George. What are you?'

There was silence for a minute, then Toby heard them start laughing. They'd probably been drinking vodka. They always drank vodka when they rowed. They enjoyed it. They'd enjoyed the rows too, laughing all through them.

'You wanted that car, so you just went ahead and got it. Never mind asking me – no, why should you?' Alice went on after George had said something. 'Well, you know what they say, George, don't you? Big car, small prick. Useless bastard. I'd have had more fun with a ripe banana!' Alice let out a whoop and carried on laughing.

There was a sudden crashing of a door and then silence.

Toby didn't know why he had suddenly remembered that row so clearly. They'd had so many. Almost every night for years they'd gone along with things quietly until they had a row like that.

He had reached Blackfriars Bridge and was crossing it when he remembered that Gran had not come out of her room that night. She'd usually come out and they sat on the stairs together while they listened to Alice yelling at George. Gran sat and laughed with her hand over her mouth, nudging Toby with her elbow. Alice had sometimes yelled really dirty things at George. That night had been different because Gran hadn't been there to make it all seem like a joke. She'd stayed in her room and didn't say anything the next morning either, as far as Toby remembered. Alice left one morning almost a week later, in a taxi. She was wearing a new red trouser suit and huge gold-coloured earrings.

Toby never thought that the rows would lead to anything. The rows hadn't meant much to him except they were better than watching telly. Gran had thought so too. He never believed Alice had really meant to clear out, until she actually left. George had never lost his temper with Alice or tried to smack her one. It was just the way Alice was. She liked shouting. She'd shouted at Toby and Gran as well sometimes. She and George often laughed like crazy people in the middle of her shouting because they were drunk. Gran said it was a game they played. And usually the night afterwards they had gone off to bed early and locked their door.

Toby stood in the middle of Blackfriars Bridge and stared back along the way he'd come. There were now a lot of people about. There were groups of tourists, couples walking arm in arm and children eating ices. Everyone seemed to be talking to someone else and laughing, all except him. He started to feel angry as he stood there. Angry at Alice for leaving home. Angry at George for clearing off to live with Maureen Stokes. They were his parents but they'd acted like a couple of slobs for most of his life. They'd been useless. They had mucked up everything. They'd never really bothered to see that his life was all right, because they hadn't cared about their own. Here he was in London and he had nowhere to live and no job. He didn't know what he was supposed to do now that he'd come all this way. He didn't want to end up like they had. Nothing had worked out so far. He'd stayed in that dump of a house in Mimosa Crescent because he thought he should. He hadn't really wanted to. He had lost his friend Alicia after he thought he was settled with her. He wanted Gran to be still alive and felt angry at her for dying. He knew he was being childish but it just wasn't fair, any of it. He felt like throwing his rucksack into the river and then his duffle-coat, and after that he'd take all his clothes off and throw them away and run up and down shouting all the swear-words he'd learned off Alice until someone took some notice of him. But he was sixteen and couldn't do that. He wasn't a child. Though he was still under-age. It was the 1960s and he was supposed to be a child. If the authorities got hold of him he'd probably be herded into some home for juveniles and left to rot. Life was utterly stupid, Toby thought.

After a while he walked back off the bridge and headed towards the Strand. He kept on walking, trying not to think about anything. He didn't want to think about Alicia and the house in Pudding Lane. Though he kept taking out the card Henry Wickham had given him and staring at it. He wondered why he'd been given it. It seemed an odd thing for Henry Wickham to have done. There were two telephone numbers on the card. Henry Wickham's name was printed in fancy lettering across the top of it.

By late morning he had walked all the way across to Camden Town, back to Mimosa Crescent. He hadn't planned to go back there, he'd just walked feeling fed up and sorry for himself. Number 17 looked exactly the same as when he'd left it, just as rundown. He stood on the opposite side of the crescent staring up at the windows. From the downstairs front flat came loud pop music. He wondered if Basil with the spotty face still lived there, where old Mrs Cranks had lived. He saw no one entering or leaving. He still felt angry and worked up and wouldn't have minded throwing a brick through one of the windows as Betsy Molesworthy had thrown a brick through their front door. The street was quiet. Not a single car came along it while he stood there. He thought about the night he'd found Lillian and Olive beside the rubbish bins and had invited them up to his room. He'd liked Lillian. Olive had made him laugh at first but then he'd felt sad for her. They could have become his friends. He could have helped them. That night seemed a long time ago. If he'd got a job he would still be living at Calcutta Mansions. Lillian and Olive might have come back. He could have begged Mr Braithwaite to offer them a room.

Toby carried on walking past the house, turning left at the corner into the High Street. He tried to make his mind go blank. It didn't do any good, thinking. It made his head throb. Opposite was a fish and chip shop, with tables and chairs inside. He reckoned he might as well treat himself to some food with what money he had left from the wallet he'd found. He could spend all the money on food and sod everything else.

He was half-way across the High Street when a sports car appeared out of nowhere. He drew back but the car's bumper clipped him on the leg, ripping his jeans open. The car didn't stop. Toby found himself sitting in the gutter. His leg was grazed but it wasn't bleeding. A few people stopped to stare but no one came to help. A fat woman with a shopping trolley and a mangy-looking dog stood on the pavement. The woman kept shaking her head and clucking her tongue but she said nothing. While she stared the dog cocked its leg and peed against the trolley. The woman walked off when Toby tried to speak to her. Toby stood up, pulled his rucksack on to his back from where it had half fallen off. After a minute he started to run. He didn't stop running until he'd passed Euston Station, heading west. As he ran he felt as if he would explode. He longed to leap up into the sky and zoom onwards and upwards until there was nothing around him except stars and planets and silence and if he shouted out the dirtiest words he could think of no one would hear him. After he'd crossed Euston Road at the lights he slowed to a walk. He found a square and went in to lie down on the grass in the sun.

As he'd done before he slept on a bench in the gardens beside the Embankment that night. There were a lot of people sleeping in the gardens. They were all ages. There were a few who even had sleeping-bags and had laid them out in between the bushes. They seemed quite well dressed. They were young and made a lot of noise and drank out of huge green bottles.

Half-way through the night a few of them got up and wandered down to the entrance of the Underground where the Salvation Army handed out soup and bread. Toby didn't bother. He didn't feel very hungry when the time came. There were a large number of old men and a few old women carrying plastic bags who went past him towards the soup-van. For a while he sat up and looked at their faces, hoping that he might spot Lillian and Olive. He didn't. He was surprised at how many people were sleeping in the small park. He lay back on the bench once it went quiet. Covered by his duffle-coat and using his rucksack for a pillow, he started to think about Alicia. He still couldn't believe that she had lied to him about her past. What Henry Wickham had told him hadn't been true, he knew that. It couldn't be true. Alicia wouldn't have made up what she had said about her life. He should have refused to leave without first seeing her. He felt he had lost Alicia just as he'd lost his flat at Calcutta Mansions because he'd been George's son and stupid. He lay and thought about Alicia. He couldn't stop thinking about her. He kept seeing her face smiling at him. Eventually, hiding his face under his coat, he had a cry and felt a little better after that.

He seemed to have been sleeping for a long time, when he woke up with a start. A figure was bent over him and he felt a hand inside the front of his jeans. The zip on his jeans was open. Toby yelled out and sat up. The hand withdrew. It was an old tramp. The man was grinning down at him with his tongue pushed out between his teeth. 'I only wanted a feel,' the man whispered. 'Go on, give an old fella a treat, son. We can go in the bushes if you're shy. I've got money – look, here – there's a quid in it if you let me have a suck. I won't hurt you. You'd like it. Got no teeth, see.'

Toby scrambled to his feet. He grabbed his duffle-coat from where it had fallen to the ground and then picked up his rucksack. He started to hurry off down the path. He looked back once. The park seemed very bright from the street-lamps. Some others had stood up and were watching. He could hear laughter. The old man was standing with his arms held out. He had a bottle in his left hand and had started singing 'Roll Me Over'. Toby ran out through a side-exit into Victoria Embankment. His face felt so hot he reckoned it would burst into flames. He thought he'd been having a wet dream before he had woken up. He had a hard-on. He stopped and looked about him and could see no one. He dropped his things on to the pavement to zip up his jeans. It took a long time. The zip got caught and pinched his skin and hurt like hell. After a while he began to giggle and then swear and he wanted to cry too but he couldn't. His skin was tingling all over and he was shivering. After pulling his coat on he headed along to the steps that led up on to Hungerford Bridge. When he was half-way up the steps it started to rain.

Once he'd crossed to the South Bank he spent the rest of the night sitting on the same steps he'd sat on before, staring down into the river and trying to decide what he should do, to make his life better. He couldn't think of anything. He was sick of sleeping rough. If he carried on sleeping rough he might end up like that old tramp, or worse. Just before dawn he fell asleep with his head against the wall, his duffle-coat across his legs and chest. The rain had fallen for only a short while. The river shone and hardly seemed to be stirring in the queer light, once the clouds had moved away. No one disturbed him. The sound of the river was like Gran's voice. It whispered to him softly and he curled himself up tight and stayed there until long after dawn.

The next day he was watching a young girl with a man who looked a bit like George, when he saw Lillian Pike. The girl didn't look much older than Toby. She had a suitcase and had opened it out on to the pavement near the cinema further along on the lower level of the South Bank. The girl wore a purple dress which was covered with pieces of lace. Her blonde hair was covered with flowers. The suitcase was filled with earrings hanging on black cardboard. The man had helped her set up her display. They had a big sign, with prices on. They both sat down on the damp concrete with their legs crossed, staring into the sky while people walked past. No one stopped to buy anything from them. Every so often the girl would call out. 'Love and Peace!' she'd yell, and then laugh.

There were a lot of people wandering in and out amongst some bookstalls, waiting for the cinema to open. Toby sat on a low wall beside a modern statue. He'd bought two cheese rolls from the café and sat there eating them, enjoying the feeling of having a lot of people around him. He looked straight at Lillian without recognizing her at first. She was standing very still in the shadows under Waterloo Bridge, just past the bookstalls, staring out across the river. She was wearing the same clothes he'd seen her in at Calcutta Mansions, but she looked much thinner. There was no sign of Olive. Lillian was alone. Now and then as Toby stared Lillian drew up her hands and covered her face with them, lowering her head. Then she'd look up, uncovering her face, staring about her as if she was expecting to see something. She looked straight at Toby once, but made no sign that she knew who he was. Every time anyone moved close to her she turned her back to them and stayed very still as if she was scared they'd speak to her. Most people didn't seem to notice her. Toby jumped down from the wall, shrugged on his rucksack over his duffle-coat, and walked across to where she stood. As he drew close he said quietly: 'Lillian?' After a moment he said her name again.

She didn't seem to hear him. Then she half turned, backed off and peered at him with a frown but said nothing.

'It's Toby,' said Toby. 'From Calcutta Mansions. Do you remember me?'

Lillian kept on staring into his face. Her lips moved as if she was talking to herself. Her eyes were bloodshot. Below her eyes there were dark areas of skin and a bruise that had swelled her right cheek. 'Calcutta?' she whispered. 'India?' She reached out with a hand, then drew it back quickly. 'Do I know you, sir?' she asked. 'Have you come to see about Ollie? My name is Miss Lillian Pike. So lovely to meet you.' She held out her hand again then suddenly, looking scared, she drew it to her face. Turning, she started to walk away.

'You stayed in my flat,' Toby said loudly. 'With your friend Olive. Mr Braithwaite made you leave. Don't you remember?' He didn't know what else to say.

Lillian stopped and became very still. Then she turned back, stepped closer and peered into his face with her eyes narrowed. 'Toby?' she said softly. 'Toby Todd? Is that you, dear boy? Is it really you?' Then she added, whispering: 'Angel of mercy, there you are in the flesh.'

She started to weep. She wrung her hands together and kept saying 'Dear boy, dear boy' until she stopped weeping. Wiping her eyes and staring towards the far side of the river she said: 'My darling Ollie isn't well. She's grown so weak, every day that passes. I am so worried. I was considering the dangers, you see, taking her across there, to the hospital. I don't know what is wrong.' She pointed across the river. Both her hands were shaking. Beneath the woollen scarf she wore on her head her hair was wet. The straw hat she'd worn on top of the scarf when Toby had first met her was squashed, as if someone had sat on it. The feathers on it were crushed and grubby.

'Where is she?' Toby asked, looking about him. He couldn't see Olive anywhere.

'I left her in a safe place,' Lillian told him. 'She's sleeping. She sleeps like a baby, my darling does. No one bothers with her. I thought some kind person here might offer us some money for tea. But no one. . . .' Lillian stared around her, making a helpless movement with her hands, then wiping them on her old fur coat. The coat had large bare patches down both sides as if someone had plucked the fur from it.

As they walked together along to where Lillian said she'd left Olive, she took hold of Toby's arm. She clung to it. She couldn't walk very fast.

'My dear boy, I never thought I would ever meet you again. Such providence. Such joyous chance. What are you doing here?

Do you have a bookstall in this salubrious place, like these other good people? Some here are so kind, so generous. They have helped Ollie and me. They've shown benevolence. I hate to ask, to beg. I never needed to, years ago. My resilience seems to have flown away.'

Toby told her that he had been sleeping rough, that he'd lost his flat at Calcutta Mansions.

Lillian stared at him for a long time, then nodded and sighed. After a few minutes she said: 'Ollie lived there, you know, before the war. Did I tell you that? It wasn't called Calcutta Mansions then. Those were the happy years for my darling, so she related. I am filled with foreboding, Toby Todd. I fear Ollie might be dying. She says nothing. She smiles and struggles to keep life in her dear bones. What must I do? I cannot let her go. We have been together for so long I haven't thought of anything else for days. What must I do for her dear sweet self?' She started to cry again, holding her hand up to her eyes as they neared where Olive was.

Olive was sitting on a patch of empty ground between some buildings. The ground was littered with rubbish and abandoned car tyres. There was grass growing on it and a stunted tree. She sat on a small earth mound, her back against a wall. When they reached her she was asleep, her head tilted forward on to her chest. She was snoring. She still wore several coats. She had a Tesco bag on her head. Beside her was another Tesco bag filled with what looked like folded-up newspapers.

'She sleeps so soundly,' Lillian whispered as they stood looking down at her. 'Anywhere we stop, she drops off like a new-born baby. Poor darling, she is simply worn through. Her body fails her. She speaks little now, when she is awake. You mustn't be offended if she stares at you. She stares but has nothing to say. I understand. She stares at me with love.'

Olive woke up then and raised her head. She kept her eyes on Lillian after one glance at Toby. She looked panicky.

'It's all right, Ollie. There now. This is dear Toby. Don't you remember? He helped us once. He's a kind, dear boy. He's here to help us again. It is providence, Ollie. Providence.'

Olive, saying nothing, squinted up into Lillian's face. Lillian knelt down at Olive's side. Drawing out a filthy handkerchief from her coat pocket she wiped Olive's mouth where she'd dribbled. Leaning forward Lillian kissed Olive gently on the forehead. Toby sat down nearby. Olive went back to sleep. Lillian began to talk.

They had hidden in someone's garden behind a hedge in the

next street the day they'd run from Calcutta Mansions, Lillian told Toby. She had been filled with anguish. She was terrified that Toby's landlord had sent for the police. She had had to calm herself down. Olive had forgotten everything as soon as they'd run away. After a while a man had come out of the house and yelled at them to clear off. Since then they'd been walking and wandering the same streets they'd always stayed close to. They had spent a lot of time in the City, as Olive loved looking at St Paul's and had usually felt safe there. They'd been in a hostel for homeless women for a time. Lillian started to have nightmares, so they'd left. It was after that that Olive began to show signs of feeling ill.

'It's time she had a proper home, a roof, a place of rest,' Lillian said. 'I have no hopes for such a thing. We are growing too old, dear boy. There's little comfort now for ladies like us on the streets. There is too much violence and malcontent. Everywhere we wander people have become intolerant. It's touching Ollie badly, poor darling. She hasn't the strength. That was why I took her back to the house, you see, when we met your dear self. I thought perhaps we might find a little haven there. I need to find my darling a home or I might lose her. I might have to give her up. But she never complains. Sometimes her old sparkle comes back. She did enjoy rhyming words for you. It was her little game. Some days she laughs.'

Lillian hung her head. Taking off her crushed hat and the scarf beneath it she scratched her head so roughly she grunted. Her hair was thin. Underneath it the skin looked red and sore. 'My poor darling is just too tired,' she whispered after putting back her scarf and hat. 'Her life ebbs, dear boy. I do fear it does. We are the abandoned creatures of life's indifference.'

Lillian seemed worn out herself when she stopped speaking. She sat stroking one hand with the other. Toby told her about Alicia Wickham and the house in Pudding Lane. As he told her he kept touching the card in his pocket that Henry Wickham had given him. An idea had begun to form in his head. The idea just came to him as if it was being put there by someone else. It excited him. He wondered if it was Gran's Angel, guiding him. Perhaps it was the Angel who had made Henry Wickham give him the card. He could try to telephone the number on the card that read 'home'. Alicia might be there. Henry Wickham had said that Alicia had been living with him. Toby didn't know but he felt so strongly all of a sudden that if he could speak to Alicia she might be able to help. He started to hear Gran's voice inside his head as he sat there quietly with Lillian. He hadn't heard Gran's voice in his head for so long it made him shiver. Lillian had stopped stroking her hand. She was rummaging in Olive's bag of newspapers.

'Never pass up chances to help others, my lovely,' Gran's voice said. The voice sounded a long way off, like a whisper. 'Chances come along and you have to grab hold. That's what life is for. My Bertie taught me that.'

When Toby told Lillian that he thought there was someone who might help, Lillian trembled. She stared at him with her eyes shining. She seemed unable to say anything. Toby got to his feet and stared about him. On the other side of the patch of empty ground was a telephone-box. He searched in his rucksack for some money and told Lillian to stay where she was while he tried to make a telephone call.

'I will. We'll just sit here with our hopes. We've nowhere else to go,' Lillian said, smiling at Olive still asleep. 'The sunshine is so good for Ollie. It's a blessing. Look, there's colour in her face. Can you see that? Sunshine is a blessing, don't you agree?' As she spoke she twisted her hands together, not looking at Toby once.

Toby ran across to the telephone-box. Shaking a little, he dialled the number on the card, pushed in a coin when someone answered, but said nothing. There was silence at the other end too. Then a man's voice said abruptly: 'Who is this?' Toby knew straight away that it was Henry Wickham. He put down the receiver.

It was early evening when Toby tried to call again. He had run along to the cinema café and brought back sandwiches and take-away coffees for Lillian and Olive. They stayed sitting on the spare ground for most of the afternoon. Lillian slept for a while, lying in the sun on her side. Then she walked with Toby across to the river's edge to look at the passing boats. Olive just sat where she was, staring up at the sky and humming to herself. She seemed happy just to remain sitting. She ate half a sandwich but didn't touch the coffee. She stared at Toby with a frown for so long Lillian told her again who Toby was.

'She used to walk all day sometimes,' Lillian said. 'And often for most of the night. She enjoyed walking so much. We walked about the City together. We admired the grandness. We marvelled at creation. Now Ollie sleeps, if I let her. She's like an old cat, soaking up the warmth of the sun.' Then she added: 'She's forgotten who you are, poor darling.'

When Toby tried to call the number again it was almost dark. The number rang for a long time. He was about to put down the receiver when someone answered. Again he said nothing after he pushed in the coin. Then a voice said: 'Who's there? Is anyone there?' It was Alicia.

'This is Toby,' said Toby.

There was a long silence and then Alicia said in a breathless voice: 'Oh my dear, where are you? I haven't stopped thinking about you, every day since. . . . Are you all right? Please tell me. I've been so dreadfully worried!' Her voice sounded shaky.

As quickly as he could Toby told her about himself, then about Lillian and Olive, that Olive was ill. Then he told her that he didn't believe what Henry Wickham had told him. He spoke so quickly he was worried she didn't understand him.

Alicia was silent for a few minutes before she spoke. He heard her breathing. She wheezed. 'Look,' she said. 'Don't ask me to explain. Make your way over to the house straight away, with your friends. I insist that you go there. I know you'll remember where it is. I'll leave a key at the back, under a pot. I must hurry. Henry and Myra are out. I'll slip round there now with the key. Don't worry, it will be quite all right. I'll explain everything when I see you. Bless you for calling. Bless you. I shan't even ask where you got this number from. It can wait. Let yourselves in. I'll get back to you as soon as I can. I just can't . . .'

The pips went, and then the line was cut off. Toby had no more money. He stood beside the telephone-box for a long time before he walked back to where Lillian and Olive were sitting. Alicia had sounded odd. There'd been something odd in her voice, as if she was drunk. Yet she had told him to go to the house as if she had meant it. Toby's stomach churned.

Lillian acted nervous and jittery when Toby told her that he might have a place for her and Olive to stay. Though he wasn't sure about it yet. It might work out, he told her. 'It's a fair way to walk,' he said. 'Will Olive be all right if we walk there? It's up in Hampstead.'

'Yes, dear boy, Ollie's had a good rest. She should be dandy. Oh dear, are you quite certain about doing this for us? I don't want tribulations, not now. Will it be safe?'

Toby shrugged.

Lillian stared at him. Then she looked away. 'You are too kind, sir,' she said. 'Too kind.'

Lillian helped Olive to her feet. Olive suddenly said loudly, staring at Toby: 'Are you a sodding policeman?'

'This is dear Toby,' Lillian said, holding on to Olive's arm. 'He's going to help us, Ollie.'

Olive frowned and then she stared up at the darkening sky. 'Moon,' she whispered. 'Moon, June, loon, soon, tickle your toes and tell.' Then she peered straight into Toby's face and grinned.

A few of her front teeth were missing, Toby noticed. The rest of them were black.

'Yes, Ollie. That's right, dear girl,' Lillian said loudly. She leaned over to Toby and whispered: 'That's the first time she's rhymed for weeks. She does remember you. Now there's a thing!'

Toby didn't think Olive looked ill. Her eyes had shone when she grinned at Toby. Her whole face shone. Even the sores on her chin had healed up.

Lillian holding her arm through Olive's, and Olive carrying her bag of newspapers, they set out slowly towards the steps leading up on to Waterloo Bridge. As they walked Olive started to hum under her breath. Then she grinned and said loudly, peering around Lillian: 'I know you, you know. You're not no policeman. I'm not ruddy stupid.' After a pause she added: 'Give us a hand-out, Harry, you wicked old bastard,' and laughed.

'Manners, Ollie, manners,' Lillian said. She glanced at Toby and tried to smile. Her lips quivered. Her eyes looked huge. 'I'm so grateful to you,' she whispered. 'She's talking because you're here. Harry was Ollie's brother, I believe.' Then she added in a normal voice: 'This is providence indeed. You've been sent to us poor mortals. Someone showed you the way to where we were.'

'I am here, you know, Lil. I'm not bleedin' dead yet,' Olive suddenly said loudly. 'Soft old tart.'

Lillian slipped her free arm through Toby's and drew him close to her as they walked. Olive didn't say anything else. She was sucking on her teeth. Around them the street-lamps had come on. Coloured lights that were strung up above the Embankment wall swung back and forth in the breeze. It was still quite warm. Out on the river, passing them, a ferry-boat blew its whistle. Across the water Toby could hear Big Ben striking the quarter-hour.

7 The Truth of the Matter

Toby peered into the kitchen through one of the windows at the back of the house. It was almost midnight. The night was as black as pitch. The street-lamps along Pudding Lane didn't seem to be working again. He made Lillian and Olive stay out front while he checked that everything was safe and until he found the key. He moved quietly past the windows to the back door. Beside it, half hidden under a small bush, sat a plant pot upside-down. He felt underneath it. A key was there. As quickly as he could he unlocked the back door with the key and stepped up into the kitchen, feeling his way across the floor to the doorway that led into the hall. He didn't switch on any of the lights. He felt sure the house was empty, but for a while he stood in the hall and listened. When he unbolted the front door and opened it he ran down the steps and along the short drive, crossing the grass to the side-gate. Lillian and Olive were still standing outside the gate where he had left them. They were holding hands. They both looked scared and exhausted. They were trembling.

'It's all right,' he said. 'No one's here. You can come inside.'

Neither of them said anything as they followed him back into the house. Olive looked as if she was ready to collapse. Lillian had her arm round her. Olive looked about with her mouth wide open. Lillian frowned and looked so worried that Toby couldn't help smiling.

The three of them had taken hours to cross the city. Toby had wanted to run all the way but had to walk as slowly as his friends. Olive had needed to sit down every so often. She soon got out of breath but she didn't complain once. She kept grinning at Toby. Sometimes she winked at him and sucked her teeth so loudly Lillian kept telling her to be quiet.

Toby had led them up Charing Cross Road, along Tottenham Court Road, past Euston Station and then on to Camden Town, before they stopped for a rest. It was the only way he knew how to get to Hampstead. There'd been a lot of people about on foot and passing them in cars. Their journey was slow but no one bothered them. Whenever they'd seen a group of people ahead, Toby had got them to cross to the other side of the street and carry on from there. He was worried that Olive might shout out at someone. Lillian had told him that Olive often shouted at people in the street. Lillian was used to it now. Olive never meant any harm. She enjoyed yelling things. If someone yelled back she'd laugh and wave at them, but sometimes she gave them the finger.

By the time they reached Camden Town both Lillian and Olive had slowed down. They rested along a side-street, sitting on the pavement in a bus-shelter.

'Are we going to Mimosa?' Olive asked Toby. She hadn't stopped staring at him for most of the way and grinning. After a while she let go of Lillian's arm and took hold of Toby's. She ignored Lillian. Toby told her he was taking her to a house where she might be allowed to stay for a while. Olive looked at him as if she didn't understand. Lillian sat without saying anything. She didn't stop smiling, but her face had grown pale and she was having trouble with her breathing.

After so many streets, Hampstead Heath looked dark and enormous. Without moonlight the trees and bushes looming up around them seemed a bit menacing. Toby got lost once they moved up on to the Heath from a road leading off Haverstock Hill. Lillian held Olive's hand. They stayed very close to each other. The whole area looked so different that Toby started to panic. But he had been there before at night. Once they had passed the ponds he recognized Parliament Hill. Half-way across it he had a strange feeling they were being followed. He looked back but there was nothing to see except the trees and bushes and the pink-tinted clouds in the sky. The hill was deserted. The feeling that there was someone close to them, watching, was so strong Toby started thinking about the pigeon man. He wondered if he had been watching them. Yet nothing happened. No one appeared. He hurried them down the slope through the long, wet grass and across to the small, almost hidden entrance into Pudding Lane safely. They saw no one else at all.

They stood quietly in the hallway once Toby had shut and bolted the front door of the house behind them. The house creaked from a strong wind that had sprung up outside. Toby still didn't turn on any lights. Their eyes had adjusted to the darkness on the Heath. Everything looked the same as it had when he had left the house. He tried to open the study door but it was locked. There was no key in the lock.

'You have brought us to a palace, dear boy,' Lillian suddenly said. 'Are you sure this will be proper? It's such a grand house. I am overwhelmed.'

'Grand,' said Olive loudly. She started to rhyme but Lillian told her to be quiet. Olive turned her back and stood still with her fingers in her mouth. She closed her eyes.

'If we go back into the kitchen we can turn the lights on,' Toby said, taking Lillian's arm. They both followed him, slowly. Olive kept her eyes shut even after Lillian put her arm through one of hers. She bumped into the door-frame and cried out as they entered the kitchen. Each of them jumped. Lillian sighed but said nothing.

In the kitchen with the hall door closed and the lights switched on Toby started to relax. The room seemed warm and friendly even though it was almost empty of furniture. The table and chairs were still there by the back door. One of the chairs lay on its side. Beside the chair sat a small box filled with groceries. There were tins of fruit, Irish stew, bread, butter and a tin-opener. He thought Alicia must have left the food there when she'd come with the key. He helped Lillian sit Olive down at the table. 'We can have something to eat, then I'll take you upstairs,' he told Lillian. 'There's a bed up there you can use.'

As he took the food out of the box Lillian began to cry. She just stood in the middle of the kitchen behind where Olive was sitting and covered her face with her hands. Her body shook. She let out little sounds. Her crushed straw hat slipped off her head and fell to the floor. Toby hurried across and put his arms round her, trying to ignore her strange smell. 'It'll be all right,' he said. 'Don't get upset. You'll be safe here. I'll look after you.'

Olive gazed around the kitchen, twisting and turning in her chair and humming. She took no notice of Lillian. 'Squat,' she suddenly said very loudly. 'Squat, pot, rot, hot, not, pop the question, sailor, and loan us a dollar.' Then she added: 'Lost me ruddy bag on that sodding hill. Dropped it. All me newspapers. Sod you, Lil.'

Lillian wiped her eyes on the sleeve of her coat and patted Toby on the arm, smiling down at him. 'Manners, Ollie, manners,' she said, glancing at Olive. 'You forgetful, dear old darling. Never mind your newspapers. We're here now.' Then she said to Toby: 'I am sorry, dear boy. I do get weepy. I am a little overcome. Such providence. It seems undeserved.'

'Soft old tart,' Olive muttered.

'You sit down,' Toby said to Lillian. 'Look after Olive.'

Olive stared at Toby with her mouth open. 'Call me Ollie,' she said loudly. 'Or call me Madam.' Then she laughed. She sat with her elbows on the edge of the table and with her hands clasped together. Her eyes sparkled from the overhead lights. She seemed fully awake. She'd pulled the Tesco bag from off her head and folded it up on the table in front of her. Toby tried not to stare at the jagged scar across her forehead. He didn't think it looked like an operation scar. It was too uneven. In the light both Lillian and Olive looked old and frail and shabby. They were very dirty. They both smelled in the close air of the kitchen. Toby started to worry about what Alicia would think when she saw them. But Lillian and Olive were his friends. He was trying to help them. Alicia would understand. As he carried on preparing a meal, finding a saucepan on top of the cooker and heating up the stew, he felt as if he'd slept for hours and he was now wide awake. He felt excited. He kept listening for sounds, wondering if Alicia would come back, now they'd arrived. Thoughts whirled about inside his head. His body tingled. Nothing seemed very real.

Lillian and Olive ate as if they hadn't touched or seen hot food for weeks. Toby sat watching them, not feeling hungry at all. He'd found plates and cutlery where they'd been before. The food Alicia had kept in the cupboards was gone. The cupboards were bare. Olive kept glancing up at him as she forked food into her mouth, chewing with her mouth open. She seemed to have trouble using a fork, so he found her a dessert spoon. She grabbed it off him and carried on eating, not even glancing at him as she took it. A lot of her stew ended up on the table and down the front of her coats. When she'd finished, Lillian took out her filthy handkerchief. She cleaned Olive up and tried to wipe the table. Lillian was shaking. Her face looked grey.

'She's not used to such luxury,' Lillian said quietly. 'I am so sorry.'

'Bleedin' right I'm not,' Olive muttered. 'Don't get hand-outs every day. Harry didn't neither.' She grinned at Toby and then said: 'Rum tum tum, thank you Mum' and laughed, spitting food on to the table.

Lillian sat patting Olive on the arm, smiling across at her.

Once Lillian had also finished her meal Toby led them both upstairs to the room he had slept in. Olive took Toby's hand as they climbed the stairs. The bed was still there. Lying on it were some blankets and cushions Toby hadn't seen before. There was a candle in a holder beside the bed on a chair, with a box of matches.

'You can both sleep up here if you like,' Toby told Lillian. 'I'll stay downstairs in case Alicia comes back.'

'Queen of Sheba, Mother,' Olive muttered, staring at the paintings that were still stacked along the walls. 'It's a bleedin' art gallery, Lil. Hoity-toity.'

Toby left them, after Lillian reached out and squeezed his arm and nodded. She went to speak but looked away and shook her head. Olive was almost asleep on her feet. She was still grinning. She kept picking at her teeth with her fingernails. Her fingernails were long and black with dirt.

'Ollie can have the bed,' Lillian whispered to Toby. 'I'll have the floor, dear boy. Such comfort. We are both so grateful.'

'Grateful,' said Olive. 'Right you are, Lil.'

Toby closed the bedroom door and stood outside, listening. He could hear Olive murmuring and then Lillian answering and then there was silence. Quietly he moved back down the stairs in the dark. He sat on the bottom step, leaning against the banisters. He thought he could stay awake for ever, thinking about his friends, knowing that Lillian and Olive were safe in the room and that they would be warm and snug. He remembered how much he'd enjoyed helping people back home. All those days when he had done his rounds lending a hand. He'd never found anyone a place to stay before.

'Snug as two bugs in a mattress,' Toby whispered, and grinned. Gran was always saying that. He sat and thought about the people he had met since he'd left home, the things that had happened to him. He wondered if Peter from South America was happy with his friend, if he was dancing in that far-away place called Bali. He thought of Annie and Adam, wondered if she was still screaming out of her window at night and wearing her eye-patch. Faces kept coming to him as he leaned against the banisters. It was as if he could actually see them gathered there in the hall. There was old Mrs Cranks with her budgerigar Ringo on her shoulder, beside the door. There was young Mr Grundy with no clothes on and Betsy Molesworthy with her flowers and George holding hands with Maureen Stokes. They were all still out there somewhere, living their own lives. His mum Alice might even be happy in America with the man she had met. George might be happy with Maureen Stokes. Toby felt happy himself. He wrapped his arms round his knees and smiled his slow smile as the faces faded. He listened for any sounds but the house was quiet. The wind had died down outside. After a while his eyes grew so heavy with a need for sleep that he curled himself up and lay back on the stairs. It wasn't very comfortable but he felt warm, thinking of Lillian and Olive in the room above him and Alicia knowing he was here. He wanted to sleep but he wanted to keep awake too. He needed to keep seeing all those faces in front of him again, smiling up at him. But he was alone.

He woke with a start. The hallway was grey with pre-dawn light. When he sat up and rubbed his eyes the first thing he saw was Alicia, standing in the open doorway of the study. She was smiling gently at him. He scrambled to his feet and ran to her. They hugged. She felt very bony in his arms. For a moment he thought he was dreaming.

'I never gave up hope that you would come back, my dear,' Alicia said. Letting go of him and stepping away she looked into his face. They stared at each other for a long time. Toby felt a warmth in his chest, a longing, as if he had been away and had come home. Alicia was nodding her head and smiling.

'I know, my dear, I know. I can sense what is in your heart,' she said quietly. 'Erihapeti is here. She wanted your return as much as I. She is surrounding us with her special rapture.'

Toby followed Alicia into the study. Alicia turned and looked over her shoulder towards the doorway and nodded twice. 'Yes, yes, you may leave us now,' she said.

The study was exactly the same as it had been before. Nothing seemed changed. There were even the remains of candles in their holders on the small tables. The curtains were open. A faint light filled with dust was streaming in across the floor. Alicia moved across to sit on the sofa. There was no sign of Bella.

'Your friends,' Alicia said, looking up at the ceiling, 'are they . . .?'

Toby nodded. 'They're in the room I slept in,' he said. 'I think they're still asleep. I hope it is all right letting them up there.'

Alicia nodded.

'Of course, my dear,' she said. Then she added: 'That shall be your own room, Toby, once we have everything sorted. I've thought of it as your room ever since you left. Come now, sit down. There is such a lot to tell you.'

Toby crossed the room and sat down in the winged armchair.

Alicia had large, ugly bruises on her arms. She tried to cover them up with her hands. The skin round her left eye was yellow and slightly swollen. Noticing Toby staring, she lowered her eyes.

She was holding her hands in her lap, twisting a handkerchief round her fingers. 'They're only bruises,' she said, then looked up and shrugged. 'Nothing broken. The flesh does heal. Even at my age.'

'What happened?' Toby asked.

Alicia looked away from him towards the windows. The streaks of dust-filled light had disappeared. A patch of sky above the trees at the edge of the Heath was a delicate azure.

'Oh, my dear. I shouldn't burden you. I wanted merely to offer you shelter, not tell you my own woes. Nothing is ever what it may seem, Toby. Remember that. Each of us has our small deceptions. I try to hide reality, to pretend it does not exist. I did that when you were last here. Yet I do so want to tell you the truth, if I may.'

She was quiet for a while, reaching up with her handkerchief to wipe her eyes. 'Well, my nephew tried to get rid of you. Doesn't appear as if he succeeded, does it?' Alicia said. 'Telling you I was touched in the head was just his ploy. They talked about you, once you'd gone. Henry lied to you. Let me explain.'

She blew her nose with the handkerchief and leaned back on the sofa, still staring out of the window.

'Some time after dear William died and the inquest was forgotten I suffered a slight nervous breakdown. Antony had been gone some time by then. I was put into a hospital. Oh, I was not terribly ill. I needed rest and quiet. They fed me happy pills and cared for me. The food was excellent. It was rather a lovely experience being fussed over every day. It was a private sanatorium, down in Kent. I was there for two months. The house had been locked up and everything seen to by Henry and Myra. In fact it was they who had suggested that I go away. They seemed most kind and concerned on the surface. They were so for some time. I'd foolishly contacted them. I trusted them to take over my affairs. I hadn't heard from Antony. I didn't know where he was. Later, a postcard came from some Middle East city. It had nothing written on it except his name. So I knew he was alive.

'While I was away Henry and Myra moved from their flat in Kentish Town to one a few streets away. They'd scrimped and saved to do so, I imagine. It was part of their idiotic plan. While I was convalescing they took over the house, sold furniture and got rid of so many of our possessions that William and I had collected over the years. I never found out about it, of course, until I came home. Before long they were driving down to Kent to begin pressing me, very politely, to let them have the deeds to the house. It was all quietly done. Most civilized. I imagine they talked to the doctors, but nothing was said to me directly about that. I was in no fit state to do much. I dallied, my dear. When I was due to leave the sanatorium they invited me to stay with them. I agreed. They had a spare room. I was still on medication. I took little notice of what was going on around me.'

In stops and starts Alicia told Toby the whole story. Once she was staying in their flat Henry and Myra had pressured her more and more about her having the house turned over to them. Alicia couldn't possibly need it any longer, they told her. There was no one else, there were no other relatives in the country to involve. Family members had all moved abroad soon after the war, even to as far away as Australia. Alicia steadfastly refused to sign over the house, she told Toby. But she'd become trapped, in Henry and Myra's flat, unknowingly for a time, as she was still unwell. Once Alicia felt fully recovered, Myra started to make vague threats and eventually used certain force. She grew violent sometimes. Myra had a vile temper. Alicia thought she was deranged.

'It's Myra, you see. She's behind it all. She always detested the rest of the family. She was quite paranoid about it. Henry was the only one who never made good. They'd always struggled, in comparison, she and Henry. Myra resented that. Henry's father, William's brother, was a wastrel. He left Henry nothing when he died. The rest of William's family were all rather well off. William had come from a very large family. Inherited wealth. The idle rich. Myra turned into a rather vindictive, jealous person very early on after her marriage to Henry. I never liked her. Henry of course is a weak man. He always was. He went along with Myra's plans to better themselves. A little reluctantly, I think, but he seems to admire her strength, or what he sees as strength.

'That morning I met you I had woken up at four. I'd actually climbed out of bed and knelt down to pray for some solution. Henry had been steadily selling my household possessions. He'd told me he was going ahead to have the place demolished, despite my protests. Myra told me I was not responsible, that they were thinking of my future. The house and the land are worth a fortune, of course. Henry had plans. Or I should say Myra had suggested plans, to have a block of luxury flats built here. Myra started terrorizing me, day after day. She waited until Henry was out of the way and then turned on me. I think she enjoyed it.'

Alicia stood up and went to stand at the window, looking out. She was trembling.

'You came into my life as if you had indeed been sent, child. I had moved back here out of protest, hoping that by doing so I might stop what was happening somehow. I was trying to decide what to do, while they were away in Italy. They thought I'd do nothing. I didn't wish to involve a solicitor. I've avoided them as William tried to do. Oh, it was so absurd, I put up with so much. So much pressure from Henry and nastiness from Myra. Selling my things. They thought it would weaken me. I lived on the edge, as they say. Well, my dear, you threw Henry and Myra into confusion when they found you here. Especially, for some reason, because you are so young. They'd not expected that. So they told you those preposterous lies to try to get rid of you. So childish and tiresome. They had to think up something very quickly. I should never have kept the truth from you. I thought you were too young to listen to my troubles.'

Alicia turned and looked at Toby with an expression he didn't understand.

'I knew you'd be back. That day you left, they took me off, Myra threatening me with everything she could think of. She locked me in the hall closet at the flat, would you believe it, after Henry had come back here to the house. Such nonsense. I almost found it laughable. I wasn't scared any longer. I kept thinking of you. I've had the house deeds safely deposited all along, at my bank. The house is still mine. The bruises were the result of what you might call a show-down between Myra and me. She's hit me before. She has an atrocious temper. She loses it often. They thought they were winning, you see. They thought I was slowly giving in to them. I almost had, up until you appeared. I've been so alone. They took full advantage of that. Oh, they kept telling me they knew best, that what they were doing was sensible. I knew no one to talk to about it, no one to turn to. They made certain of that. I've not heard from Antony for longer than I let you think. He's completely disappeared. I feel he is lost now. But you are back. And you've brought your friends.'

Alicia walked over to Toby and leaned down. She kissed him on the forehead.

'I want you to promise that you will stay. Your friends too, if they choose to. If you are living here, then Henry and Myra might give up. They're not really evil. Just terribly greedy and ambitious. There's so much money involved. I was far too vulnerable. It's been a battle, my dear. A stupid war of nerves between us. Utterly ludicrous, all of it. Your being here will put an end to it. I feel certain of that.'

'I'll do anything I can to help you,' Toby said, staring at her bruises.

Alicia took both his hands in hers and smiled. 'Bless you,' she said. 'Bless you, child.'

She got up and went across to the door, looking out into the hall.

'I have to keep the house, you see, while I'm alive. For William's sake,' she said. 'He would have wanted me to. He'd be horrified to see it now, so naked. Empty. Some days I felt quite helpless to do anything to stop them selling our things. I did try to fight, but when one is alone. . . . I cannot afford anger at my age. There were days when I feared that Myra wished me dead. She became so spiteful. Horrid. I didn't have a collapse that day, when Henry made you leave. I heard them talking about what Henry had told you, after you had gone. They treated me as if I was quite out of touch. Myra hit me across the head in frustration, with her fists.'

'You should have gone to the police,' Toby said.

'No, my dear, that is something we would never do in the family. We have never bothered the police about family matters. There's never been reason to.'

'That was stupid,' said Toby. 'I would have done.'

'I dare say you would have, Toby,' Alicia said. 'I was brought up in a different world. A world of status and class and convention. Brainwashing. All nonsense, of course. But one cannot simply ignore background. We are each brainwashed at an early age, to do what our parents do, believe what they believe. It is almost impossible to break from one's past, from how one has been taught to behave.'

'What will happen now?' Toby asked.

Alicia shrugged. She came back into the room and sat on the edge of the sofa.

'We shall simply wait. Wait and see. I feel filled with fighting spirit, now you are here. The timing is excellent. They are both going back to Italy early tomorrow morning. Myra has some connections there, I believe, as well as Henry's business dealings. They buy and sell antiques. I have been acting suitably contrite and passive towards her. Since I heard from you I even hinted that I might be changing my mind. I was most careful about what I said. Myra suddenly became kind and almost gentle in reaction. Fussed over me. Such bigotry. They'll think I'm out walking, now. I often leave Bella behind. Bella does belong to Myra, child. I suppose I lied to you about that. I'm sorry.'

Then she said after a silence: 'I never told Henry you were my son, Toby. Myra told Henry to tell you that. They discussed it in front of me as if I were deaf. Myra was so keen to get rid of you. She's always acted rather terrified of youths your age.'

'Why?' Toby asked.

Alicia stared at him then looked away.

'That's a mystery, my dear, even to me. They were both disturbed by your being here. Let's just leave it at that, shall we? Best to, I think. I don't really understand them. I never did. I do believe they are cowards at heart. Ambitious cowards, if there is such a thing. They want the house and all the money it would bring. But they fear trouble just as much. Their reaction to your being here convinced me that you might be the answer, if you came back. I knew in my heart that you would. Erihapeti told me so. She is a rare treasure.'

'She's a bit like my Gran's Angel,' Toby said.

'Yes, isn't she? Just like your Gran's Angel. We never did talk about that, did we? We must, once the dust has settled. I do believe you are here to stay. We shall be such good companions. Good chums. We can help one another. I hope you don't imagine I am trying to use you. I have become immensely fond of you. You are a treasure too.'

'I thought about you a lot,' Toby said. 'You're a bit like Gran. Except you're posh.'

Alicia laughed. 'Your friends are welcome, Toby,' she said. 'They have shelter here, if they want it. I've often thought about taking in ladies who have need. It appears that I have done so. Though I didn't quite expect. . . .' She paused, frowned, and then carried on: 'Lord knows, I have the room. Charity is difficult. One has to be tactful. I hope your two ladies will not be offended if I offer them a place to stay. There'll be no conditions or rules. We'll arrange for new furniture. A fresh start.'

'Lillian wants a place for Olive,' Toby said. 'Olive's a bit touched in the head. I hope it'll be all right. Lillian said Olive's ill, but I don't think she is.'

'What are their names, Toby, their surnames?'

Toby told her.

Alicia nodded. 'I don't suppose it matters,' she said. 'Of course it doesn't. It sounds fussy, wanting to know. Brainwashing again.' She laughed. 'I was sounding like my dear mother. She would have wanted to know who they are descended from. Are they gentry? she would have asked, in her deeply suspicious voice. I am sure she must have prayed every night to gentle gentry, meek and mild. She was terrified of mixing out of her class.'

Toby heard a sound in the hall. He got up and peered through the doorway. It was Lillian. She was standing half-way down the stairs. Her hair hung down across her face. She had wrapped herself in a blanket.

'Dear boy,' Lillian said in a loud whisper, gesturing to him. 'I'm afraid Ollie's had a little mishap. She's wet the floor. I am so sorry. Are there any rags?'

Alicia had followed Toby out into the hall. When Lillian noticed her she drew back, holding a hand up to cover her face. She was about to turn away and go back up the stairs when Alicia called out: 'Hello! You must be one of Toby's friends!'

Lillian lowered her hand and tried to smile but didn't move.

Alicia stepped over to the stairs and held out both her hands.

'Do come down and join us. Don't feel shy. I'll make some breakfast for us all. Is your friend awake? Did you sleep well?'

Lillian stared. For a moment she looked as if she couldn't decide what to do. Then she started to move slowly down towards them, taking each stair as if she was frightened she might fall. 'My name is Miss Lillian Pike,' she said in a shaky voice as she descended. 'So lovely to meet you.'

Toby looked at Alicia. Alicia was smiling gently. Lillian looked like some strange sort of spook, Toby thought. Her legs were bare. They were covered with dark stains and scratches. Her lips quivered. The bruise on her cheek still looked swollen. Her hair, covering most of her face, was matted and greasy.

'It's quite all right,' Alicia said after a moment. 'You are more than welcome here.'

Lillian stood staring away from them again, still half trying to hide her face. Just as Alicia spoke there came the sound of a crash from above them and then the sound of Olive, swearing. Olive's face appeared round the corner of the upper hall. It withdrew quickly when she saw faces looking up at her.

'I've stubbed me bleedin' toe,' Olive called out. 'Where's the ruddy bog, Lil? I'm busting for a shit.'

Alicia kept on smiling. She took hold of Toby's hand and held on to it tightly, drawing him close. She'd started to tremble. After a minute she said in a bright voice: 'Well, it should be a glorious day.'

An hour later Alicia and Toby were clearing up the mess Olive had made on the bedroom floor when they heard the front door being opened. Lillian and Olive were both in the kitchen eating a cooked breakfast. Alicia had brought eggs and bacon and more bread. Toby had cooked the breakfast. He had closed the kitchen door and told Lillian to keep Olive in there until he came back. Lillian had hardly stopped saying sorry to Alicia. Olive had been caught short in the night. No one had showed them where the bathroom was. Olive's waterworks were upset. Olive had woken up and thought she was back at Mimosa Crescent. She'd dreamed that Mr Braithwaite was coming after her with a knife.

'You stay there,' Alicia whispered to Toby. 'It'll be Henry, no doubt. He must have found a spare key. Wait for a couple of minutes and then come down. I may need you.'

Alicia had gone pale but she patted Toby on the arm and smiled before she left the room. Toby stayed close to the door, which Alicia shut behind her. There was a long silence, then Alicia cried out.

Toby pulled the door open and ran along the landing to the top of the stairs. In the gloomy hall he could see a figure standing with his back to the stairs. The figure was very tall. He had his arms round Alicia. For a moment in Toby's panic he thought it looked as if the man was strangling her. Toby shouted and started to leap down the stairs two at a time.

The man turned.

Toby came to a stop half-way down. Alicia was smiling and weeping, her hands clasped together in front of her. The man was smiling too.

Alicia hurried forward across to the foot of the stairs, gesturing to Toby. Her face looked radiant. 'It's Antony!' she cried. 'Antony, my son. He has come home!'

8 Miss Lillian's Story

Olive told Toby that she'd never really had an operation on her brain. She had made the story up. She'd got the scar when some youths had attacked her years ago, one night on Clapham Common. 'Don't tell Lil I told you, son,' she said, grinning at him. They were sitting in her and Lillian's new room, at the top of the house.

'Why did you lie to her?' Toby asked.

Olive just shrugged.

'Gawd knows. It was a long time ago. I talked a load of cobblers in them days when I met Lil. It was the gin, I suppose. Lil got me off that muck.'

'She loves you,' said Toby.

'Reckon she does, silly old cow,' said Olive. 'Don't know why. Love's a load of bollocks. Look at the way dogs carry on. Just the same. Gives me the gripes.'

Olive talked to Toby when Lillian wasn't about. Lillian was having a bath. Alicia had told each of them to have as many baths a day as they wanted. She'd bought Lillian and Olive special oils for their skin, and shampoo. Toby's friends had started to look a bit different already, after only two weeks. They didn't smell any longer.

Lillian and Olive had a room to themselves at the top of the house. The room had rugs on the wooden floor. There were two beds and a wardrobe. Alicia had been to a local charity shop and bought dresses and other clothes for them. A window set into an alcove looked down on to the garden and across rooftops. Toby was sitting beside the window on a rocking-chair while Olive sat on her bed. When Lillian had first seen the room and was told it was for her and Olive she had burst into tears. Olive didn't say anything at all. Toby had told her several times now to stop calling Alicia 'Duchess'. Olive had become rather cheeky. She was forever swearing. She didn't seem the same person Toby remembered meeting at Calcutta Mansions. Her favourite word was bollocks. She said it all the time. She had stopped rhyming and refused to leave her room except to go to the bathroom. If Toby was still about when she went, she would sit on the toilet seat with the door open and call things out to him. 'Bleedin' luxury, son, ain't it?' she'd yell.

Toby brought most of their meals up on a tray. Alicia didn't seem to mind. At least she didn't say anything. She didn't talk much to anyone except Antony. When Olive went downstairs Alicia smiled gently at her but said very little. She talked more to Lillian. Olive sat and glared. She went to sit with Alicia only the one time.

Toby couldn't believe how much had changed in the two weeks since Antony Wickham had come home. Though the house was still mostly empty of furniture they each had their own rooms, with beds and wardrobes bought from second-hand furnishers. Toby had helped Alicia clean the rooms they were using. The others were left as they had been. He had been out shopping with her a few times. The furniture was delivered all in one day. Lillian had tried to help with the cleaning but she'd acted weak and had to keep sitting down. 'I keep coming queer all over, dear boy,' she told Toby. 'Such providence is a little too much for my old soul.'

Antony had brought all the bedding to the house. It was brand new. He told Toby he loved to buy sheets and blankets. Antony and Alicia spent hours alone together shut in the study after he turned up. They didn't stop talking. Antony didn't say a lot to Toby, and nothing to Lillian and Olive. He seemed mysterious and very shy. He'd bought a lot of luggage with him, which was in the room next to Toby's. Nobody was allowed in there.

Myra and Henry had gone off to Italy without knowing that Antony was back, or that Toby was in the house again, along with his friends. Alicia had made sure of that. They were due back in a week.

'I lied like a trouper to them,' Alicia told Toby. 'I was so contrite, Myra was most civil to me. I dare say they'll be in for a shock on their return.'

At first Alicia cooked special meals for Lillian and Olive, going up to their room to see them several times a day. She sat and chatted to them about William and how things had been, just as she had talked to Toby. Often Toby joined them. Lillian sat leaning forward hanging on to every word Alicia said. Olive didn't listen at all. She stared out of the window and sometimes turned on the little transistor radio which Alicia had bought Toby, holding it up to her ear with her eyes shut. She listened to Radio One and told Toby she thought the disc jockeys sounded sexy. She ignored Alicia mostly, hardly speaking to her at all as she'd done when she went downstairs the one time. Lillian kept saying sorry, as if it was all her fault that Olive acted rude. Alicia just smiled. 'Jolly good,' she said in a far-away voice. Whenever she said that, Olive laughed. Olive never called Alicia 'Duchess' to her face, only to Lillian and Toby.

'I don't know what has come over Ollie,' Lillian admitted to Toby one morning. 'She was never like this on the streets. We have been shown such kindness. We are ladies drawn up out of the mire. Olive should be grateful. At least she talks now. Her rhyming was a trial.'

'Perhaps she doesn't like it here,' said Toby.

Lillian sighed. 'She will stay here for me,' she told him. 'My Ollie knows where she is better off. We never had such luxury, dear boy. It is a blessing. We are so grateful. We are lost and languishing ladies no longer.' And she laughed.

After the first week Alicia stopped going upstairs altogether. She kept asking Toby to encourage his friends to come down to the study. Olive refused. 'I been down there once,' she said. 'Bleedin' cheek. It's a load of bollocks.'

Lillian didn't want to leave Olive alone, so Toby sat in the study with Alicia during the evenings and read to her as he'd done before. He always read from Dickens. Sometimes Antony was home, but more often than not he was away from the house until late. Toby hardly saw him. He had a small car which he used to drive Alicia to the local supermarket to buy food and necessaries. Alicia never invited Toby to go with them. Toby stayed in the house and worried. Alicia had taken money out from her bank to spend on steak and fresh vegetables, huge cheeses and dozens of eggs. The kitchen cupboards were overflowing. She fed all the best food to Lillian and Olive. She never ate much herself. Antony ate out at restaurants. Alicia bought a washing-machine and taught Toby how to use it. Then came a refrigerator. Alicia kept talking about buying a television set. Toby felt guilty.

Toby wasn't sure what to make of Antony. He was very quiet, though he smiled all the time just as Alicia was doing now, and sometimes he looked a lot like her. He was tall and thin and pale and had the same green eyes. There was something odd about him, but secretly Toby thought Antony was the most perfect-looking person he had ever seen. His fingers were long, his hands very narrow and pale and he used them a lot when he talked. He was a bit theatrical, just as Alicia was. Antony had asked Toby about his family but said nothing about himself, why he had suddenly come home without warning. Alicia said nothing to Toby about Antony either. They acted secretive. Toby felt a bit left out, but Antony was Alicia's son. Yet after the times when she had been shut in the study with Antony Alicia would stay in there with the door open and Toby heard her crying. Toby went in to sit with her, after Antony went off in his car.

'Oh, my dear. It's all been too exhausting,' Alicia told Toby. 'It is rather a shock, Antony coming home. Even Erihapeti has been staying away. She said there were too many people around me. I'm not complaining, mind. We are sorting ourselves out, I dare say. Antony has not had things easy as I thought he might. I am trying to understand his needs again. But it has left me feeling so ancient. I shall tell you, child, once the dust has settled. I cannot speak of it now. I'd hoped the two of you might have become good chums. Such a thing seems rather remote in the circumstances.'

She never explained what the circumstances were.

Antony was mostly at home during the day. He and Alicia sat in the garden when it was warm, on deck-chairs, talking. Toby would go up to sit with Lillian and Olive in their room.

'It's a bit of all right here, ain't it?' Olive said to Toby. 'Bit like living in a bleedin' hotel. My bro' Harry would've felt like some bloomin' king or something, living here. The rich have it all, don't they? Ruddy ponces.'

'Alicia isn't rich,' Toby told Olive. 'She's spending a lot of money feeding you. She's going to a lot of bother.'

'What's the Duchess want?' Olive asked him on another day while he was sitting with her. 'What's she up to? That's what I want to know. She's after something.'

Lillian was fast asleep on her bed. She and Olive both slept a lot during the day. Olive sometimes snored so loudly at night Toby would hear her from his room on the floor below.

'She doesn't want anything,' Toby told her. 'It's because you're my friends. She's being kind. She likes to help people like I do.'

'Load of bleedin' bollocks,' said Olive, scratching at her head under her scarf.

'Don't you want to stay here?' Toby asked.

Olive stared at the wall. She wore scarves on her head now instead of plastic bags. Alicia had bought her three silk ones. One had a picture of St Paul's all over it in psychedelic colours. Sometimes Olive wore all the scarves at the same time. Alicia had also bought her some trousers and a huge woolly jumper. Olive had told Toby she hated wearing dresses. She had asked for a pair of men's boots and had got them as well. She wore the boots without socks.

'I'm here because Lil wants me to be here, that's all,' she said. 'That's why. Don't you say nothing, son. Never wanted no bleedin' charity. Didn't ask for it neither. I'm no charity case. I've looked after meself all me bleedin' life.'

'Alicia's not forcing you to stay,' Toby said.

'Dead right she's not. You ain't got to rub it in. I'm here for Lil, soft old tart. I'm grateful. It's just me way. Can't be anything different than what you are, can you? That'd be lying, son. Olive Pinch ain't no liar, not much she ain't.'

'Why did you make up rhymes all the time?' Toby asked.

Olive shrugged. 'Enjoyed it,' she said. 'Made me stop thinking. Thinking don't do no good.' Then she laughed.

Toby wasn't sure he liked the new, talking Olive. And Lillian had grown quiet since they'd been in the house and Olive had changed. Every time Olive said something rude, Lillian would look away and her lips would quiver. Olive ate everything that Alicia sent up to them but often Lillian wouldn't touch the food at all. Lillian slept so much during the day Toby wondered if she was ill. She didn't look ill. Neither of them did.

'Did you really live in that house in Camden Town?' Toby asked Olive.

Olive stared at him. She stared at him a lot, with a blank face. She didn't like Toby asking questions, but she always answered.

'Me husband bumped hisself off there, son. Took a load of pills. Never did get over the war, poor old bastard. Got the shakes. The big war, that is, not that ponce Hitler's balls-up. I lost it, you see, after my old man died. I pretended to Lil that I couldn't remember half the ruddy time. It was easier. She would keep trying to drag me back there. Nearly drove me barmy. I suppose she was only doing what she reckoned was best. Trying to help. Soft old tart.'

After a minute she added: 'You should mind your own business, son. You ask questions and you might not hear what you want to hear. Flaming right, that.'

'Friends are supposed to tell each other things,' Toby said.

Olive just kept on staring.

'Told Lil you was after her body that night we was in your room,' she said. 'That lad will be wanting his jollies off of us, I said. Young lads are randy little buggers. I should know. Made a mint when I was young out of young lads. Sodding sex. Gives me the gripes.'

Toby felt his face grow hot. He looked away, out of the window. 'It wasn't like that,' he said. 'I wanted to help.'

'Didn't bleedin' need your help,' Olive told him, grinning. 'We was all right, Lil and me, till you pushed in. We got by all right. You should have left well alone. Who do you think you are, a ruddy social worker? You're only a boy. You got eyes like a girl. You're still wet behind the ears, son. Bleedin' cheek.'

'Lillian's my friend,' said Toby. 'I thought you were too.' He kept looking out of the window.

'Ain't got no friends,' Olive said. 'Don't want none. It's a right load of bollocks, friendship. Told Lil that too. No such thing. I got by on the street, you can count on that. Never needed no one till Lil came along. She's made me soft in the head like she is. Silly cow. Always blubbing.' Olive laughed again and looked across at Lillian, who was still asleep on her bed. 'Soft in the head,' she muttered.

She glared at Toby.

'Why don't you sod off. I want a sleep like Lil's having. Hanging about here. What's your game? You must like old bints like us, is that it? Turns you on, does it? Bleedin' charity cases we might be as you think but you're a head-case, son. Go on, get off and leave us to get some kip. I shan't be here long, that's for sure. Duchess will get sick and tired of me. They all do. Ruddy charity. It's barmy.'

Olive lay down on the bed and rolled on to her side, facing the wall. Toby sat for a moment watching her back. She started sucking her thumb. After a few minutes she was snoring. Toby got up out of the chair and tiptoed from the room, shutting the door carefully behind him. He went down the hallway to sit on the main stairs for a while. The house seemed too quiet. He wanted to feel angry at Olive but he just felt sad. He suddenly thought of his Gran and wanted her to be with him.

'How old are you, Toby Todd?' he whispered. After a long time he answered: 'I'm one hundred and four. I'm only a youngster.'

Every time Lillian met Antony in the house she would hang her head and turn away and say nothing at all. She acted a bit nervous of him. Antony just stared at Lillian with a little smile as if he didn't know what to say to her either. Toby had wanted them all to be friends but it didn't seem to be working out that way. He had dreamed about them sitting down around a table like a family, just like he and Gran and Alice and George had done back home. Sometimes at Christmas even Betsy Molesworthy had joined them for turkey and stuffing and Brussels sprouts, though it had always ended up in a fight between Alice and George. Lillian and Olive carried on eating in their room and Antony was never home for meals. The only time Alicia seemed to eat was when she took a tray into the study and sat in there reading. Toby ate his meals alone in the kitchen. In the evenings he sometimes sat on the back step watching the fading light of the day through the trees.

One morning Lillian joined Toby in the kitchen for breakfast, before anyone else had stirred. 'I fear my dear Ollie wants to go back out on to the streets again, poor darling,' she said. She had sat down at the table, and watched him going back and forth from the cooker. 'She said she hated my bringing her here, dear boy,' Lillian went on. 'She's been acting so badly. I don't know what to do.'

Toby sat down opposite her. He had cooked her two eggs on toast and a slice of bacon. Olive had said the next time she came downstairs was when she was leaving, but not to tell Lillian.

'Do you want to leave?' Toby asked. He watched Lillian as she started to eat. She ate carefully and slowly as if what Toby cooked her was the best food she'd ever had. She didn't answer until she had cleaned her plate.

'Dear boy, dear boy,' she said slowly, looking down at her hands. 'We cannot stay here for ever. I don't wish to leave. I rejoice every given day that we have found a refuge from hardship. If only Ollie would start to enjoy it.'

She started to weep. Toby reached over and put his hands over hers. She so often burst into tears that it made Toby feel as guilty as he felt about Alicia using up her money on food. 'It'll be all right,' he said. 'You're my friend.'

Lillian smiled at him and wiped her eyes with the sleeve of her frock, pulling away from him. 'I was certain my Ollie was ill,' she said quietly. 'I don't wish you to think I was lying. Ollie does lie sometimes. I thought she needed a place. A quiet corner where she might feel welcome and recover from ailments. I am not sure, I feel so confused. I don't think she has any ailment.' Then she added: 'Your kind, dear friend, do you think she wants us here? Now that her son has returned to the fold?'

Toby shrugged. 'I don't know,' he said. 'She doesn't talk much at the moment. She's worried. There's things going on.'

Lillian stared at him for a long time. 'I do fear I shall lose Ollie,' she said. 'We were ladies fallen on hard times, wanderers along the stony pathway. We were joined as one. Ollie told me last night that she hates it here. She would rather die on the street, she said, than rot in our room.'

Toby had also cooked Olive some breakfast. He was just going out through the kitchen door carrying it on a tray when they both heard Olive yelling. When Toby got to the bottom of the stairs Olive was standing at the top leaning over the banister, peering down. She had nothing on except her trousers and the three scarves tied around her head. Toby tried hard not to stare at her breasts. They looked dark and stained. She didn't even try to cover herself up.

'My belly thinks me throat is cut, son,' she called down to him. 'Get a move on!'

As she shouted the words, Alicia came rushing out from the study and stood staring up at Olive. Alicia often slept the night on the study sofa. She stared at Olive without smiling and didn't even glance at Toby. After a moment she turned back and shut the study door with a thud.

'Get her,' Olive muttered. She was still staring at the tray Toby was carrying. 'Knew a bleedin' landlady like her once,' Olive went on as Toby climbed the stairs towards her. She was talking loudly enough for Alicia to hear. 'In Blackpool it was, just before I met the old man. Years ago. Mean old bitch she was and all. She used to number every sodding section of bog paper, then charge us extra. She was a duchess. The whole ruddy country's overrun with them. It's all bollocks under the bridge to me.'

Toby walked the rest of the way up the stairs without looking at Olive. She grabbed the tray from him when he reached her and turned her back, clomping across the landing in her boots to the stairwell that led up to their tiny attic room. Toby went to say something to her but closed his mouth. She wouldn't have listened to him. He watched her until she had moved out of sight. When he turned away and looked down, Lillian was standing in the hall staring at the study door, wringing her hands.

Two nights before Myra and Henry were due back from Italy Toby found Lillian sitting at the kitchen table in the dark. It was after three o'clock in the morning. Lillian never went into any other part of the house apart from the kitchen, except the bathroom on Toby's floor. Toby had woken up feeling thirsty and gone downstairs to heat up some milk. He nearly cried out when Lillian raised her head. She'd been resting it on the table-top. 'Dear boy, is that you?' she whispered. 'I couldn't sleep. Ollie was snoring so loudly. Most nights I can't sleep. I come down here. Ollie has announced that she is going back to where we came from. She told me tonight she didn't want me around her any longer. She wants to go off on her own. I feel such a loss, in my heart. What must I do? I cannot let my poor darling back on the streets alone.'

Toby fetched a glass of water and sat down. 'Do you want me to come with you?' he asked. 'We don't have to stay. Alicia will understand. I thought it'd be all right for you here.'

Lillian didn't seem to have been listening. 'If I let Ollie go off alone I shall lose her dear self,' she said. 'She has not been her true self here, I must tell you that. Did I tell you? I have never heard her being rude before. She just rhymed and hummed her tunes. She was contented with her lot. I don't understand. Ollie is my loved one. I must do what is best for her.'

They sat in silence for a while. Somewhere nearby outside a party was going on. Toby could hear laughing and loud pop music. The music kept getting even louder and then it stopped and started up again.

'I lost my dear mother, you know,' Lillian suddenly said. 'Did I tell you that too? She was the reason I became a rover, a gypsy. I ran away, ran away like the clappers.' She stopped talking, wiping her mouth with a handkerchief. The clothes that Alicia had bought Lillian were mostly too large for her. But in a dress covered with a flower pattern, her hair combed and the bruise gone from her clean skin, she had grown to look more and more like Gran in Toby's eyes. He shivered suddenly there in the dark. It was almost like he was back home and he and Gran were sitting in the kitchen having a midnight snack and a chat. They'd often done that when Gran couldn't sleep from her arthritis. She had woken him up so many times for a chat over hot milk, when George and Alice had been fast asleep.

'I called my mother Mutter,' Lillian told Toby. 'When I was a child she would tell me: Don't mutter, child. Speak up, she'd say. Pronounce your words or the world will denounce you! You are English! You must speak it. She was a wondrous person, Mutter was. My father died when I was a young girl. We lived in a small village in South Devon, beside the sea. Oh the sea, the shining silver water, dear boy. Such solace. Shaldon, the village was called. We had a small cottage. My father had laboured so hard. Do you mind if I tell you about Mutter? She has been so much in my thoughts.'

Toby shook his head, and smiled his slow smile.

Lillian smiled back at him sadly. After a time she said: 'I never had a noteworthy life. It was mostly ordinary. We were small folk in this huge world. We were of no importance to the grand design. When my father died we kept on at the cottage. I grew up and found a job locally, as a typist. Mutter taught me to type. She was so skilled. We managed. We drew so close as those years went past. The village was quiet and peaceful. Once a week we would venture across the river to Teignmouth to do our shopping. My school days were over so quickly. My world was with Mutter. We were alone against the tides of chance, after Father passed on. He'd been ill for a long time. He died quietly. We had his poor remains buried, and he was gone. So quick. It drew us inward, Mutter and me. We saw so few people. There were kind souls who reached out from the village, but Mutter liked to keep to herself. She had done, all those years there with Father. She was used to that. They'd made no friends, no close friends, dear boy, all their married life. They had both been born in Poland. They'd not liked England, or Father hadn't. Mutter confessed to me after he had passed on that she'd gone along with his dislike of England only to appease him. She'd been fond of England but had disliked changing the family name. That had never pleased her. Such sacrifice. Such devotion.'

Lillian paused. She stared up towards the ceiling, then out of the window. Toby watched her face.

'I was thirty-five when Father passed on. I'd never wanted to leave either of them. I'd never met anyone I thought I might marry. But then I did, just like that. Overnight, dear boy. His name was Radley Miller. He was a fine figure of a man. He had been at sea most of his life. He was a great deal older than I was. He began to court me. Mutter seemed to approve. Though she never once invited him to the cottage for supper as I'd hoped she might. She never spoke of him, inside the house. Radley and I walked beside the river-mouth. We held hands as courting couples do. Oh, he never acted as if he wished for more. He was a gentleman, I thought. There was no question of us being alone anywhere. I never even knew where he lived at first. Life was so different back then. There were rules. But we became a team, Radley Miller and Miss Lillian Pike. We got to know other couples. Radley seemed to know everyone. He wanted to know them. He opened up a world to me that I'd not known about. I began to spend all my free time with him, when I wasn't at my employers. Dear Mutter didn't complain. She said nothing. Weeks went past. I suppose I was falling in love, with Mr Radley Miller and all the world.'

Lillian's hands began to shake and she looked down at them.

Toby stared at them too. They were covered in plum-coloured marks, and wrinkled.

From outside, across on the Heath, they suddenly heard voices shouting, then a scream. The voices grew closer, then faded away.

'I spent more and more time with Radley,' Lillian said. 'We would visit the local cinema, then walk along the Teignmouth sands afterwards in the moonlight. Other couples might join us. I was so innocent, dear boy. I suppose, looking back, that Radley Miller must have known how innocent I'd been. I felt I was living just for that man. Meanwhile I was leaving Mutter alone often, and for long periods. One night Radley took me home to his little cottage, miles away down the coast. I stayed the night. In the morning when I awoke in his arms there was a terrible storm raging. Radley told me the storm had raged all night. I hadn't noticed. I had discovered love. Love of the flesh. Such a powerful thing. So strong. So dangerous. Radley had been gentle and patient. I thought only of him and his attention. He drove me home in style that morning in his horse and buggy, once the storm had passed. The sun had come out. Dear boy, dear boy, had I known what was in store!'

Lillian stopped talking as through the windows they could see a blue light that kept flashing. They heard more shouting. Toby got up to have a look but could not see anything because of the trees. People were shouting loudly, then they stopped. The music of the nearby party had faded to silence. Toby looked back at Lillian, who had put her head in her hands. He moved back to the table and sat there, reaching out to her. Lillian looked up as if she'd just had a fright. She leaned forward, clung to his hands, pulling them close to her.

'Radley left me in Teignmouth. He told me he had business there. I walked back the long way, across the bridge and around to the village, feeling like a young girl. Trees and bushes had been uprooted in the storm. The sea looked yellow. I remember it all so clearly. The sky had been a strange vivid orange.

'I found Mutter lying on the hard kitchen floor, below a wooden ladder. She must have been trying to shut one of the windows high above the cupboards during the storm and had fallen. Her body was quite cold. She had been dead for hours. Then I panicked. To this very day I don't know why but I covered her with a shawl and placed a cushion beneath her head as if she were only sleeping. I left the cottage and started to walk. It had begun to rain. I walked for hours, looking for Radley Miller. I couldn't remember how to reach his cottage, though I tried. Eventually some kind soul took me to the local police station.

'After that, everything closed in. Mutter was buried. I remember that only vaguely. No one came to the funeral except a neighbour. I don't remember her name. Burying Mutter took up all our savings. I was left with the empty house, and grief. No one came. I never heard from Radley Miller again. I never found him. Weeks later it was, I began to feel desperate. One night I was certain that Mutter came into my room to stand at the foot of my bed. She accused me of abandoning her. She pointed at me and wept. Then she came back, night after night, for a week. She spoke to me in Polish. She was so angry.

'After that I fled. I can't remember how I really felt. I knew I'd been frightened. I remember packing a small suitcase of Father's. I caught a train up to London, using what little money I had. I found cheap rooms in Whitechapel. I hid myself away.

'I lost the rooms when the money was gone. I was asked to leave, just as you were made to leave your own lodgings, dear boy. Since then I have lived on the streets, and off them, and from charity. There are years I cannot remember. Blank times when I wandered and fought for peace. It never came. I kept wandering, seeking sustenance. It was a long time before Ollie came into my life. I grew old. I never went back to the village. I never went back to see about a headstone for dear Mutter's grave. I was too ashamed. Now it's too late. Now I could never return.'

Lillian's body shook but she didn't cry. Her hands felt cold in Toby's. She doubled over as if she was in pain. Toby got up from his chair and knelt down on the floor beside her, holding her against him. It was quiet outside now. There were no sounds at all inside the house. Toby stroked Lillian's hair until she had stopped shaking and became still, leaning against him.

'It all happened long ago,' Lillian whispered. 'Long ago. Life has moved forward. I've had my life now. I am old. I found my dear Ollie. I've known divine love that only women can share. Now I fear losing herself. I don't know what I must do. Ollie is so strong, so wilful. I cannot stop her from leaving me.'

'Did you ever tell her your story?' Toby asked.

Lillian just shook her head. She jerked herself away from Toby, then squinted down into his face, looking for something in it she wanted to see.

'You must return home and look for your own mother soon, dear boy. You must seek her out before it gets too late. She is your mother, however you feel about her now. You must not lose her the way I lost my own. You must promise me that. You must not let her die abandoned.'

She took hold of Toby's hands and held on to them so tightly it hurt. She raised them to her lips and kissed them, looking away from him towards the windows.

Toby helped her up from the table. Lillian was so worn out she almost fell as he helped her across to the door. She didn't say anything else. Toby didn't know what he could say to her to make her feel better. He felt he should say something but didn't know what or how. In the hall he put his arm round her waist and helped her climb the stairs. She seemed to be half asleep once they had reached her room at the top of the house. No one else appeared. He opened the door quietly.

Lillian stepped away from him, about to enter the room. Then she turned and patted him on the arm. 'You are too kind, gentle sir,' she whispered. She didn't look at him.

Toby closed the door behind her, putting his ear to it and listening. He heard nothing. For a while he just stood there, unable to move away from the door. He suddenly felt that someone else was standing behind him on the small landing. He whirled around to look, but there was no one there he could see. Faint moonlight, or light from the street-lamps along Pudding Lane, was coming in through a small window at the end of the short landing. There was a sweet smell in the air, like perfume. It was a smell like crushed rose petals that reminded him of Gran. He listened. The whole house seemed still. He could hear his own breathing.

Just as he reached the hall below he looked right, suddenly sensing that there was someone else in the hall with him now, at the far end, leaning against the banister beside the stairs. He blinked, trying to see more clearly. It was very dark but he could make out a figure standing there. As he stared he saw that the figure was a woman. She was wearing a long white dress that touched the floor. The dress was covered in ruffles. The woman wore white gloves, which covered her arms up to her elbows. She held a glowing cigarette between the fingers of one hand. Jet-black hair hung down to just below her shoulders. Her face was as white as the dress. She didn't move. Toby stayed where he was. He could feel his heart start to thud and his mouth went dry. He glanced towards his room. There were no lights showing under any of the doors. The woman began to move slowly towards him, her arms held out as if she was walking on a tightrope. Toby began to back away. The figure was nothing like Gran's Angel. There was no silver light. The face didn't smile. The eyes looked dark and empty. He started to feel panicky.

'I'm afraid I have startled you,' the woman said. The voice was deep and husky. 'I am so sorry. You are quite safe, with Lola.'

Toby stared. There was something familiar in the voice but he knew he'd never seen the woman before. As she drew closer Toby kept his eyes on her face. Lola smiled, reaching out with a hand towards him as if she wanted to touch him but was afraid to. Toby kept on staring with his mouth open, suddenly recognizing the smile.

The woman was Antony Wickham.

9 Lola and the Secret Life

Toby heard the news the next morning on a small transistor radio that Alicia had given him. Olive had started claiming that the radio was hers. He'd taken it back from her. The pigeon man had been murdered.

The newsreader didn't call him the pigeon man. He didn't call him a tramp either but used a long word that was a polite one for someone who was homeless. The old man had been found on Hampstead Heath. No one had come forward to claim what was left of his body. They described his clothes and the strange purple cap he'd worn. The cap had been lying below the body. It was thought that he might even have been nameless as well as homeless. The body had been found hanging upside-down with its hands and feet nailed to the trunk of a tree, near one of the ponds below Parliament Hill. Beneath the body on the grass were five pigeons lying in a circle, each with a broken neck. There were no clues as to what had happened. Three youths and a girl had discovered the body in the early hours. They'd been questioned and released, but the girl was still in hospital suffering from shock. The body had been mutilated. Pieces of it were missing.

Toby knew straight away that it was the pigeon man, as soon as he heard the news. He'd not been able to get to sleep after meeting Antony dressed up as Lola in the hall. He'd crept into Lillian's and Olive's room just after dawn and taken the radio from where Olive had left it on the rocking-chair by the window. Neither of them had woken up. He thought that listening to the radio might stop the thoughts that had been rushing around inside his head about Lola and Antony. He'd been unable to stop thinking. After some music on the radio he didn't like, the news came on. He was lying on his bed and sat up, remembering the flashing blue light and the shouting voices. It must have been while Lillian was telling him her story in the kitchen that the pigeon man's body had been found.

Toby went straight over to the Heath as soon as it grew light. No one else had stirred in the house. He'd heard Olive snoring. Antony did not come out of his room. Alicia never got up until ten.

There was a small crowd of people standing about close to where the pigeon man had hung from the tree. The trunk of the plane tree was covered over with plastic sheeting. The area was cordoned off with a long strip of plastic, held up by stakes in the ground. A policeman on duty beside the tree told Toby to clear off after he stood there for a while staring. Toby heard a woman with a black poodle telling a man with an Alsatian that the body had been taken away hours ago. The pigeons had gone. The sky was heavy and grey with low cloud, for it had rained most of the night.

For the next couple of days the newspapers took hold of the story. All sorts of reasons were offered for the death. There were suggestions of black magic and Devil worship. No one came forward to give any information. Toby read reports in newspapers that Antony brought home and left on a table in the hall. One report said that the police were baffled. They were planning a door-to-door inquiry.

No one came to the house.

Toby carried on listening to the radio news but nothing new was said. There was a threatened miners' strike and fears of power cuts. Nurses were on a work-to-rule and were refusing to empty bedpans because of staff cuts. An old lady of ninety-two had been found brutally raped and half beaten to death inside a caravan at Southend.

The plane tree on which the pigeon man had been found was cut down and taken away. There was a local outcry over that, and a small demonstration on the Heath. In the local newspaper Toby read a letter from a Councillor Betty Grieve who complained that the destruction of the tree was an abomination. It was the last mention Toby found to do with the murder. There wasn't a thing written or said on the radio about what had been done with the pigeon man's body or where it was to be buried. Eventually the cordon was taken down from around the tree-stump. People avoided the area. Toby went back there several times.

Alicia didn't say anything to Toby about the death. He knew she must have heard about it. She seemed to have been avoiding him since Toby had met Antony dressed as Lola. She smiled at him every time he came downstairs and one time stared at him sadly for a while, then rushed off into the study and closed the door.

Olive had started going on about seeing a ghost in the hallway every night. 'This old dump's haunted,' she told Toby. 'Places always are where rich ponces live. It gives me the sodding willies.

It's all decked out in a fancy shroud and it moans. Its face is a sight. Enough to make you go blind.'

Toby tried not to laugh. He said nothing to her or Lillian about Lola. He didn't mention the murder either, as he knew it would upset Lillian too much. He tried to ignore Olive. Every time they saw each other Olive stared at him with a sour look and was often rude. Toby spent most of his time with Antony.

When Toby came back to the house from the Heath the morning after he had heard Lillian's story and then the radio news, Antony was sitting in the study with the door wide open. He was wearing a red dressing-gown and pyjamas. It was still very early. He gave Toby a brief smile when he looked in. 'Hello, my dear,' he said softly. His voice was different. He had not called Toby 'dear' before.

Toby stood in the doorway and he and Antony stared at each other for a long time. Toby felt his face growing hot. His mouth went dry. He felt a bit odd after what had gone on. He didn't know what to say. Antony got up from the wing-chair where Toby usually sat and came out into the hall as Toby started to walk away. He walked past Toby to the stairs and then looked back, not speaking, beckoning Toby to follow. Toby did, after a moment. Antony didn't speak again until they were inside his room.

'Mother thinks the world of you, Toby Todd,' Antony said after he'd closed the door behind them. 'She said you've saved her life. She asked me to speak to you. She's rather overwrought and worried about avoiding you.'

Toby didn't reply. He was staring about the room. From the ceiling hung hundreds of pieces of silk. The silk pieces were all different colours, attached to the centre of the ceiling stretching downward and out to the walls, where they met other pieces of silk that hung to the floor. Lengths of silk hung down over the inside of the door, hiding it once it was closed. The whole room looked like a rainbow-coloured tent. The windows had been covered over with even more silk, but these pieces were larger and darker in colour. There was little furniture in the room. There was a round bed covered in huge cushions and an armchair. On each of the walls hung small paintings. The paintings were all of men wearing swim-suits. They looked like body-builders. There was a wardrobe, a small desk and chair, and small lamps sitting on the floor. Antony went about turning them on. Each of the lamps had a pink bulb. The room looked as if it was from a dream. It was the strangest, most beautiful room Toby had ever been in. Antony sat down on the chair in front of the desk and gestured to Toby to sit in the armchair. Toby had been staring at everything with his mouth open.

'This is Lola's room,' Antony said quietly. 'She likes the colours. They aren't exactly to my taste.'

Toby sat down and stared up at the silk. There were so many pieces hanging from the ceiling they changed the shape of the room. The silk moved slowly in a draught as if it was alive. From the middle of the ceiling hung a single light-bulb with the largest shade Toby had seen. The shade was pink and dotted with small holes. It had long tassels hanging from it. Across the floor were scattered plain white rugs that looked like sheepskin but weren't.

'Mother wanted to explain to you, Toby,' Antony said to him quietly. 'But she's asked me to instead. She is rather upset that you saw me last night. I told her about it. She fears you might wish to leave. Mother is terribly conventional.'

'Has she always known?' Toby asked.

Antony grinned and looked away.

'About Lola? Yes, of course she has. Though she's always hoped I only dressed up in private.'

'Is that why you went away?' Toby asked.

Antony didn't answer. After a while he said: 'Mother told me she wanted you and me to become friends. Good chums, she said. She lives so much in the past, my dear. Another age. Sometimes I think she still considers me to be a normal little boy. I never was. It was never easy for her, accepting Lola. Father hated her.'

'But you're Lola,' said Toby.

'I am, and I am not,' Antony said. 'Oh dear, that sounds pompous. I don't mean to be. Lola has her own life. One day I plan to become Lola all the time.'

For a while they sat there in silence. Toby could sense Antony staring at him, but he kept his eyes on the floor. There was a red stain on one of the rugs. The room was very clean and smelled faintly of roses. On the desk sat a coffee- and tea-maker. Steam was rising up from it. Antony stood up and fetched two cups and saucers from the inside of the wardrobe. The wardrobe was huge and filled to overflowing with clothes. Toby could see drawers and small cupboards inside it when Antony opened it up. The doors were covered with carvings of birds. Antony made two cups of coffee, added cream and sugar and handed one to Toby.

'Mother told me too that you knew that poor man they found on the Heath,' Antony said. 'What an extraordinary business. She was quite horrified. If you don't mind my asking, how did you meet him?'

Toby talked. He didn't know why he was able to talk so easily. It felt odd, but he didn't think anything was wrong, being here. He longed to ask Antony questions about Lola but didn't want to seem rude. He talked about the pigeon man until there was nothing left to tell. While he talked, Antony sipped his coffee, sitting on the edge of the round bed. He kept nodding the whole time Toby spoke.

'Have you thought about informing the police?' Antony asked when Toby stopped.

Toby shrugged and then shook his head.

'I should think it a silly idea anyway,' Antony said. 'Best to keep quiet. What a world we live in. Some days I feel positively normal.'

Toby smiled his slow smile. As Antony said that he threw his head back and, for some reason Toby didn't understand, it was funny. He felt warm from the coffee. He thought he could sit here in this room all day. It felt safe, like being inside a cave when everything outside was in the middle of a storm.

During the next few days as the news about the pigeon man began to fade from the radio news, Toby went up to Antony's room every morning for coffee. Alicia stayed shut in the study, resting. Not once was Antony dressed as Lola. He told Toby that Lola came out only at night, the way things were. He made her sleep during the daytime. She needed her rest. He explained that Lola had been inside him ever since he was a little boy. She had only truly appeared, he said, once Antony was old enough to buy all the things she wanted. She had grown up with him. She shared his body. He had a man's body but Lola didn't mind. He and Lola loved each other like brother and sister.

'Lola needs beauty to live,' Antony said. 'Or she has done. She adores clothes and colour and gentleness. She hates confusion. When there is trouble she usually hides herself deep inside me and won't come out. She loves Mother.' He watched Toby's face and then said slowly: 'I suppose you think I'm mad.'

Toby shook his head and then shrugged. He started to feel a little uncomfortable. He didn't know what he thought. 'It's the way you talk about her as if she's someone else,' he said.

Antony nodded, smoothing the cover of the bed. The cover was made of blue silk. 'Mother has been very protective,' he said. 'Apart from her, only my closest friends know Lola. She won't appear for just anyone.'

'Olive told me she sees her when she goes to the toilet at night,' Toby said, grinning. 'She thinks she's a ghost.'

Antony smiled. After a silence he said: 'Mother went on about taking in lodgers before I went away. I never imagined she would, not at least. . . .' He stopped speaking and glanced towards the door.

'They're my friends,' said Toby. 'I've been trying to help them.'

Antony stared at him for a long time. 'You are a curious little person,' he said, still smiling.

Toby, feeling his face go bright red, suddenly said: 'I think Lola's the most beautiful person I've ever seen.'

He looked away when Antony kept staring at him. Antony's smile had made Toby come out in goose-bumps all down his arms. He shivered. He didn't know why he'd said that. It sounded pretty stupid.

'Are you cold?' Antony asked. 'I've an electric fire somewhere.'

Toby shook his head.

'Lola would like to meet you properly,' Antony said after a while. 'She has been asking about you. Would that be all right? I don't wish to scare you off. Mother has convinced herself that you are about to flee, now my ghastly secret has been revealed.' Then he laughed.

'Olive reckons she's going back on the streets,' Toby said. He didn't know how to answer Antony's question about Lola. 'She doesn't like being here.'

'She is so wonderfully vulgar,' said Antony, and laughed again. 'Some of my friends would find her quite irresistible. Though she's rather a burden for Mother. That's partly why Mother's been rather vague with you, I'm afraid. She can't cope with Olive.'

'Olive's all right mostly,' Toby told him. 'She used to rhyme her words all the time, before we came here. She'd say a word, then come out with others that sounded the same. She spoke funny little sentences. She told Lillian she'd had an operation to take away a bit of her brain. She was lying. Lillian and Olive are good friends. Or they were. Olive's been bad-tempered since we've been here. She hasn't liked it much.' Toby wanted to go on talking. But he'd begun to feel nervous again. He sat and stared at the floor.

'Would you like to come to a party, Toby?' Antony suddenly asked. 'With me? Or I should say with Lola. She wants to take you out to thank you for taking care of Mother.'

'When is it?' Toby asked, looking up.

Antony told him.

Toby blushed. It took him a long time to answer. 'That's the same day as my birthday,' he said. 'You must have known. I'll be seventeen. I haven't told anyone.'

Antony clapped his hands and his eyes opened wide. 'I swear I didn't know, Toby,' he said. Then he added: 'Pure coincidence. How delicious! What do you say? It can be our little secret until then, if you want. Is that all right?'

Toby nodded. They grinned at each other. Suddenly the room became filled with sunlight. It streamed in through the cracks between the silk at the windows.

Over the next few days Toby found himself in Antony's room for hours at a time. Antony made him laugh. He had travelled all over Europe with Lola. Lola liked to entertain people and make new friends when she came out. She had once danced on tables in a café in Paris when she had taken over the place and no one knew Antony. They knew Lola was a man, Antony explained, but no one cared or even wanted to know Antony's name. It hadn't mattered. Lola had appeared in a stage play in Berlin, she had performed dances in night-clubs and been paid for it and had had three marriage proposals from rich men.

Toby told Antony about Peter from South America who had also danced, about Annie with the eye-patch from Ireland and Mr Braithwaite, even about old Mrs Cranks and her budgerigar, Ringo.

Antony kept clapping his hands and saying 'Oh, how delicious!' and laughing. Toby felt flattered. Antony seemed so interested in him Toby told him everything about his life.

Antony explained to Toby that sometimes Lola would come out when he was Antony and it became difficult to control her. She was so feminine and sometimes loud. Usually she came out only when Antony dressed as her and put on the make-up. He told Toby how he treated his skin so that it looked like a woman's, or a well-cared-for man's. How he shaved off all his body hair and spent hours taking care of Lola's real-hair wigs and her clothes. He took special tablets too, which helped. He'd found the tablets in

Holland. His wardrobe was filled with clothes that Lola wore and clothes that Antony wore. Antony took them all out to show Toby. It cost him a fortune, but Alicia had made certain for years that Antony had enough money for him and Lola. Antony wouldn't talk about why he had gone away. He never spoke about his father. He mentioned Myra Wickham once, and then grew angry and silent.

Toby was properly introduced to Lola late one night. Meeting Lola was like meeting a different person. Toby knew that Lola was Antony dressed up but the change bewildered him. Antony didn't allow Toby into his room while Lola was getting dressed. She took a long time. She need solitude for the change, he said.

Toby joined Lola every night, after the first time. When everyone in the house was asleep he would step into the hall and wait outside Antony's door, having knocked once. Then Lola would open it and invite him in. She spoke very quietly at first. She spoke the same way that Antony spoke, but somehow it was not his voice. The sound of Lola's voice made Toby's skin tingle all over. His heart thumped when she smiled at him.

'Antony is my guardian if you like, darling,' Lola said. 'He is a dear, sweet man. Isn't he? I am so pleased you and he are chums. Alicia wanted that. She is rather distracted, Toby. You mustn't think that she is deliberately ignoring you. She awaits the return of the wicked Wickham witch. She's most distressed at the moment. Myra will be back soon enough. Myra is everything that is grossly vile in this world.'

Lola liked to sit and sip champagne on Toby's visits to her. She wouldn't let Toby have more than a taste of the champagne from a cup. Toby didn't think much of it. It tasted sour. He tried hard to imagine that Lola was Antony dressed up, but after a few times he started to think of Lola as being another person, just the way Antony talked about her. Lola began to fill his dreams at night. He kept wanting to see her during the day as well, but Antony would not allow it. Antony kept telling him that Lola was resting, that she needed her sleep. Into Toby's dreams Lola came to him with her arms open and they would dance and he would hold her to him and they would kiss.

One evening when Antony was out, Alicia invited Toby to join her in the study. He was half-way down the stairs when Alicia came out into the hall from the kitchen and looked up at him. 'Do come through and sit with me, my dear,' she said, moving across to the study door. She only glanced at him and didn't smile. She looked pale and tired and seemed to walk with a stoop. Toby followed her.

Once he was sitting in the winged armchair and Alicia was on the sofa she said quietly: 'I wish to apologize. I have been neglecting you disgracefully.'

'That's all right,' Toby said.

Alicia looked at him for a long time. 'I've been unable to get myself to talk to you for days, my dear,' she said. 'Now I feel I have so much to say, I don't know where to begin. I feel we should talk about Antony, but there is something else. It has been playing heavily on my heart.'

For a while she was silent. 'It is about your friends,' she said eventually. 'I don't know quite how to put it. I don't wish to offend you.'

Toby didn't answer.

Alicia's eyes were watering. She nodded. 'Olive isn't quite what I had expected,' she said. 'I feel selfish and mean, but I cannot seem to. . . .' She stopped and stared towards the door.

'It's all right,' said Toby. 'Olive's been talking about leaving. She doesn't like it here.'

'Oh child, I don't wish to send her packing. Really I don't. I wanted so much to help your friends. You do understand, don't you?'

Toby nodded and smiled at her. He stood up and went to sit beside her. 'Olive's been a real pain,' he said. 'She's upset Lillian too. She keeps talking about going back out on the streets. She's told Lillian she wants to. She doesn't want Lillian with her. She keeps swearing. Do you want me to say something to her?'

After a moment Alicia shook her head.

'No, perhaps not. We'll just let things be. If Olive is indeed planning to leave, well then it's best if we remain silent on the matter. I feel such a foolish old lady. I'd imagined things would have been rather different. I so wanted them to be, you know. I have grown so fond of you, young man.' She stared down at her lap, and was trembling. 'The way you have befriended Antony recently has moved me deeply. I dare say I should have explained about him. I tried to tell you again and again, in my mind. But it all sounded quite preposterous. Then your hearing about that poor man on the Heath. I could tell you'd heard. I know it must have upset you. I heard the news too, my dear. Antony and I discussed it. So very distressing. I knew straight away who the man was. I couldn't speak to you of him. I'm so sorry.'

'I heard it on the radio,' Toby said. 'As soon as they said he'd been found, I knew who it was.'

Alicia took hold of his hand and held it in her lap. 'I so wanted you to feel safe and unbothered here,' she said. 'I thought this could become a haven for each of us. I so detest complication. I wanted to help your friends but I can't seem to warm to Olive at all. Though I am more worried about you.'

'I'm all right,' said Toby. 'I like it here.'

'Do you? Do you really, my dear?' Alicia asked, looking into his face. 'I have been rather upset that Antony let himself reveal his secret, about Lola. Secrets never remain buried as they should.'

'I'm glad I know,' Toby said. 'You could have told me. It wouldn't have made any difference.'

Through the open doorway of the study they heard Olive upstairs, laughing. She shouted out something, then was quiet.

'Yesterday, my dear, Lillian asked me if you were all right,' Alicia went on. 'She seemed quite confused. She thinks you are avoiding her because of Olive.'

'I've been with Antony,' Toby said.

Alicia stared at him and he blushed.

'I cannot tell you how relieved I am that you accept him. He has been desperately lonely. But you must not neglect your friends.'

'I thought we might have been like a family,' Toby said in a quiet voice. 'I know that's stupid.'

Alicia squeezed his hand and then let it go. She dabbed at her eyes with a handkerchief, then smiled. 'Very little turns out the way one expects,' she said. 'I never imagined I would ever see Antony again. He said he had come home as Lola had begun to worry about me. Bless her. He knows everything that has happened. We have talked. We are waiting for Myra and Henry to appear. I have felt rather ill from tension over the past few days. I expected them back last week. I dread their arrival, I really do. I've suddenly begun to feel like the frail old woman I suppose I am.'

'I'll be here,' Toby said. 'They won't try anything now. I won't let them. And you're not old. You just think you are.'

Alicia laughed. 'Bless you,' she said. 'Bless you for that.'

For a while she talked quietly about Antony. She had known since he was a teenager – even earlier – that he was different. It had taken her a long time to begin to accept him. She had thought he was unbalanced but had never taken him to see a specialist, as

William had suggested. Over the years, as Lola began to appear more and more often, she had learned somehow to accept things as they were. She had even helped Antony with Lola's clothes, to keep everything away from William, who had not really wanted to know about his son's difference from others. Antony had always disappointed William, Alicia said.

'William left things to me, child. For years I managed to keep them apart. It was so lonely, for Antony. I do believe that that was what created the animosity between them. The arguments, when they did see each other. I realized eventually that Antony could not be anything other than what he was. He is two people. Simply that. I know it must be frightfully difficult for you to accept. I am so glad now that I was able to accept it, and cope. I often thought that I had gained a daughter in Lola, she became so familiar. I even grew to like her somewhat. She isn't so different, of course, from Antony.'

When Antony had arrived back unexpectedly she had helped him during the night to decorate his room the way Lola wanted it, so that Toby and his friends wouldn't know. They'd had the bed delivered while Toby was out walking with Lillian. Olive did not appear during that time.

'I made him promise not to leave his room while Lola was out,' she said. 'Not while you were here. But Lola is a rather wilful person. Quite the opposite to Antony in that way. I am aware that the world might call him insane, or whatever the words are nowadays that are used for people like him. He is quite happy, despite his aloneness. He does have some close friends, I believe, who are like him. He has never had any problem at all, accepting Lola. The world would condemn him, shut him away somewhere, I dare say, if the truth came out. I made it my duty to protect him. One is fortunate, having money for such things. When he went away I believed that one day I should hear of his fate. Hear that he had been confined, treated as if he were ill. I have never considered that he is.'

'Why did he leave?' Toby asked.

Alicia didn't answer straight away.

'He was, or had become, tired of hiding. Of course it also had a lot to do with how his father died. The one thing I cannot accept is that he wishes Lola to take over. He wants to live openly as her. I doubt it will ever happen. So he travelled to places where he thought it might. He fears now that he has failed.'

'Lola's beautiful,' said Toby.

Alicia smiled sadly and nodded. 'Isn't she,' she whispered. 'I have missed them both, to be perfectly honest.' For a moment she covered her eyes and then rubbed them. Then she stood up and walked across to the french windows, peering out.

'I am so grateful to you. I still believe that you were sent here to me. Just like your Gran's Angel was sent to her. You have enriched my life.'

'I haven't really done anything,' said Toby. 'I brought Olive. She hasn't made you happy.'

Alicia turned her head to look at him, then carried on staring out into the front garden. 'I don't know how on earth to cope with Olive,' she said. 'She is quite beyond my comprehension. I know there are hundreds, perhaps thousands out there, homeless and bruised. Just like her. Like your pigeon man. It causes an ache in my heart when I think of them. I have had so much comfort in my life, and so much shelter. When I was young I never even thought about poverty and what it might do. I took my life for granted. Erihapeti helped me to see things differently. She has been rather annoyed at me for wanting to be rid of your friends. She stands beside my bed at night when I cannot sleep and lectures me. She is a dear soul. She is so simple. Uncomplicated. I am not simple, not in that way. I often wish I were.'

Toby didn't really understand what she was saying. He stayed silent.

'I shall make some supper and take it up to your friends,' Alicia said, turning back into the room. 'Don't worry, I shan't ask Olive to leave or anything silly like that. Things do have a way of working out.'

She walked over to where Toby had stood up and placed her hands on his shoulders. She kissed him on each cheek and stared into his face. 'If you do choose to go if or when your friends do leave, then I shall not fuss,' she said. 'We don't *own* each other. But I should miss you as dearly as I have missed Antony. And Lola. They will miss you too, I dare say. I shall say no more about that. But you will always have a place here, while I am alive. And always a special place inside my heart.'

Then she left the room quickly, not looking back.

It was later that night when Henry and Myra turned up at the house.

Toby spent a couple of hours with Lillian and Olive up in their room before he went downstairs to bed. Olive had done nothing but argue with everything Toby said to her. She'd gone on about Alicia, calling her Duchess. How the rich ruled the world. Lillian ended up in tears. Toby wondered if Olive had been drinking. He knew there was no alcohol in the house except in Antony's room. But the room was always kept locked when Antony wasn't there.

Olive had been trying to get Lillian to clear out. 'She doesn't want us here, Lil. I can tell,' she said. 'I don't bleedin' know why she lets us stay. Rich old cow. It's like a sodding prison. Let's get off, Lil. I miss the streets.'

Lillian said she didn't want to leave just like that. Alicia had been kind to them both. They couldn't just go. They should talk about it to Alicia, if Olive wanted to.

'Bollocks,' Olive kept saying. 'She'll just act posh. I don't want none of her charity no more. I told you, she wants something off of us. You get nothing for nothing these days.'

'You're wrong,' Toby said. 'How do you know? You won't even talk to her.'

Olive stared at him, looking him up and down. 'Talk, pork, fork, hawk, sew up your lips with a blister, mister!' she said loudly. Then she added: 'Wet behind the ears, you are, little runt. We don't want none of your chat either, do we Lil? What's he doing here, sodding little blimp. Tell him to sod off, Lil. Go on, he gets on my tit.' She turned her back to him and stared at the wall.

Olive went on like that the whole time Toby was in the room. When he left, Lillian was not able even to glance at him. She covered her face with her hands and turned her back as well.

Toby was lying on his bed staring at a watermark on the ceiling when he heard the front door open and slam shut and then voices. The watermark was in the shape of a face when he'd first seen it weeks ago. It had changed. Now it looked like some type of animal with a long snout. At first, when he heard the voices, Toby didn't move. He thought it was Olive but then realized that it wasn't because he could hear her snoring. The voices were very loud. He got off the bed and went to the door. The lights were on in the hall. The voices sounded like several people all speaking at once. When he reached the stairs and looked down he could see that the study door was open. The voices came from there. A woman was shouting. Then a figure came rushing out from the study. It was Myra. She made as if she was about to run up the stairs. She came to a stop and glared when she saw Toby peering down at her. He recognized her straight away though she looked different somehow.

'You can collect your things and get out now,' she called up at him. Her voice was cold and harsh. 'If you know what's good for you. You've no right being here.'

'I'm not going anywhere,' said Toby.

Myra began to hurry up the stairs towards him but he started down towards her and she stopped. Toby walked slowly, not taking his eyes off her. He didn't feel scared of her. He felt angry. Myra began to back away as he came close to her. She started to look a bit confused. She glanced over her shoulder towards the study. Just as she did so the door slammed shut.

'Listen, you little delinquent,' Myra said. 'You've no idea what you've stirred up, have you? I'm not having this crap, the house filled with tramps, do you get my meaning?' She went to take hold of Toby's arm but he jerked away.

'I know all about you,' Toby said. 'Alicia's told me. I know what you've been trying to make her do. And hitting her. You're a liar.'

The study door opened and Henry came out into the hall. He glanced at Toby, then looked away. Toby rushed past them and into the room. Alicia was standing in front of the curtains by the french windows. She was trembling but she smiled at him.

Henry followed Toby into the room. 'This is all quite impossible,' he said to Alicia. He ignored Toby. 'I thought we had come to an agreement.' He spoke very politely.

Toby moved across to Alicia and stood beside her.

'I have made no agreement with anyone, Henry. We are both fully aware of that,' Alicia said.

'Don't bother to argue with her!' Myra yelled out, having followed Henry into the room. Her voice whined. She glared at Toby. 'There's no point. The doctors said that if we choose to we can have her committed.' Myra walked straight across to Alicia and stood in front of her with her arms folded. 'Where are the others?' she said loudly. She spoke as if Alicia was deaf.

'I have told you, Myra,' Alicia said quietly. 'My friends are upstairs. They are sleeping. They live here with me now. Just as Toby does.'

'Utter nonsense,' said Myra. 'You've gone too far this time. Tramps off the street? You're demented, Aunty!'

Henry had closed the study door and was standing leaning against it. He was frowning at the floor.

'You will have to get rid of them, won't you?' Myra carried on. 'I'll help you. Then you'll come back with us. We have really become quite tired of your attitude. We shan't be going away again, leaving you. Will we, Henry? Everything's fixed. Isn't it, Henry? Tell her, tell her about Italy. We're selling this place, just as we planned. You aren't responsible, Aunty. You aren't well.'

Henry stayed silent.

Myra turned and stared at him until he looked up. 'Well?' she shouted.

Henry muttered something no one could hear.

'Oh, for Christ's sake,' Myra yelled. 'You're so bloody useless.'

She grabbed hold of Alicia's arm and tried to drag her towards the door. Alicia half fell and cried out. Myra pushed her, letting go. Toby leaped forward and shoved Myra in the back. She turned on him, lashing out at him with her hands. 'How dare you touch me!' she shouted.

Toby was too quick for her and ducked out of the way. Her face looked as if she'd gone mad. Her hair hung all over it. In a moment they were shouting at each other. Toby kicked Myra in the leg when she tried roughly to pull Alicia up off the floor. Henry shouted at Myra. Myra had begun screeching. She let go of Alicia's wrist and managed to hit Toby over the head with one of her fists. Toby kicked her again and she swore. Henry had left the door and was trying to get hold of Myra by the arms, shouting at her to calm down when the study door opened. None of them heard it open.

It was Lola who walked in. She was wearing a red dress that was so tight it clung to her. She had on black net stockings and high heels. On her head there was a huge felt hat with a veil that hid her face. In one hand she held a cigarette in a holder. Toby stared at her with his mouth open. She looked like a film star. Lola stood posing just inside the room and stared across at Myra. She started laughing. The room suddenly grew quiet. Henry stared at Lola with a dippy smile starting to appear on his face. He was still holding Myra's arms and he suddenly let them drop. Myra just stared. Lola walked slowly across the room to Henry and reached out, patting him on the cheek. She was inches taller than Henry.

'Who the hell are you?' Myra said loudly.

Lola ignored her. 'Dear cousin Henry. How very sweet of you to call by,' she said. Then she turned her head, peering at Myra. Myra didn't move.

Before she spoke again Lola took the cigarette out of its holder, crushed it in an ashtray that sat on one of the small tables, threw the holder on to the sofa and looked up with a smile.

'And Myra too! How perfectly divine. After all these years. How are you, darling? I see you've met Toby. Isn't he a little stunner? I remember how much you used to adore surrounding yourself with teenage boys. Toby and I have become such good friends, aren't I the lucky one?' She stared Myra up and down, then frowned. 'But, my dear, what on earth have you been doing to yourself? Your hair. Oh, you must let me have someone do something with it. I am shocked. Letting yourself go – one cannot afford to at your age. Really, Myra, but really. . . .'

Lola turned her back and moved across to Alicia, who had got to her feet and was trying to look calm. Myra carried on staring with a puzzled look on her face.

'Hello, Mother darling,' Lola said. 'Are you all right, treasure?' She leaned down and kissed Alicia on each cheek.

Alicia didn't move. She was staring at Henry. Henry looked shocked. Lola glanced at Toby and winked at him. Slowly, as everyone watched, she reached up and took off her hat and veil, placing it carefully on the winged armchair. No one spoke. To Toby it seemed that everyone was nailed to the floor. He had a strong urge to giggle.

'Now then,' Lola said quietly, staring at Henry and then at Myra. 'I think it's time for you pair of nasty, smelly little prats to leave. Don't you?'

She moved back to where Myra stood. Without any warning she hit Myra so hard across the face that Myra staggered and fell against Henry. Henry shouted but Lola turned on him quickly, grabbing his arm and twisting it behind his back so that Henry yelped. He didn't try to struggle. Lola marched him across the room out into the hall before he realized what was happening, pushing him towards the front door. In a minute she came back into the study and went to grab Myra's arms. Myra twisted out of her reach and hurried past her, calling out Henry's name. Lola followed. Toby heard Lola saying something in a low voice and then she laughed and the front door opened and slammed shut.

Toby looked at Alicia. She had her hands clasped in front of her mouth as if she was praying. She was smiling broadly.

Lola walked back into the study and stood staring at Alicia. Even after the scuffle with Henry, Lola looked perfect, in Toby's eyes. Her face was flushed. She looked magnificent.

'Lola always did despise those two cretins,' Lola said to Alicia in Antony's voice. Then she pulled off her wig.

Toby wanted to rush across and throw his arms around Antony but he still couldn't move. Antony and Alicia were looking at each other and grinning. Toby suddenly sensed that they wanted to be left on their own. They acted as if they had forgotten he was there. As he went to leave the room they didn't even glance at him.

Lillian was sitting at the top of the stairs. She sat there staring down at her hands clasped in her lap. She was wearing the nightdress and dressing-gown that Alicia had bought her. The dressing-gown was about three sizes too big. It was purple with a high collar. Toby climbed the stairs and sat down beside her when Lillian looked up.

'Oh, dear boy,' Lillian said and then started to cry. For a while she couldn't say anything else. When Toby tried to take her hand she pulled away from him. It was a long time before she seemed able to talk.

While Toby and the others had been shouting at each other in the study Olive had got dressed, thrown some other clothes into a plastic bag and, wearing all three of her scarves and her men's boots, had run out of their room. Lillian tried to follow to bring her back but Olive hurried down the stairs and was out into the night through the front door before Lillian managed to reach the downstairs hall.

'My darling has left me for good,' Lillian whispered. 'We are two ladies of the town no longer.'

The two of them sat on the stairs in silence. Toby could hear voices coming from the study and then the sound of Alicia laughing. Lillian pulled out a sodden handkerchief from a pocket of the dressing-gown. She blew her nose so loudly, Toby jumped.

'She never even said goodbye,' Lillian muttered.

10 Celebration Time

Antony drove Toby in his blue Mini to all the places Lillian told them Olive might have gone. There was no sign of her anywhere. They looked for her for hours every day and at night, driving around the West End and Charing Cross and over in the City. Lillian did not want to leave the house. She thought Olive might come back. She began to sit in the study with Alicia. Alicia was showing her how to knit. Now that Olive had gone, Lillian and Alicia had become friends. They were rarely apart.

'She sat and wept so much, I had to do something with her,' Alicia told Toby. 'She showed such grief. Knitting is excellent for calming the spirit. Erihapeti suggested it.'

So far Lillian had knitted small, multicoloured squares of wool. Alicia planned to sew them together to make a shawl. Antony went out to buy the wool. He brought back so much of it that Alicia suggested they could start their own business.

Every evening the four of them sat down to a meal in the study. Lillian even helped Alicia to do the cooking now she had recovered from the shock of Olive's leaving her. She told Toby she did not want to go after Olive herself.

'It's in the hands of fate, dear boy,' she'd said. 'My wandering has come to a close. My old bones tell me that. I had to let her go. There comes a time when the heart has to make a turning.'

Lillian talked about Olive every day. She worried about her so much at first Toby told her quietly that Olive had never had the operation on her brain she had claimed to have had. He thought she was quite able to look after herself. He hoped the news might make Lillian worry about her less.

'I knew. I knew all along she had not told me the truth,' Lillian said. 'It was simply my dear Ollie's way of saying how much she needed me back in those other days. That was all. I should not have told you about it. I so wanted you to feel for her as I do. She often came out with untruths, as we wandered and searched for sustenance. For a long time she believed she had cancer. Did I tell you that? She worried that I would abandon her. My poor darling drew strength from me until I had no more to give.'

Every morning Lillian sat by herself in her room for two hours. She told Toby she wanted to sit up there and think of Ollie and send out little messages to guide and protect her. For the rest of the day she sat with Alicia. Sometimes they sat together in the garden in deck-chairs. Alicia read passages aloud from Dickens and Trollope and travel guides and articles in *The Times*. If Antony had to go out, Toby found himself alone. He didn't mind. Like before, he felt he was waiting for something but did not know what. At night in his dreams Gran's Angel would stand beside a gate and she'd beckon to him. He could see Alice, surrounded by the silver light, standing in a doorway nearby, holding her hands out towards him. Sometimes Gran's face might appear, then slowly fade away. Toby would start to hurry forward towards where Alice waited, but then the dream faded and he would wake up with a start, reaching to the ceiling with his arms. George never appeared in the dreams at all.

Alicia told Toby that Antony had fainted when Toby left the study the night Myra and Henry had turned up.

'I almost called you back, my dear. I am so glad I didn't. Lillian needed you. If you hadn't been there she might have run off after Olive. I would not have made a new friend. Lola has never come out before, when trouble was present. Not as far as I know. I fear she has become stronger than Antony realizes. He was so pale and weak when he came to. He remembered everything, of course. We laughed about it.'

While Lillian had a rest in the afternoons Toby kept Alicia company. Sometimes he read aloud to her, but often she fell asleep, then woke up and pretended she had been listening. Toby could see that she was worn out from what had been going on. Some days he would cook meals or take each of them breakfast on trays up to their rooms. Antony did not keep his room locked any longer. Toby tried to explain everything to Lillian about who Lola was, once Olive had been gone a week. Lillian didn't say a lot about it. Toby wondered if she had understood.

'He is a dear, kind boy,' Lillian told Toby. 'He returned to care for his mother. I do so approve of that. There is so little kindness in this world.'

Lillian did not mention her own mother again to Toby, having told him her story. After a while, as she started to spend more and more time with Alicia, Lillian didn't talk about Olive either. She sat with Alicia and they would talk. Some days they went across to the Heath together for walks, arm in arm. Toby wondered what they talked about. He watched them sitting together in the garden, their heads together, chatting away and sometimes laughing as if they had known each other all their lives. They didn't act as if they needed him. He thought he might have felt jealous but he just felt relieved. It left him free to be with Antony, and Lola. Just as Lillian had begun to spend all her time with Alicia, Toby wanted to be with Antony, to sit in Antony's room, even when Antony was away from the house. Toby would fall asleep on the round bed. He would make tea and sit reading in the armchair. Sometimes he just sat and stared at the silk as it moved in a draught. The room was quiet and peaceful and gave him a calmness. Antony never told Toby where he went during the day. He was often away from the house for hours. He didn't ask Toby to go with him on those trips out.

Antony had taken Alicia back to Myra's and Henry's flat and found it empty. Alicia still had her own key. Her clothes, some books and other possessions she had there had been left in cardboard boxes just inside the front door. There was no note or letter for her. Most of the furniture had gone. The flat was abandoned. Alicia told Toby she thought they had probably returned to Italy.

'They never knew about Lola, you realize,' she'd told Toby after she and Antony returned with her things. 'I have no idea what they must have thought.' Then she laughed. 'It has all been rather a farce, don't you think?'

Toby hugged her.

Antony had nothing to say to Toby about Myra and Henry. He acted as if the whole matter wasn't important, that it was closed and ended. Toby kept watching through the windows for the next few nights. He felt sure Myra and Henry would come back. But the days passed and there was no sign of them. Pudding Lane stayed empty, as it always did. He would sometimes see a figure walking past, heading for the Heath, usually with a dog on a lead. One night a group of skinheads ran past, kicking a football and laughing. They were each wearing a British flag wrapped round their waists and their legs were bare.

Toby missed Olive. With her gone the house seemed so quiet. He kept expecting to hear her voice shouting out. Every time he went up to the top of the house to see if Lillian was all right, he imagined he would see Olive perched on her bed glaring at him. Driving through the streets at night when he and Antony had searched for her, Toby had the feeling that Olive hadn't been real. He saw nothing in the streets that made him want to go back there. He supposed that Olive had been living rough for so long that nothing else suited her.

Antony took Toby to a small men's boutique just off Regent Street and bought him clothes. Brand-new jeans and bright jumpers and shirts, a real sheepskin overcoat and even a pair of leather boots that Toby had admired in the window. Antony seemed to have plenty of money. He paid for everything by cheque and went bright red when Toby thanked him. Toby had his hair trimmed and washed in a large store in Regent Street. The barber called him Sir.

'Don't say anything to Mother,' Antony told Toby in his quiet voice. 'She'll say nothing. It's something I want to do to pay you back. You've done so much for her. She has found new purpose.'

Later that day as they were crossing Regent Street, heading towards where Antony had left the car, Antony put his arm round Toby's shoulders. Toby looked up into Antony's face and somehow it was Lola looking back at him.

In the evenings after the four of them had sat together in the study for a meal which Lillian and Alicia had made, Antony disappeared upstairs. Eventually, as Antony suggested, Toby followed. Lola would stand outside her door, waiting for him. They would spend the evening together, Lola reclining on the round bed and Toby sitting in the armchair. Toby read aloud from novels Lola kept in her wardrobe. The novels were all romances with lurid covers. Toby didn't think much of them after reading Dickens. He didn't say anything. Lola would sit listening with her eyes closed, wearing one of her long, rustling dresses. Sometimes she started to laugh and giggle and mutter: 'Oh, my dear. Too much for a white lady.'

Alicia telephoned every veterinary clinic in north-west London. She was trying to find out what had happened to Bella, Myra and Henry's dog. She even contacted Battersea Dogs' Home. Alicia worried about the dog every day. She feared that Myra might have had Bella put down out of spite. The kennels where Bella had been boarded knew nothing except that she had been collected and paid for the day after Myra and Henry had come to the house. Bella seemed to have vanished, just as Myra and Henry had vanished.

'I do hope she is all right,' Alicia said to Toby. 'I feel almost certain they would not have taken her with them. Myra treated the poor darling abominably.'

But just as Toby and Antony could find no trace of Olive, Alicia discovered nothing about Bella. In the end she decided that somehow they must have taken her across the Channel with them. People did that all the time, she said, if they thought they could get away with it. Alicia had planned to have Bella at the house, as she had become fond of her. Antony offered to buy her a puppy. Alicia wouldn't agree to that. 'It isn't the point, my dear,' she told him.

She suggested contacting the police about Olive. To offer a description of her, try to trace where she had gone.

Lillian wasn't keen. 'My Ollie has gone,' she kept saying. 'There's nothing we can do. She wants her life away from me and I must accept that,' she told Toby when they were alone.

Since Olive had left, Lillian seemed to have changed, in Toby's eyes. She was brighter and calmer. Her hands had stopped shaking all the time. Colour had come back into her face. She still cried a lot, but she rarely stayed up in her room for long and often helped Alicia about the house. One afternoon Toby found her watering some new plants in the kitchen, singing to herself and smiling. She never stopped talking to Alicia. 'It's providence, Toby. Providence, dear boy,' she told him. 'My life has turned yet another corner. I am the homeless wanderer no more. Such blessing. Such bliss.'

Yet Toby knew she missed Olive more than she let on. Sometimes he found her sitting on Olive's bed, weeping and trembling. She had not let anyone go near Olive's bed or change the sheets since Olive had left. Toby wondered if Lillian was waiting for Olive to return. He didn't think Olive would come back.

Antony told Alicia about Toby's birthday. Secretly Alicia and Lillian baked a fruit-cake and covered it with chocolate icing and seventeen blue candles. On the morning of his birthday, exactly three weeks after Olive had run away and Myra and Henry had been banished by Lola, Toby was woken up in his room by singing voices. When he opened his eyes Antony, Alicia and Lillian were standing at the foot of his bed singing 'Happy Birthday'. Lillian was holding the chocolate-covered cake. The candles on it had been lit and for a minute before Toby was fully awake he thought he saw Gran standing there too, then Alice with George and Betsy Molesworthy and one-armed Cyril. They were all standing around the bed smiling at him as they sang. When he blinked, the others had gone and there were only his three friends standing there. They were laughing as they finished the song. Alicia started singing 'For He's a Jolly Good Fellow' and very soon Lillian was weeping. On the foot of the bed there were three presents wrapped in silver paper. Someone had tied gas-filled balloons to them, so the balloons were suspended in the air, the long strings attached to them festooned with tiny flags, each with Toby's name on them. Toby didn't know what to say. He sat up and stared and grinned and kept swallowing. He was scared he'd start crying. One by one each of them walked up to him and kissed him, placing a present in his lap. Antony had carried a small table from the study to sit the cake on so that Toby could blow out the candles.

Alicia gave him an ancient, leather-bound edition of *David Copperfield*. She said she'd had it sent from a shop in the Charing Cross Road. Toby had never seen a book like it before. It was more beautiful than any of the books in the study. The dark-red leather and the edges of the pages were embossed with gold.

'I'd been foolishly hoping to find a signed copy somewhere,' she told him. 'No such luck, I'm afraid! I dare say such a thing would be quite beyond our reach!'

Lillian had knitted Toby three pairs of navy-blue socks. Each sock had his initials at the top, in red wool. They were too large and a peculiar shape but Toby didn't mind. He hugged Lillian until she was out of breath and had to sit down on the edge of the bed. 'I'll keep them for ever,' he told her.

'Dear boy, you dear boy,' Lillian kept saying. Her eyes were already swollen from crying. She was so overcome by it all that Alicia had to thump her on the back when Lillian started to cough and couldn't stop.

Antony's present was a solid gold watch that not only showed the date but the year, and it had an alarm.

Toby burst into tears and couldn't look any of his friends in the face. Alicia fussed over him and got him to blow out the candles on the cake to calm him down. Then she bustled out of the room with Lillian to take the cake down to the kitchen, leaving Toby alone with Antony. Toby climbed out of the bed and put his arms round Antony, hugging him, hiding his face in Antony's jumper. They stood there for a long time saying nothing. Toby felt he was the happiest person alive.

After a few minutes Antony stroked Toby's hair, then kissed him on the top of his head. Toby looked up. Antony pulled away, his face bright red. 'I've told Mother that Lola wants to take you out this evening,' he said quietly. 'I didn't say where. Lola has a gift for you, but she'd rather give it to you herself, later on.'

Toby stood staring at Antony. Antony had turned his face away.

They spent the day quietly. Antony did not leave the house. In the afternoon after a grand lunch of freshly cooked beef and asparagus tips and roast potatoes followed by ice-cream they sat out in the garden. Toby read to them: a passage from *David Copperfield*, where the young Copperfield is sent to Yarmouth to live in the boat-house with Peggotty, Dan, Mrs Gummidge and little Emily. Lillian clapped her hands when he had finished.

After that Alicia sang a song. It was called 'Let the Great Big World Keep Turning'. She sang so beautifully that Toby asked her to sing it three times. Alicia told him that the song was very special. 'It has been my undying favourite, Toby,' she said. 'I declare the words are perfect for friendship such as ours. If only my loved one were still here. Down all the years William used to sing it to me so movingly.'

Toby got Alicia to write the whole of the chorus into the frontispiece of the book she had given him, and sign her name. 'Famous at last!' she said, laughing. In the end he asked Lillian and Antony to write their own names there too. Antony wrote Lola's name as well as his own.

Lillian recited a long, rambling poem. She kept forgetting the words and having to start all over again. She made the poem twice as long as it really was by the time she finished. It was about a little girl growing up in an orphanage and wanting to become everything she saw around her. There were dozens of verses. Lillian kept stuttering and stopping but she carried on. At the end of the poem the girl died and was transformed into all the things that she had ever loved in her short life. Lillian said her mother had taught her the poem. It was the only one she knew off by heart.

'Or that you cannot remember, dear girl,' said Alicia, and they both laughed.

Through it all Antony stayed quiet. He kept staring at Toby. Whenever Toby looked back at him, Antony would avert his eyes. Antony sat on the grass beside Alicia, who was in one of the deck-chairs. While Alicia sang she had reached down and taken Antony's hand and held it in her lap.

The late summer sunlight was so warm it seemed as if autumn was still far away. The leaves on the trees were beginning to turn. Across on the Heath they could hear dogs barking joyously and laughing voices. For a moment Toby was reminded of the pigeon man and his death but he pushed the thought away. He didn't want the afternoon to be spoilt, or for it to end. He wondered if Gran was watching him from wherever she might be. He felt that he had never been as happy, that if the afternoon did last for ever his heart might burst.

As the day wore on and the sunlight coming down through the trees began to fade, Antony went back into the house and brought out a huge tray, on which sat Toby's birthday cake. Then he returned to the house three times, bringing out more trays covered with lighted candles in holders which he set about in the garden on tree branches and on the grass so that the whole garden became filled with flickering light. He wouldn't let anyone help him.

When he had finished, Alicia handed Toby a bread-knife to cut the cake. The garden grew slowly dim as the sun started to set and from cloud that had gathered in the sky. The candles flickered in a breeze that had sprung up, but each one of them stayed alight. They sat and ate the birthday cake and Alicia produced more sherry so they could toast Toby's health. Toby made a toast to Olive and then a toast to his Gran. After a while he made a toast to the Angel who had come to her the night she'd died.

'The everlasting Angel,' Alicia said softly, raising her glass towards him. 'She is forever near, watching over us.'

It was the best birthday Toby could remember having.

At ten o'clock that night Toby was sitting in the armchair in Antony's room watching him shave his legs for the umpteenth time. He used a small razor that worked on batteries. Antony took three hours to get ready. He kept taking off his stockings to check his legs in the mirror, then using the razor again. Toby sat staring at Antony's legs trying to decide if they looked more like a man's or a woman's. He couldn't decide at all but he liked looking at them. Antony let Toby watch him put on make-up. They were both still a bit drunk from the sherry. By early evening the four of them had got through three and a half bottles of sherry since the party had begun and Toby had been sick all over the grass. Antony had made him have a hot bath and then a sleep while he dressed himself up as Lola.

Alicia was upstairs at the top of the house sleeping in Olive's bed to keep Lillian company. Lillian had drunk so much sherry she started singing songs with the rudest words Toby had ever heard. They shocked him. Alicia didn't stop laughing. She and Lillian had helped each other into the house and went straight up to Lillian's room still laughing like schoolgirls and holding on to each other so they wouldn't fall over. Toby had never imagined that Alicia would ever get drunk. He felt a bit disappointed in her. After his bath he went up to see if they were all right. Each of them was lying on a bed fast asleep, so he covered them with blankets and went to tiptoe out. Just as he opened the door Alicia stirred and said his name. He looked across at her. She lay with her eyes open, beckoning him to come across to her. Toby glanced at Lillian, who still seemed to be asleep. He moved across and crouched beside Alicia.

She took his hand in hers, then kissed it. 'I am sorry, my dear,' she whispered. 'Afraid I got a little tiddly. So naughty. Lillian is a bad influence!' Then she smiled up at him and added: 'I have such love for you in my heart. I feel so happy that you and Antony are chums. Bless you. You enjoy your evening.'

Closing her eyes she settled back into sleep. Toby left the room, closing the door behind him as quietly as he could.

The party they were going to was being held in a flat in St John's Wood. Antony would not tell Toby anything about it or who would be there. Toby was dressed in his new jeans and a red shirt with a high collar and a navy-blue jumper. He was wearing the leather boots Antony had bought him and the gold watch. Once Antony had finished dressing, Lola stood there and stared at Toby and licked her lips, then poked her tongue out at him. She wore a vivid blue dress that shimmered. It flared out at the knees. She wore shoes with six-inch heels, black stockings and a long red silk scarf that hung down from her neck. Toby could not take his eyes off her. She'd become the most beautiful person he had ever seen.

'You look quite edible yourself, darling,' Lola told him, grinning. 'The girls will simply die. You'll be a star. Have you ever had a date before?'

Toby grinned and felt his face grow hot. He shook his head and looked away from Lola down to the floor. 'Not with anyone like you,' he said quietly.

'Cheeky minx,' Lola said, laughing.

Lola walked across to him and smoothed his hair, brushing his shoulders with her fingers. She had long red fingernails which Toby had watched Antony putting on with a kind of glue. She wore a large gold ring on one finger, but no other jewellery.

'Don't be nervous,' Lola said to him softly. 'No one will bite you. You'll be with me. They will all know who you are. You are Lola's friend.'

Toby trembled when Lola touched him.

Eventually Lola said she was ready. To Toby she looked stunning and nothing at all like Antony. Antony had disappeared somewhere, as if he had left the room. Lola had taken his place. Toby had tried not to think of Lola's wanting to take him to the party. He'd thought she would have forgotten. Now that the moment was here, he was so scared his mouth had gone dry. He kept worrying that he might wet himself and someone would notice once they got there and laugh at him.

Lola leaned down and kissed him lightly on both cheeks. 'Come on, tiger,' she said. 'Let's go break some hearts.'

As they walked down the stairs Lola put her arm through Toby's. Toby couldn't stop grinning.

He felt a bit foolish sitting in the front seat of the Mini letting Lola drive. But he didn't know how to do so. Lola didn't appear to mind. She hardly stopped talking most of the way down through Belsize Park. The wig she wore was made of human hair, she told him. It had cost a small fortune. The wig shone from the street-lamps, which lit up the inside of the car. The hair had come from Japanese women who had died young, Lola added. 'You're to meet my best friends, darling,' she said.

She drove so fast Toby held his hands together in his lap, squeezing them tightly so his fingers began to go numb. The Mini swerved in and out of the traffic as if it had a mind of its own. Lola acted as if she always drove fast. They went through two amber lights and the tyres screeched when they rounded corners.

'I've known the girls for years. We grew up together. I have a confession to make. You mustn't tell Alicia, pretty promise? I feel guilty enough as it is.'

Toby nodded, not taking his eyes off the road. He was terrified they were about to crash. He didn't want her to see he was scared so he kept a smile on his face.

'I was in London for most of the time Alicia thought I was abroad,' Lola went on. 'I was having a love affair with a man. His name was Jason. He'd left his wife. Antony couldn't face things after William died. He couldn't cope with Alicia's grief. So I took over. It was what Antony wanted. He is a dear, sweet man. I came out and stayed out. Jason and I had a little love-nest in Mayfair, until he left me. He went back to his wife, as I feared he would. After that, Antony and I did travel. I wanted to tell you, as you may hear Jason's name being bandied about. He may even turn up. He hated being normal.' Lola laughed.

'Oh,' said Toby. He tried hard to think of something to say. His mind had gone blank. He felt confused but he kept on smiling. He sensed Lola looking at him but he stared out through the window. He hoped Lola wouldn't mention Jason again. As she'd told him, Toby felt like someone was sticking pins into his skin.

They slowed down and moved along a road beside a canal. After a minute Lola added: 'You really are like a sponge, aren't you? You take everything in and carry on smiling. Antony said you were a curious little person. I hope the girls won't eat you up. You're a treasure.' Then she laughed again.

The flat was on the third floor of a brick block of flats four storeys high. The door had an entry phone. Lola produced two bottles of champagne from the back seat of the Mini after they'd found a parking space. She gave one of the bottles to Toby to carry. Lola pressed the entry phone button and the buzzer sounded straight away. Just inside the entrance was a tiny lift with wooden doors. The walls inside it were covered in carpeting the same colour as the carpet on the floor. By the time the lift had taken them up two flights Toby could hear voices calling out and high-pitched laughter. A Shirley Bassey record was playing so loudly he wondered why he hadn't heard it down in the street. The hallway outside the lift where they left it was decorated with gigantic bunches of pink and blue carnations. The flowers were in huge vases that stood against the walls along the floor. Pieces of coloured silk like the ones in Lola's room hung down from the hall ceiling.

'We've arrived!' Lola suddenly called out in Antony's voice and Toby jumped.

Lola didn't notice.

One of the doors off the hallway burst open and two women in identical pink ballgowns rushed out. They threw their arms round Lola and shrieked. They had pink hair and long black eyelashes and looked terribly old. Lola told Toby before they entered the flat that they were twin brothers and called themselves the Cartland Catalysts. They had a night-club act in an underground wine-bar in the West End.

From then on it was as if Toby had entered another world. Inside the flat dozens of women stood about, some in ballgowns and some dressed in fluorescent miniskirts and tank tops. Each of them wore a lot of make-up. They were all stunning to look at. Lola took him around and introduced him to so many he couldn't remember all their names. The flat was enormous. It had so many rooms he stayed close to Lola at first, though he kept getting asked to dance and was offered drinks and food and everyone wanted to whisk him off to other rooms until he started to feel dizzy from smelling so much perfume. After a few glasses of champagne he started to feel quite relaxed. Before long he had lost Lola and found himself sitting on a plush sofa in between someone with big breasts and a beehive hairdo and another who told him she was Shirley Bassey's elder sister. Dusty Springfield and Shirley Bassey records seemed to be the only music being played from a stereo in the corner of the main room. A few of the women were dressed to look like them. Everyone was very polite. Toby wasn't left alone for a minute. They each seemed to know who he was and that Lola had brought him. It was a while before Lola came back to him. She sat beside him on the sofa after the woman with the beehive got up to dance with the Cartland twins.

Lola shouted in his ear above the noise that every person at the party was a man and that some of them lived all the time as women and were dancers or entertainers in clubs around the West End. By that time Toby had drunk so much champagne he didn't really care. He'd never seen so many beautiful women. They all looked like film stars in his eyes. No one acted drunk and there was so much laughter that being there felt like nothing he had ever felt before. He danced with Lola and then he danced with Shirley Bassey's elder sister, who was called Rhonda. She told him he was terribly cute and gently bit both his ear-lobes. He danced with a Dusty Springfield lookalike and then someone who told him she had real breasts and that he was 'a very bona young stud'. Then he was taken out arm in arm to the kitchen by the Cartland twins who piled food on to the plate they gave him and made him eat everything on it by picking pieces up and pushing them gently into his mouth. One of the twins stood there and sucked on a peeled banana which had two small apricots attached to the bottom of it. She kept shrieking with laughter after she bit the top off.

In every room of the flat there were some of the most glamorous-looking women he had ever seen. He couldn't fully believe that they were really men. It was what being in Hollywood must be like, he thought. Some of them spoke in really high-pitched voices and made even Lola look a bit dowdy. One woman draped in a pink ostrich-feather boa and wearing a dress covered in diamonds taught him how to do the Charleston and he found himself in the middle of the floor in the main room dancing with her while everyone stood back to watch. There was so much noise and with the music playing he didn't have to say anything. He just smiled and nodded and laughed and kissed hands that were offered to him and he thought he had died and gone to heaven.

After what seemed to have been hours the music stopped playing and everyone began to gather in the main room. The shrieking voices died down. Toby found himself alongside Lola. She had put her arm round his shoulders and played with his hair with her fingers while she was talking to someone next to her who was dressed completely in black and had a veil across her face. She called herself the Other Miss Garbo. She'd kissed Toby on the mouth in the kitchen.

Lola leaned down to Toby and whispered in his ear: 'Our hostesses are about to appear,' she said, and winked at him.

For a moment the lights were switched off, then they came on, very low. There was a blue spotlight aimed at the door leading into the outer hall. From the stereo came a fanfare and some music like church music and in through the doorway suddenly swept a man dressed in a top hat and tails. In his arms he was carrying a woman dressed as a bride, with a long train made of lace. She carried a bouquet and screamed out 'Here we are again!'

Everyone started catcalling as the music grew louder. The man carried the bride into the centre of the room and, as he lowered her, he swept her around in a half-circle so that the bridal gown and train spread out across the floor. They stood there holding their arms up high and looking about them smiling and laughing and then they blew kisses. Lola leaned down and whispered to Toby as loudly as she could that the party was to celebrate their marriage. The two friends, Alec and John, had been together for twenty-nine years. Just as she stopped whispering there was another fanfare and a man dressed as a butler carried a three-tier wedding-cake into the room and placed it on a table just inside the door. Then Dionne Warwick's voice filled the room, singing 'Here Where There Is Love', and everyone was moving suddenly, rushing up to the bride and groom and kissing them and shrieking 'Congratulations, darlings!' and the bride was suddenly standing right in front of Toby and she curtsied low and leaned forward to kiss him on the mouth. Up close to Toby she looked ancient and had bright-red lipstick that had smudged and a mole on each cheek on either side of her nose. Toby bowed and the bride grabbed him and pulled him to her and started to dance round and round the room so fast that Toby was almost lifted off his feet. The bride was terribly strong. She had huge hands. Her legs were short. She kept trying to push one of her legs in between Toby's as they danced. His face got covered with her red lipstick.

The party went on for hours. The dancing didn't let up at all. No one bothered to turn the music down even after it was well past midnight. Toby saw two guests having a fight in the kitchen. They tore off each other's wigs and were hitting each other across the face and screaming so loudly he felt his ears popping. A short while later there was a sudden rush of people out of the main room. Gathering around the door that led into the bathroom, some were crying out 'Oh God, it's not boring Brenda again!'

When Toby looked he saw blood on the bathroom floor and a girl in a purple dress was lying there with her head beneath the sink. Lola dragged him away into another room and didn't say anything, but later he saw the girl being carried out of the flat on a stretcher by two ambulance men. The ambulance men were laughing. One of them wore a pair of women's knickers on his head.

It was getting close to dawn when people started to leave. None of the neighbours had come to complain. Toby stood on the balcony which led out through french windows from the main room, his arm round Lola's waist while they watched lots of kissing and hugging down in the street. People were staring from windows opposite and laughing. Soon after that Lola said she wanted to leave too and gave him a knowing smile. There was no sign of the hostesses when they looked for them to say goodbye. The bridal gown lay in a heap on the floor near the kitchen. Beside it was a top hat. On top of the hat was a huge mound of chocolate ice-cream. As they went into the hall Toby could see into the flat opposite. The same party seemed to be going on in there. One of the Cartland twins seemed to be doing a striptease.

Outside it was cold but clear. Lola took Toby's hand. She said she wanted to take him across the road into Regent's Park so she could give him his birthday present. Toby still felt drunk from all the champagne.

They walked down the short street and across another and were soon crossing a bridge over the canal. There was no one about. They walked a long way, deep into the park. Lola seemed to know exactly where she was going. She headed for a gap in the inner circle fence. She rucked up her dress around her legs as they clambered through. Beyond the fence was one of the small artificial lakes. Beside it were several rowing-boats. Still holding Toby by the hand, Lola started to run, pulling him along after her until they had reached the edge of the lake. Then she got Toby to help her push one of the rowing-boats into the water, and before Toby really knew what was happening they were pushing out into the middle of the lake and above them the sky was clear and he could actually see the fuzzy shape of the moon. Lola did the rowing. She stopped and let the boat drift, once they were in the middle of the water. It was very quiet. The water looked like it was made of glass. It was freezing cold.

'I've wanted to come out here so often at night,' Lola said, whispering. 'Jason never would. He was a bore really. Most normal men are.'

They sat there not speaking for a long time. Lola did not take her eyes off Toby. Every now and then she leaned forward slowly so that the boat didn't rock and touched his face with her fingers. Then she reached up and out of the top of her dress she pulled a small gold-paper-wrapped parcel and handed it to him without saying anything. Toby undid it. Inside a velvet-covered box was a fountain-pen.

'It's solid gold, darling. I hope you don't mind such extravagance. Mother will think it vulgar. I found it in Regent Street. Such a dear, sweet little man served me. He asked me out. I wanted you to have something that would stay with you all of your life, to remember Lola by. Happy birthday, treasure.'

'Are you going away?' Toby asked her.

Lola looked away from him, shaking her head. 'You might, Toby,' she said. 'Tonight you probably started to grow up.'

Toby put the pen back into its wrapping and laid it in his lap. He leaned forward and took hold of Lola's hands. He hadn't understood what she meant. 'I love you,' he said.

Lola just smiled.

Toby leaned closer to her and tried to kiss her on the mouth. Lola went to pull back, then rested her arms on his shoulders. They kissed for a long time. Afterwards, Lola wiped the lipstick off Toby's lips with her handkerchief, then off his face from where the bride hostess had kissed him. She told him he was a naughty boy. Toby didn't want the kissing to stop.

By the time they had got back to the edge of the lake, tied up the boat and walked across the park and out of it to where Lola had left the car, it was just beginning to grow light. Lola did not speak as they drove up along Haverstock Hill and turned towards Pudding Lane. Toby fell asleep, his head bumping on the window beside him.

He was still asleep when he heard Lola cry out. She had stopped the car. Toby opened his eyes. They were outside the house. He hadn't even realized they'd got there. Lola was opening the driver's door and after leaping out started to run across the road towards the gate before Toby fully realized what was going on. He hadn't noticed the two fire-engines standing further along the lane. There were figures moving in and out of the front garden. He clambered out of the car and ran across after Lola, who was already through the gate and talking to two firemen whose faces were covered in soot. He saw one of the men try to pull Lola back as she broke away from them, running up the path towards the front door. She came to a stop at the steps and just stood there, her arms at her sides. Smoke rose up into the early morning sky. There were hoses lying all across the path and across the grass. Blackened wood was piled up all over the garden.

Sometime during the night while he and Lola had been at the party a small fire, caused by what the firemen thought to have been an electrical fault, had started in the downstairs rooms. Before anyone had noticed, the whole house was ablaze. A body had been found in an attic room. A woman had been found lying on the grass in the back garden. She was already in hospital. The body had been taken away an hour ago. No one knew who the women were. Immediate neighbours had not been at home to identify either of them. Someone further up the lane had called out the fire brigade.

Lola was still standing beside the steps. She was weeping loudly when Toby reached her. One of the firemen had run after her and was holding her arms.

11 Looking for Olive Pinch

Toby had pulled the winged armchair to the windows in the study and was sitting there looking out. It was raining. The sky was dark and heavy and he could see nothing of the Heath. He had been sorting through Alicia's books, taking them down from the shelves and packing the undamaged ones into boxes Antony had sent over. The study smelled of damp and smoke and age. The ceiling was blackened and slightly buckled in parts. It was the only room in the house apart from the kitchen that had not been ruined. Antony had borrowed a foldaway bed and bedding and it sat in the middle of the floor. Toby was sleeping there at night. The upstairs bedrooms were in such a bad state he spent all his time in the study, as Alicia had been doing when he had first met her. Antony was staying with friends who had been at the party. He had been on Valium from the doctor and had not been able to face entering the house since the fire. His and Lola's clothes that were undamaged had been collected from the house after the funeral.

Over three weeks had gone by. Everything still felt false. Toby had gone through the days feeling as if he was dreaming. The doctor explained that this was normal. It was the same doctor who had looked after Antony. He had offered Toby some pills too but he didn't want to take them. As each day passed he felt a little better. He kept hearing Gran talking to him in his head. Her voice kept coming to him after he fell asleep. He would wake up in fright only to hear her as if she was sitting in the room with him. She told him that he was grown up now. He needed to sort himself out. She'd never said anything like that while she'd been alive. He had spent days tidying up downstairs once the firemen were satisfied that the house was not dangerous to live in. Toby didn't have anywhere else to go. He didn't want to stay with any of Antony's friends. They had all wanted Toby to stay with them but he felt too nervous at the idea. Everyone had been kind. But he needed to stay in the house; to feel close to Alicia, where it was familiar. Despite the damage and the damp from the water that had put the fire out, and the smell. It seemed right that he remained there until Antony was well enough to take over.

His feelings for Antony confused him. When Antony had been with him since the fire all he thought about was when Lola would appear. Sometimes she seemed more real than Antony. Each time he thought about her he started to feel as if he was out of breath. The feeling came and went like little waves and his heart would thump. He'd never been in love before and wasn't too sure if it was really love that he felt. He didn't know what love really was. All he sensed was this longing to be with Lola every minute, to be near her. It was the only time since the fire when he didn't feel unreal and guilty from what had happened.

Alicia had died in the fire. Toby and Antony had rushed off in the car to the Royal Free Hospital and all the way there they thought that the woman who had been found in the back garden was her. But it was Lillian who had escaped. Alicia's body had been found on Olive's bed in the attic bedroom. She had died of smoke inhalation. In her hands she had been clutching a photograph of Antony and the copy of *David Copperfield* she had given Toby. Antony went to identify the body. It was after that that he collapsed and had been put on medication until the funeral was over. Alicia had been buried in a plot beside William. Only Antony and Toby were at the private service in a local church. Antony had wanted no one else to be there.

Just after the service had begun Toby turned his head and saw a group of Antony's friends from the St John's Wood party entering the small church. Each of them was dressed in a black maxi. A few of them wore long black veils in their hats and elbow-length black gloves. They had come in so quietly that Antony didn't notice until Toby nudged him. Antony turned to stare, but he was still groggy from the Valium. He didn't even smile. Toby recognized Rhonda, who'd said she was Shirley Bassey's elder sister. She raised her veil and pouted, waving to him briefly with her fingers. The Cartland twins were there in identical black frocks and feathered hats. They were both weeping. A couple of them kept blowing their noses the whole time the vicar was speaking. When Antony stood up to place a single lily on the top of the coffin and to read the words from Alicia's favourite song, 'Let the Great Big World Keep Turning', there was so much sniffing coupled with loud gasps of grief that Toby couldn't hear Antony's voice. Once the service had ended they all clustered around Antony at the back of the church. They kissed him and called him their poor darling and dabbed at their eyes with huge lace handkerchiefs. Each of them kissed Toby on both cheeks and hugged him but said very little. They left the church quietly one by one until Antony and Toby were alone with the vicar, who had shaken hands with each of Antony's friends and thanked them for coming. He seemed unaware that they were all men. The vicar had approached Antony after they'd gone and said how spiritual was the friendship of women.

Toby was unable to cry at the funeral. It didn't seem all that genuine to him except when Antony spoke. Antony did not want any hymns sung. The service was over quickly. The vicar hadn't known Alicia, though he said he had met William. Toby sat through the service remembering Gran's funeral. The vicar at Gran's funeral hadn't known her either; had even mispronounced her name. At least this vicar didn't muddle Alicia's name. Her full name was Alicia Victoria Edwina Wickham, and when the vicar said the name it didn't sound like he was talking about the Alicia Toby had known. Antony held Toby's hand. They held hands all the way through the vicar's talk and then afterwards at the cemetery once they were by themselves. Antony asked his friends not to come with them to the cemetery. He wanted the burial to be as brief as the church service. He said Alicia wouldn't have wanted a lot of fuss. The pallbearers were from the funeral parlour which had organized everything.

For the rest of that day they walked in Regent's Park. They did not talk about the party in St John's Wood, nor about the boat ride out on the lake. They hardly spoke at all. They sat and watched the waterfowl on one of the lakes. They walked round the perimeter of the park until they were so tired they sat down on a bench overlooking the zoo, observing a crowd who were watching two elephants being walked up and down their compound. There were few people about as the day grew cold and damp. Toby remembered being there before. It seemed a long time ago. Antony took hold of Toby's hand and held it in his lap. They sat leaning against each other as the sky above them slowly darkened until it began to rain.

It didn't stop raining for days. Now that Toby had sorted out Alicia's books, the shelves in the study were empty. Some days he walked for hours on the Heath. He and Antony had been back to visit Alicia's grave, and to visit William's. One day Antony drove them down to Brighton. They spent a few nights in a hotel owned by a friend. They walked on the West Pier, drove to Lewes to have lunch at a country pub. The days were balmy and calm. Antony did not allow Lola to appear. He did not mention her at all. Toby didn't ask why. They were just happy to be together. After they returned to London Antony left Toby at the house, and drove away back to his friends in Swiss Cottage where he was staying.

Toby was waiting for Antony to arrive. They were going to look for Olive. Lillian had been asking for her every day, when Toby went to visit. Lillian was due to be released from the hospital in two days' time. She had minor burns on her hands and had been treated for exhaustion and breathing in too much smoke. There had been complications with her chest but she had survived. She had known straight away on Toby's first visit that Alicia had died. Lillian had tried to get back upstairs to Alicia after having sat in the kitchen, where she'd fallen asleep at the table. She hadn't smelled the smoke. She'd been waiting for Toby to come home. She didn't know how the fire had started. It had been confirmed to Antony that it was an electrical fault. No one was to blame. The house was so old and nothing had been done to improve it for too many years. Toby told her everything he knew, yet Lillian blamed herself. She wept and wrung her hands, going over and over what she should have done to save Alicia. The fire had spread quickly and she'd passed out half-way up the stairs and had then had to crawl back down on her hands and knees all the way to the kitchen door after she came to. By which time the fire was raging.

The police had been to see her, Lillian told Toby. They had asked endless questions. She had asked them if they would try to find her friend Olive Pinch. They had not done anything about it. She had heard nothing from them since. They had just turned up and asked their questions and had then gone away. Toby put his arms around Lillian and for the first time he cried, for Alicia and for Antony, for himself and for Lillian. He had wanted each of them to live in the house together, Olive too, as some kind of family he could belong to.

Antony had heard nothing from Myra and Henry, despite announcements of Alicia's death being in all the newspapers. Toby had not known that William had been so important. There were articles about his death, alongside the news about Alicia. There were photographs of her and William together. It was mentioned on the radio. Antony said they'd shown a photograph of Alicia from her theatre days on the six o'clock television news. Reporters came to the house. Toby didn't answer the door. Antony advised him not to.

Antony was sitting in the car looking straight ahead when Toby ran out to join him. The sky had cleared and the heavy clouds were gone. Leaves lay in damp heaps along the gutters. Antony didn't say anything as Toby got into the car. He just leaned over and kissed him on the cheek and they stared at each other.

'I've packed most of the books,' Toby said quietly when Antony had driven to the end of Pudding Lane. Antony did not glance once at the house. 'Are you feeling better?'

Antony nodded. 'I'm sleeping,' he said. 'That's better, I suppose. I worry about you.'

'I'm all right,' Toby told him. 'I've been worrying about you too.'

'Have you been to see Lillian today?' Antony asked.

Toby shook his head but didn't speak. He stared at Antony's face while Antony drove. Antony's face was pale and beneath his eyes there were dark patches. His eyes were bloodshot. Toby suddenly wondered how old Antony was. He had never asked. He had never looked old enough to be Alicia's son. Toby thought he looked old enough now.

Just before they reached Camden Town Antony slowed down and drew up beside a huge red-brick church. For a while he stared at the church with his face turned away. Then he looked back and smiled for a moment. His smile seemed nervous. 'Would you live with me, Toby?' he suddenly asked.

Toby blinked. He felt his face growing hot. It was a long time before he answered. 'Yes,' he said eventually. 'If you want me to.'

Antony was reaching over to him when Toby threw himself into Antony's arms, clinging to him so tightly that Antony started to laugh, then stopped. He stroked Toby's hair. Toby rested his head against Antony's chest. He could smell the scent that Lola wore.

'I do love you, but not in the way you might think,' Antony said quietly. 'There are so many kinds of love. Much of it isn't understood. What I feel for you frightens me a little. I don't understand it.'

They were both silent for a while. Toby could hear Antony's heart beating very fast. He closed his eyes and kept them shut.

'Mother wanted us to be close,' Antony said in almost a whisper. 'She told me that just after I came back. She was such an innocent. If we do live together, I don't expect it will be easy unless we lie. Not everyone will be as kind as my friends.'

'I don't care,' Toby said. He lifted his head. The windows of the Mini had steamed over. No one could see them from outside. He reached up, trembling, and put his hands on Antony's shoulders, trying to kiss him.

At first Antony turned his head away but then he brought it back. They kissed gently, as if they were both scared of bruising each other. Toby felt himself grow hot all over and then cold and then he trembled again and Antony put his arms around him, holding him close. It was the longest kiss Toby had ever shared.

Afterwards, as they drew apart and Toby became aware of where they were as if he had left it for a while, Antony said: 'We'll need to talk. There are things I need to explain. Things we need to sort out.'

'What things?' Toby asked.

Antony shook his head. 'There's plenty of time,' he answered. 'Let's just leave it at that for now. I shan't abandon you. We'll be together. Let's go and look for Olive, shall we? I feel I owe that much to Lillian.'

For the rest of the day they drove down every street in the West End they had driven down before, peering into doorways and along alleyways and in small squares where Toby said he had often seen people who were living rough. They parked near Leicester Square and searched the streets on foot. They checked a few run-down cafés and sat in Trafalgar Square staring at the tourists and watching for Olive in case she came by. Every so often they looked at each other curiously, as if they both wondered why they were there. They drove south across the river and searched along the Embankment, below the Festival Hall and beneath bridges. The few people Toby asked questions of either didn't bother to answer him or just stared until he walked away. There were two or three figures they saw from a distance that Toby was certain was Olive. But when he drew close, he could see he had been mistaken. One old woman shouted at him and spat when he rushed up to her and touched her on the arm, thinking she was Olive.

It was late afternoon when Antony suggested looking under the arches beside Charing Cross Station. He knew that homeless people slept there. He sometimes went to a club nearby and there were often people gathered along the pavement when he came out. The Salvation Army had a mobile soup-kitchen that visited the homeless there. Toby didn't let on that he'd slept there himself.

'There's a lot you know nothing about,' Antony said as they

were leaving the car parked on the Embankment outside the tube station. 'About me, I mean.'

'That doesn't matter,' Toby said. 'I love you. I told you that.'

Toby could feel Antony staring at him as they left the car. He didn't say anything more. They started to walk up the steps into the tube station. When they reached Villiers Street, Antony put his hand on Toby's shoulder. Sitting on a bench just to the left of the archway entrance were two women who, Toby guessed, were living on the streets. He knew that as soon as he looked straight at them. Though they were well dressed and looked clean they ignored everyone, or pretended to. One of them wore a lace stole. As he walked up to them they stared with narrowed eyes, looking him up and down, then ignored him. Quietly he asked them if they knew Olive Pinch, and described her.

'She that old bint who's always talking queer? Bald as a coot with a big scar on her bonce?' one of the women asked him.

Toby nodded.

'Nah,' the woman said. 'Ain't seen her.' Then she laughed. She leaned forward and stared closely at Toby, squinting her eyes. 'I seen you before, love, haven't I?' she said. 'You were with her a while back. I don't miss much.'

Toby nodded again.

The woman nodded as well, then stared at Toby's boots and at his sheepskin coat, sucking her top lip. She peered past him at Antony, who was standing a few yards away staring up towards the Strand as if he wasn't listening.

'He's not a copper, is he?' the other woman asked in a loud whisper, jerking her head towards Antony.

Toby shook his head.

'Didn't think he could be,' the woman went on. Then she snorted. 'Looks like a fairy, don't he, Dandy?'

The two women laughed.

After a while they said that Olive might be about if he waited long enough. She'd been hanging around near the arches for days and had taken up with some old men. She was looking after them. They'd been kicked out of a hostel.

'We look after ourselves, sunshine, us lot. Don't you think we don't,' the woman called Dandy said. She kept staring at Toby with narrowed eyes. 'You come into some money, then? Remember seeing you over the park. Who's your mate? He your pimp? You on the game now? All the kids are at it these days. Perverted, I call it.'

'Olive's my friend,' Toby told her. 'I want to help her.'

'That's right,' said Dandy. 'And I'm the ruddy Pope's long-lost sister from Rome. Here, you got money, we don't talk to strangers for nothing. You look as if you can spare a few quid. How about it?'

Toby went over to Antony. He brought back a five-pound note and handed it to the women with a smile.

'Well, then . . . too kind, I'm sure. Ain't he, Dandy?' the second woman said. 'Hope it makes you feel saintlike. You thank your fairy friend for us, as he's too proud to come over. Your Olive'll show up. If it's the same one, that is. Not sure now if she is the same one – are we, Dandy?'

Dandy dug her friend in the ribs and they laughed some more.

Toby stared. Neither of them seemed to have any teeth. He thanked them politely but they didn't say anything else. Dandy was holding the five-pound note up to the light and then she sniffed it. Toby felt them watching him as he rejoined Antony. They moved into the park opposite, where they sat down on a bench. The sun was warming the air. The pavements, still dark and wet from the rain, gave off a dank, sweet smell. The smell reminded Toby of Lillian.

They sat and waited over two hours before Toby saw Olive. She came slowly towards them from further inside the park, with two men. On her head she still wore one of the scarves that Alicia had given her. She was also wearing what looked like Lillian's moth-eaten fur coat. Toby recognized it straight away. She must have taken it with her when she'd left the house, though Lillian hadn't said anything about it. She was carrying a plastic bag which appeared to be full of empty bottles. The two men looked much older than Olive and shuffled along, staring at the ground. Olive didn't notice Toby and when he called out to her she just glanced at him without surprise and then took a look at Antony as if she had never seen either of them before. Toby hurried across and stood in front of her, then began walking backwards as Olive seemed determined not to stop. Antony remained sitting on the bench.

'It's Toby,' said Toby, reaching out to her. 'I know you remember me. It's about Lillian. She's in hospital.'

Olive stopped and squinted up into Toby's face. She didn't smile. The old men stopped with her but didn't look up. They both stared at the pavement. Olive had her arms through theirs and one of the men took hold of the plastic bag handle with his fingers as if he was worried that Toby might grab it off them.

'So what do you want, a medal?' Olive said rudely. 'I've left Lil. I got new mates now. What's she done, then? Been run over, has she, silly old cow? Rumty tumty diddle dee dee, why don't you piss off and let me be.' Then she grinned and winked at him.

Toby quickly told her about the fire and that Alicia had died and how Lillian had been asking to see her almost every day.

Olive looked back at him blankly. She shrugged her shoulders. 'So the Duchess has copped it,' she said. 'Well, I never. They all come to sticky ends, bossy tarts like her. How the mighty have fallen. What you want me for then, son? You're still wet behind the ears, aren't you?' She glanced over at Antony. 'That her son?'

'Lillian wants to see you,' Toby said. 'We could take you there.'

'Bollocks,' said Olive. 'You just leave me be, you know nothing. Them times is gone. Thought you'd come to tell me that Lil's dead. She might as well be, the silly cow.'

'She was your friend,' said Toby. 'She looked after you. Why don't you want to see her?'

'Didn't say that, did I?' said Olive. 'Where is she, then?'

Toby told her.

Olive just nodded. 'I might go. There again, I might not. Bit too far, tell the truth. Nothing to do with you anyway, son. You've told me. Now you can bugger off. You done your bit. What's between Lil and me has nothing to do with you. Ruddy cheek, if you ask me, coming down here with bother. I got me own life to think about.'

'She misses you,' Toby said. 'She's never stopped talking about you.'

'Bet she ain't, soppy old tart. Soft in the head. I told you son, didn't I? As I said, you've come to tell me, you done your bit. I want to be left on me own, that's all, son. It ain't much to ask, is it?'

She pulled the two men closer to her and moved round Toby, then carried on walking away, towards the entrance to the park. Beyond them Toby could see Dandy and her friend still sitting on their bench. They stared without expression as Olive and her friends moved towards them. Toby looked over to Antony and he shrugged. Just as Olive reached Villiers Street she turned and stared back at Toby. She said nothing and stared at him for a long time, frowning, then turned away and, crossing the street, she moved out of sight into the tube station with her friends. Toby stood staring at where she had gone.

Antony had got up off the bench and come to stand beside him. He put his hand on Toby's arm. 'You tried,' he said quietly.

'You've told her. It's up to her now.'

'She won't go on her own,' Toby said. 'If she doesn't go today, Lillian mightn't ever see her. She's coming home soon, you know that.'

'Home?' asked Antony.

Toby felt himself blushing. 'Back to the house. You said it was all right. She's got nowhere else to go,' he said. He still stared towards where Olive had gone. The two women had moved off their bench and had disappeared from sight as well. 'I wanted to help,' Toby added. 'They've both been my friends.'

The sunlight was fading. The day had moved on to late afternoon. Toby turned away and rubbed his eyes with his hands.

'We'll take care of Lillian,' Antony told him. 'Olive doesn't want to know, that's obvious. Forget about it, Toby. Come on, let's find the car.'

'Will you come back to the house?' Toby asked, looking up. 'Please. It'll be all right.'

Antony's hand was still on Toby's arm and he left it there. After a moment he said: 'I shouldn't have let you stay there alone, should I?'

Toby shrugged. 'It's been all right,' he answered quietly. 'I didn't mind.'

As they left the park and walked through the tube station entrance they saw no sign of Olive nor of the two men she'd been with. They had vanished. Antony drove back to the house in silence.

That night Antony slept on the foldaway bed. Toby slept on the floor. He woke up after a few hours and lay there staring at the ceiling, wondering what would happen next. Nothing had turned out as he had hoped it might. It still didn't seem real that Alicia was dead. Hours later he lay there listening to Antony's breathing. Antony lay on the foldaway hidden beneath the blankets. He hadn't stirred. Toby saw his mum's face staring down from the ceiling as it started to grow light. Alice was grinning at him and saying something he couldn't hear. Her face faded away slowly and he had the sudden urge to climb up on to the bed to be with Antony but was too scared to try. It had begun to rain outside. Antony mumbled in his sleep and turned over. Toby was still awake when Antony stirred, sat up, and stared down at him. They looked at each other for a long time.

'You can join me if you want,' Antony whispered, pulling the blankets aside.

It was almost lunchtime when Toby went off in a taxi to fetch Lillian from the hospital. Antony had not wanted to go. He said he'd get things ready for Lillian and fix up the bed so she could enjoy some privacy and comfort. The telephone was still working. The taxi took twenty minutes to arrive. Toby hugged Antony before he left. Antony did not hug him back but just stood there with his arms at his sides smiling gently as Toby let himself out of the front door.

All the way to the Royal Free Hospital the taxi-driver wouldn't stop talking. Toby didn't have anything to say. He just smiled his slow smile and nodded and stared out of the window. Antony had given him enough money to hand over a good tip. Since Toby had joined him in the foldaway bed that morning Antony had been acting distant. They had hardly talked. Toby had lain under the blankets and in the warmth and with Antony's arms around him Toby, for the first time in his life, had discovered what it was like to have sex. They didn't do very much except touch each other and then they removed each other's clothes and the feeling of Antony's skin had been as if Toby was touching Lola, and afterwards he had cried for a while. Neither of them had said anything during their love-making. Eventually Antony had got up off the bed and left the room to get dressed, and then he went out. He didn't return for hours. When he came back he said nothing about what they had done. Since then he had spoken hardly at all to Toby. Toby felt confused and lonely and happy all at the same time. He didn't know how he was supposed to act so he kept out of Antony's way, and walked on the Heath when Antony was at the house.

Lillian was dressed in one of the frocks Alicia had bought her and was sitting on the edge of her bed when Toby reached her ward. She had plasters on the backs of her hands and although she seemed to have lost weight her eyes sparkled when she looked up and saw Toby walking towards her. One of the nurses had baked her some biscuits and Lillian was holding them in a paper bag on her lap. They had given her a new coat. Lillian had it draped over her arm. She didn't stop smiling the whole time they were saying goodbye to the staff nurse and other patients she seemed to have become friends with in the ward. Everyone kept wishing her luck and smiling.

They found a taxi waiting just outside and Toby helped Lillian in, and as they drove off she held his hand up against her chest and wept. 'Dear boy, such tragedy,' she said. 'Yet I can't help feeling so blessed. They have all been so kind, so kind. I don't deserve such kindliness.'

Toby told her that he and Antony had been out searching the streets for Olive but had not found her anywhere, that he was sure Olive would be all right, wherever she might be. Lillian just nodded and didn't answer him, staring through the window and holding his hand tightly.

As they turned into Pudding Lane, Lillian began to tremble slightly but then she stopped and, once they had pulled up outside the side-gate to the house, she let Toby help her out on to the pavement. She stood there staring up at the windows while he paid the fare. When the taxi had gone she took hold of Toby's hand again and held it in both of hers, staring into his face and searching it with her eyes. Her eyes were watering. 'I've been dreaming of your mother,' she said. 'Such strangeness. I knew it was your mother without her having to tell me. I wanted you to know. She is waiting for you, dear boy, she told me. She is in England. We must do something about finding her, before it is too late.'

Toby nodded but looked away from her. He wasn't really listening.

'You don't understand,' Lillian went on. Her voice sounded a little panicky. 'We must go off and find her, without delay. I feel that so strongly. I have been so worried. I don't want you to lose her as I lost my dear Mutter. You must promise.'

'I promise,' Toby said. He was staring towards the house but couldn't see Antony in any of the windows. The front of the house was still scorched and blackened. He had covered two of the windows with cardboard where the glass had cracked. Piles of blackened wood remained scattered across the garden.

'Antony's inside,' Toby said. 'He's waiting for us.' But then he noticed that the Mini wasn't parked in its usual place, opposite. He shivered. He felt then that Antony had gone, that the house was empty.

'That poor, dear boy,' Lillian was saying. 'I shan't know what to say to him.'

Toby looked at her. Lillian seemed very old and frail. 'It'll be all right,' he said. 'Whatever happens, it'll be all right. The fire wasn't your fault.'

'I know. I suppose I do know that now,' Lillian said. She was staring towards the top of the house. Her face suddenly went pale and she stepped back and let out a little cry. She went to pull away but Toby was holding her and as soon as she looked back down at him her face relaxed.

'I am sorry, dear boy, for a moment I thought. . . .'

Toby looked up to where she'd been staring but didn't see anything except the dark, empty windows. Lillian took his arm and let him help her through the gate and along the path. She walked very slowly. She didn't explain what she thought she'd seen. She stared at the ground as if she was thinking.

'I'm a bit delicate on my pins,' Lillian said slowly. 'I am so sorry for all the bother I've caused you.'

Toby smiled but didn't answer. Suddenly he didn't want to go inside the house at all. He felt certain it was empty. But he helped Lillian up the steps, unlocked the door with his key and they went into the hall. The hallway was dark, the walls streaked with soot. Damp wallpaper hung down in strips. The floor was still wet. It squelched as they walked on it. Everything was covered with white dust and pieces of ceiling plaster. Toby listened. He could not hear any sounds at all.

It was Lillian who first noticed the figure appearing at the top of the stairs. No one was there when they entered. Lillian looked puzzled for a moment as she squinted up into the gloom. Then she smiled and nodded and moved forward. 'Hello, dear girl,' she said in what Toby had come to recognize as her posh voice. 'My name is Miss Lillian Pike. So lovely to meet you at long last.'

'Hello Miss Lillian Pike,' said Lola.

Lola looked at Toby and smiled at him gently. With her black hair hanging down to her shoulders and a scarlet dress that trailed to the landing at her feet she looked so beautiful and calm that for a moment Toby couldn't breathe. At the bottom of the stairs sat a pile of men's clothes. They were neatly folded. Beside them was a suitcase. The clothes were Antony's. Lola started to descend the stairs slowly, holding up the hem of her dress with one hand. As she reached the hall she turned and crossed to the study door, which was closed. As she opened it, she turned her head and gave them the most radiant smile Toby had ever seen.

'I've made tea,' Lola said. 'Come along, my dears. It's all ready. I shall be mother.'

Let the Great Big World Keep Turning

The three of them walked from the car, carrying the hamper. They'd seen a small grass-covered clearing beside a brook. Lola had taken off her shoes. She had very small feet. Her toenails were painted purple and she was wearing a silk caftan with a hood attached. The caftan was midnight blue in colour and covered with streaks of red. Reaching the clearing they sat down on a tartan blanket which Toby spread out on the grass. Lola had insisted that Lillian have the blanket across her knees in the car. It was still early, not long after dawn. It had been dark when they left London. The sunlight was thin as it angled down through the trees above them, the air cool and moist, yet the day promised to be warm. Lillian was wearing a Burberry overcoat which had belonged to Alicia and had survived the fire. All the clothes she wore had belonged to Alicia. With her hair lightly permed and make-up that Lola had applied to her face, Lillian did not look at all the same person Toby had first seen beside the rubbish bins at Calcutta Mansions. The scars on her hands were slowly healing. Lola had bought some expensive cream which she'd been massaging into Lillian's hands every day.

Less than a month had gone by. The memory of the fire and its consequences were only just beginning to fade. They were on their way to Southampton, to look for Toby's mum.

In the hamper were bacon sandwiches and boiled eggs and small fried lamb chops wrapped in foil. Lola had prepared all the food. There was a Thermos of coffee and four terracotta mugs. Toby busied himself passing out the food.

Lola leaned back against the trunk of a plane tree. She looked about her and sighed. 'Mother would have loved it here,' she said quietly. 'She adored the country.'

Lola had hired the car, along with a driver who had brought them this far, through her friends. She had got rid of the Mini while Toby had collected Lillian from the hospital. The Cartland twins had come over and driven it away. It had been Antony's car, Lola told Toby, not hers. She'd hated it.

'It was all so hectic, Toby dear,' Lola said. 'I rushed about before you came home like an hysterical wraith. The girls were thrilled that Antony was leaving. They'd never liked him.'

The car Lola had hired was a Daimler. The chauffeur was called Benedict. He didn't want to join them for breakfast. Benedict was Jamaican. He was the father of one of Lola's friends. He didn't say much during the journey. Toby had sat in the front for a while and talked about Jamaican Fred from the factory in Southampton who'd wanted to go home to Kingston but had been run over by a bus. Benedict told Toby that he was sixty-nine years old and hadn't been home to Jamaica for over thirty years. He had no desire to go back. He loved England. He wasn't too happy talking. He was waiting for a new set of false teeth, having had all his natural teeth pulled out on the National Health. His son, Lola's friend, dressed up as Aretha Franklin and mimed to her songs at a pub in Camden Town. Lola told Toby that Benedict's son was famous. Benedict seemed very proud of that.

While Lola was explaining to Toby who Benedict was and all about his son, Benedict kept glancing over his shoulder and giving Lola wide, toothless grins.

In the days following Lillian's release from hospital Lillian had not mentioned Olive at all. She had spent her time, when she wasn't resting, with Lola. The two of them had passed hours together in the study, while Lola altered Alicia's clothes so that they would fit. Lola washed Lillian's hair every day for a week. Then she took her out to a hairdresser to have it permed. They had talked, sitting out in the garden when it was warm, just as Lillian had sat there with Alicia. Lillian told Lola all about her life. Lola made Lillian laugh as Toby had never heard her laugh before.

Toby left them alone. He walked on the Heath some days, visiting the places where he'd been with Alicia, and where he had slept and wandered before he had met her. The trees were turning now and it was already autumn but the days were still warm. He watched people sitting together beside the ponds or under trees in just the same way they had been there before. He avoided the area where the pigeon man had been found. Where he walked, nothing seemed changed. Yet so much had changed inside him.

Toby explained carefully to Lillian when they were alone that Antony had become Lola and what it meant. Lillian just smiled at him and patted him on the arm. They had made up a bed for her in the kitchen. The Cartland twins had lent Lola a second foldaway bed.

'Dear boy, you dear boy,' Lillian had said. 'You already told me, once before. I do understand. I am not unaware of such things. I have had my share of life's labyrinths. Don't you worry your dear self. Lola is a charming person, quite charming. She cares for people. It's destiny. It is providence. It's the way of the world. We must accept such things.'

Toby looked at her and for a brief moment he thought that Alicia had been speaking to him, with Lillian's voice.

'I love Lola,' he told Lillian.

She took his hand in hers and held it to her and kissed it. 'I knew that too,' she said. 'You love them both. I am so happy for you.'

Lola, Toby and Lillian had gone together to visit Alicia's grave several times, taking bunches of late summer flowers. On the last visit they took a wreath that Lola had ordered. The wreath had been made up from miniature white roses. The roses were treated so that they would not fade for a long time. Lillian stood and wept at the graveside on the last visit, her arms through Toby's and Lola's. She had tried to recite the Lord's Prayer but kept getting muddled over the words. With the prayer unfinished they each stood beside the grave in silence, until a sudden downpour of cold rain had forced them to leave. Later that day, Lola went in a taxi to Alicia's solicitor, to hear her will being read. Everything had been left to Antony, and to Lola, whose name was also registered in the will. Lola told Toby afterwards that the solicitor had been rather confused. She had sorted it all out, but by the time she left the man still didn't seem to understand.

Alicia wanted the house to be completely renovated. She had left money for that to be done. She wanted the house to be home for Antony and Lola and whoever was to share their lives. The will was dated long before Toby had started living in the house.

'We'll have to respect what Mother wanted, darling, won't we?' Lola said to Toby when she'd been back at the house for a while. They were sitting together in the garden. Lillian was having a rest on her bed in the kitchen. 'I think she knew things. I think she sensed that she might die soon, when she made those arrangements. Not that she'd die in the fire. She often seemed to know so certainly about her life. I think it had something to do with that strange spirit guide.'

'Erihapeti,' said Toby.

Lola nodded. 'All she ever longed for was to be surrounded by happiness,' she went on. 'She loved you, Toby. She told me so, many times. Or rather she told Antony. She thought of you as her other son. She knew we would become good friends.'

'We're more than that,' Toby said quietly. 'Aren't we?'

Lola reached across to touch his face, drawing her fingers slowly down the side of his neck before she kissed him on the nose. Toby stared at her as she drew away. He could never quite understand how Lola had become such a totally different person from Antony. It wasn't the way she spoke. Lola's voice was almost exactly the same as Antony's, except that it was huskier and, he thought, sexy. Antony didn't sound sexy when he spoke. Just posh. It was the way Lola moved, the way she breathed, the way she looked at him; how she sat. She and Antony seemed like two people who had been in the same body. Now Antony was gone. Lola had got rid of all his things. Along with his clothes, she'd sent everything of Antony's to a charity shop. Toby stared at her and waited for her to answer. He felt scared at what she might say.

'I do want us to stay best friends,' Lola said softly after a long time. 'Special friends. But we may not be together for the rest of our lives. You must remember that. It's the inevitable sadness of life.'

Lola stood up and moved away from him, deeper into the garden. Toby got up from where he'd been sitting and joined her. Putting his arms around her he hugged her. He wanted to say how much he felt he loved her, yet he didn't know where to begin or what words to use, so he stayed silent. Lola drew up her hands and rested them on his back. Toby shivered. They were still standing like that when Lillian appeared, to tell them she'd made tea. Holding hands, Toby and Lola had followed her back into the house.

Later that night Lola told Toby that, now Antony was gone for good, she would be living life as she had always wanted to live it. Antony had wanted to live as Lola for so long. Now it was time for that to happen. She told Toby so calmly that Toby felt straight away that it was right. He had no problem accepting what she said. He would have Lola around all the time as he had longed for. He hoped that it meant she might love him as he loved her. Toby knew now that what he felt must be love.

There'd be plenty of money, Lola said. Alicia had been better off than even Lola had supposed. For years she had spent nothing of the interest that had accrued from investments William had made. Lola and Toby and Lillian could live together. They could make a life which would grow out of the past. Alicia would have approved of that wholeheartedly.

Lola and Toby settled themselves on the bed in the study, once Lillian was asleep, covering themselves with blankets, holding each other's hands until they both fell asleep. Some time in the middle of the night Toby awoke and stared at Lola's face until the room began to grow light from the morning's sun.

After they finished eating all the food in the hamper the three of them sat beside the brook for a while, staring down into the clear water. Toby told them how he and Gran had played Pooh sticks on their walks. How she had showed him what berries he could eat and that she had tried to teach him all the things he must know to live off the land. It all seemed a bit silly now, when he thought of it, though he had loved Gran. He talked about her until there was nothing more he could think of to say.

'She wanted me to be a gypsy like she'd been,' he said, grinning.

'And look how you've ended up,' Lola said, laughing gently. 'Isn't life so divinely queer.'

Toby, still grinning, started to help Lillian put everything back into the hamper. 'We'd better get going,' he said. 'Hadn't we?' He glanced across at Lola but she didn't move. She was staring at them both so intently Toby stopped what he was doing and looked back at her.

'How would you like to go to the South of France?' Lola suddenly asked. 'After Southampton, that is. For a little holiday.'

When they didn't say anything Lola added: 'There's a villa we can stay in. I've had an offer. There's a swimming-pool, a tennis-court and an Italian cook who is a treasure with pasta.'

'Goodness,' Lillian said. 'What a lark!'

'Goodness has nothing to do with it, Lillian,' Lola said. 'But we have the offer. I've already spoken to Benedict. He says he'd be quite happy to come over on the ferry with the car and drive us down there. What do you think, Toby?'

Lillian clasped her hands. Her eyes were shining when Toby glanced at her. 'I don't know,' he said. 'It's a long way.' He wasn't sure he liked the idea. 'What about the house?' he asked. 'Someone might break in. Myra and Henry might come back.'

'Oh, poo. They won't be back. Besides,' said Lola, 'I've arranged to have workmen at the place while we're away. I'm doing just as Mother wanted. If we go back to London we'll have to stay somewhere else. It's all been arranged. I couldn't bear being there with butch navvies all over the place.'

'What about passports?' Toby asked. 'I don't have one. Lillian won't have one either. It's too difficult.'

'You moaning little minnie! That's nothing to fret about,' Lola told him. 'I've already thought about it. We'll sort it out in Southampton. Trust Lola. She knows the answers. She has been *around*. So what do you think, Lillian?'

'Oh, dear girl, I would love to go. I've never been abroad,' Lillian said.

'Well then, it's settled. You're outvoted, Toby darling.'

Toby shrugged. He looked across at Lillian and grinned. Then he poked his tongue out at Lola and said: 'You had it all arranged.'

Lola leaned across and dug him in the ribs. 'Cheeky minx,' she said.

They both started laughing.

'You are both so kind,' Lillian said in a shaky voice. She was close to tears. 'I don't deserve such good fortune, I really don't. I am so blessed from your friendship.'

'There, there, Lillian,' Lola said loudly. 'None of your weeping now, dear. You'll ruin that make-up. Stiff upper lip. Mother was a great one for stiff upper lips and straight backs. Leave it to Lola. We shall go to France and start our new life with a holiday. We deserve it.'

They walked back to the car arm in arm. Toby carried the hamper. Benedict had fallen asleep in the front seat of the car, his head leaning against the window. His face was covered with *The Times*. The morning was already beginning to grow warm. Benedict was snoring so loudly that once they were in the back seat Lola had to tap on the sliding window between them until he woke up with a loud grunt.

For the rest of the journey Lillian dozed off and on, sitting in between Lola and Toby. Lola opened two bottles of pink champagne which she'd hidden in a small compartment on the floor of the car. The Daimler had dark-red leather upholstery, sliding glass windows between front and back and a sound system that played eight-track stereo music. Lola told them it was used mostly for weddings.

They toasted the future and afterwards, when Lillian began to nod, Lola drew the tartan blanket round her and settled her back with her head resting on Lola's shoulder. Quite soon Lola closed her eyes as well.

Toby sat staring out of the window. After a few minutes he couldn't stop thinking about Alice and George and seeing Gran's grave again. The thoughts came without his really wanting them to. He didn't feel that Alice was back home as Lillian believed. Lillian had kept saying over and over again to Lola that she'd dreamed about Toby's mother every night while she was in hospital. She was quite convinced that Alice was back in England and waiting for Toby to return home. It had been her going on about the dream that had decided Lola to organize the trip. Toby wasn't sure he wanted to go back home at all. He'd just gone along with the idea. He said nothing against it. Going home didn't seem so important now, after the time he'd been away. So much had happened to him. He knew he couldn't be the same person he had been when he'd left. Nothing had turned out the way he thought it might. Yet he hadn't known what to expect anyway so it was stupid thinking like that. He had almost forgotten Empire Street. The people he had helped and had talked to there, all those days and years that he'd lived with Alice and George and Gran, seemed far away from him and it felt as though he had been only a boy when he'd lived there and now he wasn't a boy any longer. He didn't feel angry with Alice and George. He didn't wonder if they had really loved him or not. It didn't seem to matter. They were his parents and they'd looked after him as best they could, but then that care had stopped. He might even have left home anyway if they had stayed together. It would be better if Alice wasn't in Southampton, if she was still in America and George was still somewhere up North living with Maureen Stokes.

As Benedict drove through towns and across bridges and past country houses along the road that was taking him home Toby felt more strongly every mile that he didn't want to go back at all. The thought of it scared him. He wanted to leave behind that boy who had walked with Gran in the woods, played Pooh sticks and sat on the stairs listening to Alice and George arguing night after night. Gran was dead. The Toby Todd he'd been wasn't there any longer, in Empire Street. He'd changed. He'd had sex. He loved Lola.

Yet another part of him wanted Alice to be waiting. He wanted George to be at home messing about in the garden shed and whistling out of tune. He wanted Gran to be there, raring to go off to the woods on another hike with her box of sardine sandwiches and her flask of tea and wearing Bert's stained cap and her corset which she'd hated. Alice would be getting ready to get off to the hospice for her shift. She'd be moaning about everything and yelling at George about things he'd never take any notice of.

Scenes moved through his head so fast Toby started to feel hot and sick. He pressed hi face against the coolness of the glass window, closing his eyes and squeezing them to try to get rid of the memories. He tried to replace Alice and George with Peter the dancer from South America who'd liked having sex with truck-drivers, with Annie from Ireland who'd screamed, with old Mrs Cranks and her budgerigar called Ringo. But as hard as he tried to see those other faces it was Gran's wrinkled face and eyes that kept moving in front of him. Alice and George were standing behind her, and then slowly the vision of Gran's Angel started to appear, surrounded by silver light. Soon all he could see were the Angel's huge eyes smiling down at him and he forced his own eyes open to try to swallow back the feeling that he was going to cry. His face was damp with sweat. As he wiped it he glanced across at Lola. She was staring at him across the top of Lillian's head. When their eyes met Lola smiled at him and slowly the eyes of the Angel were gone. He kept on staring at Lola until she started to frown. She turned away to stare through the window.

Toby gave directions to Benedict through the opened sliding windows once they reached the outskirts of Southampton. Benedict had never been to Southampton before. It was late morning by the time they arrived. Once they reached Empire Street Toby was so racked with nerves he sat leaning forward, his hands clasped between the knees of his jeans.

Empire Street was usually lined on both sides with parked cars. But the street was empty of vehicles. Lillian had woken up and was holding on to his arm, peering forward just as Lola was peering forward. Down along the middle of the street stood two long sections of trestle-tables covered with white paper and festooned with streamers and balloons and vases of flowers. Women were bustling in and out of houses carrying bowls of food and bottles of soft drink and beer. The tables were already covered with food and plates and tumblers. Far down towards the end of the second long table Toby could see old Mrs Kent, sitting in her Bath chair. She seemed to be directing all the comings and goings with her walking-stick. She kept waving the stick in the air. She was wearing a silver Lurex frock and on her head was perched a gold-coloured party hat. Her face was caked with make-up. She wore bright-red lipstick and rouge. She'd never worn make-up at all when Toby had lived in the street.

'What is it, dear boy? Is it a street party?' Lillian asked. 'I never knew they still had such things. What a lark.'

'I think it's for old Mrs Kent,' Toby said, pointing towards her. His voice sounded shaky as he spoke. He saw no one else he recognized. His house was at the other end of the street and out of sight from where they were parked. He glanced towards the cemetery where Gran was buried. It looked smaller than he remembered, overgrown with tall weeds. Someone had written the words *Make Grass Legal* on the surrounding wall, in red paint. 'She was going to have a party when she was a hundred,' Toby added. 'But that isn't for two years.'

'Well, someone is celebrating,' said Lola. 'How divine. We can join in.'

They left Benedict sitting in the car. Toby had got him to park out of sight around the corner. No one had seemed to notice them. The day had become warmer, the sky mostly free of cloud. There was music coming from somewhere close by as they entered the street. Old Mrs Kent spotted Toby before they were half-way down it. She had never missed anything going on. 'It's sonny! It's the lad!' she began to shout, waving her stick in the air. 'My goodness me!'

A woman Toby didn't recognize helped her get up out of the Bath chair as the three of them drew near. Old Mrs Kent was smiling so broadly Toby could see she wasn't wearing her teeth. 'Sonny, sonny, you've come home!' she kept calling out.

Along the street people stopped hurrying about for a moment to stare. Toby pulled away from Lillian and Lola and ran to where old Mrs Kent stood leaning on her stick. He hugged her. He helped her back into the Bath chair, something he had done so many times he hadn't even thought about doing it.

'Is it really you, lad?' she asked, peering up into his face. 'Have you come home to help me celebrate? My goodness me! What an honour!' Then she added in a loud whisper: 'I couldn't be blowed waiting another two years, sonny. Who cares if I reach a hundred. The Queen won't care. We've been having my party for two days. All day yesterday we had high jinks. Gluttons for punishment!' She leaned back in her Bath chair and blew out her cheeks as if she was exhausted by her little speech.

Toby stared about him. He could see his house from where he now stood. A couple of the front windows were boarded up. The house looked as if no one was living there. Yet the street seemed just the same as when he'd left it, apart from the party preparations. Someone had filled in all the pot-holes with earth and the trees down one side had had their branches trimmed. Young Mr Grundy had once tried to have all the trees cut down before he went senile and started to walk about in the nude. Old Mrs Kent was leaning forward in her Bath chair, squinting up at Toby. He looked back down at her, smiling his slow smile. 'It all looks just the same,' he said.

Old Mrs Kent nodded. She didn't take her eyes off him. 'It don't change much, sonny,' she said. 'Not here.' Then she added, her eyes sparkling: 'Your mum'll be as pleased as punch you've come home. Pleased as punch.'

She had always called Toby sonny, as she often forgot his name. For a moment Toby didn't take in what she'd said. He was grinning across at Lola and Lillian. They were standing arm in arm beside the trestle-table. Lola was pointing out all the different types of food. Around them women were hurrying to and fro and calling out to each other and laughing. A few were staring at Lola out of the corners of their eyes. No one spoke to her, or to Lillian.

'Your mum, sonny,' old Mrs Kent repeated loudly when Toby failed to respond.

Toby stared back at her, his eyes opening wide. He suddenly realized what she had said.

'She's here, you know. She came back over two months ago. Quite a big flutter there's been in the street. What with you gone off and George as well. It was in the local paper. They found George. He won't be back. They've been searching all over for you. I told them George had probably murdered you and buried you in the yard. I always had a wicked streak. No one believed me.'

Toby kept staring at her until old Mrs Kent blinked and looked flustered. 'Where is she?' he asked. He started to tremble. He felt a bit faint.

'Why, she's in her flat of course, sonny, down the street. Oh, you wouldn't know, would you?' Old Mrs Kent waved her stick towards the block of flats that had been built after young Mr Grundy died and they pulled his house down because it had rotten foundations. 'She always wanted to live in one of them, didn't she? Well, she does now. All on her own, bless her. She came all the way back from America on her own and you'd scarpered, both of you.' Old Mrs Kent started to cackle. 'You should have seen all the palaver. It was right comical. There was three. . . .'

Toby didn't listen to anything else. He started to run across the street. Lillian and Lola followed him. He didn't stop running until he reached the pavement below the flats. Behind him old Mrs Kent started calling out: 'Give her a shout, sonny! She's up there icing my cake! Ninety-eight candles, lad. Ninety-eight!'

The flats were five storeys high. Toby could see no one on any of the balconies. He could hear music from some of the flats. All the balcony doors were open. As he stood there Lillian and Lola joined him and put their arms through his. Toby stared up for a long time. 'Mum?' he called out. When no one appeared, he shouted the word. He took a step back, not knowing which balcony to look at, wondering if he should just go in and start knocking on doors.

Then he saw Alice. She was leaning over one of the highest balconies on the left, peering down at him with her lips pouting. Her hair was in curlers and she wore bright orange lipstick and had a cigarette dangling from the corner of her mouth. She stared without saying anything until Toby said 'Mum?' again in a quiet voice. 'It's me,' he said. 'It's Toby. I've come back.'

'Where the bloody hell have you been, you little bastard?' Alice yelled down at him. 'Do you realize I've had half the county police dragging lakes? What the bloody hell have you been up to?'

Toby couldn't speak. He could only stare at her, trying to blink back tears and wanting to laugh and feeling his face growing hot because Lola and Lillian must have heard what Alice had shouted. The whole street must have heard. Alice's face looked tanned. Her hair was dyed a dark-red colour. He hardly recognized her. She looked old.

'Who are they?' Alice called out, gesturing rudely at Lillian and Lola. They had moved away from Toby when Alice appeared and were staring up at her just as Toby was staring.

'They're my friends,' Toby said loudly. 'They've been looking after me. We're going to live together in London.' Then he added: 'Aren't you going to come down?'

Alice's eyes were on Lillian and then on Lola and then on Lillian again. Her eyes moved back to Lola and stayed there for a long time. She stared Lola up and down with a sour look. Toby wondered if she was drunk. She looked drunk. Suddenly he wanted to rush off, head back to the car and be driven away until Empire Street was left far behind. He felt ashamed and guilty and filled with a need for Alice to rush down and take him into her arms and weep. Alice turned her eyes back to Toby. She didn't smile. She didn't seem pleased to see him at all. She looked at him as if he was a stranger. But then something changed in the way she stared. Her face softened and crumpled and she drew one hand up to her chin, then removed the cigarette from her mouth and crushed it out on the balcony. The look only lasted for a moment. 'Always thought you'd end up a ruddy pervert' he heard her mutter. Then she added, loudly: 'You stay there, I'm coming down. Got words to have with you. You've been the near-death of your father and me!'

Suddenly her face was gone. Toby kept staring at the empty balcony. When he turned away and looked around him he realized that at least half the street had been listening. The street was filling up with people. He recognized most of them. He turned to Lillian and Lola and shrugged and tried to grin. His face felt as if it was on fire. Children were running about all over the place, in and out among the tables. They weren't taking any notice. Toby suddenly caught sight of Mrs Green, who thought Hitler was still alive. She was marching out through her gate carrying what looked like a toy machine-gun. She saw Toby and grinned at him and stared up at the sky. She held the machine-gun as if she was going to use it if she had to. Then through the crowd he could see Betsy Molesworthy walking towards them. She was holding a huge bunch of pink carnations in her arms. When she saw Toby she came to a dead stop and dropped the carnations and held her hands up to her cheeks. At the same time Mr Ramsdean appeared, hurrying out from The Cedars wearing his piano accordion and his Viennese hat. He did a double-take when he saw Toby. Slowly he bowed and touched his forelock as he'd always done when he saw Toby passing by. He stared at Lola and blinked.

Just as Alice appeared in the doorway of the flats and stood staring at Toby, Mr Ramsdean started to play on his accordion. He'd moved out into the street and people edged out of his way. He started to play his favourite song, which was supposed to be German. Toby had heard it a dozen times or more. The song was called 'A Star Falls from Heaven'. Alice did not bother to walk across to where Toby stood, his arms at his sides. She stopped just outside the entrance to the flats, as if she didn't know what to do or how to say anything else. Her face seemed to have sagged since he had last seen her, before she had gone away to America and written to tell George that she was never coming back. She and Toby looked at each other for a long time. Alice reached up and started taking the curlers out of her hair. She kept glancing at Lola and then back to Toby.

Lillian had moved to sit down on a wooden chair beside two women. Toby recognized them. They were from the next street. Alice had always said they were snobs. Lillian was laughing and had begun to talk non-stop. He turned his head and there Lola stood on her own, smiling gently at him. He felt his heart begin to thump. Something in her eyes made Toby walk across to stand in front of her. He took her hands in his. Lola glanced across at Alice.

The music from the accordion seemed to grow louder and louder as Toby and Lola stepped out into the street. Smiling at each other, while above them one-armed Cyril's flock of racing pigeons flew up from a nearby rooftop to circle in flight across the sky, they put their arms round each other's waists. Mr Ramsdean had finished playing 'A Star Falls from Heaven'. He had started to play a Viennese waltz. Not looking at anyone except at each other, Lola and Toby began, gracefully, to dance.